Fuzzy Logic

Susan C. Daffron

An Alpine Grove Romantic Comedy

Book 2

Published by Magic Fur Press
An imprint of Logical Expressions, Inc.
P.O. Box 383
Ponderay, ID 83852, USA

Fuzzy Logic

ISBN: 978-1-61038-023-2 (paperback)
     978-1-61038-024-9 (EPUB)

Fuzzy Logic is dedicated to my husband James Byrd,
my best friend and biggest supporter.
Thanks for everything!

Books by Susan C. Daffron

The Alpine Grove Romantic Comedies

Chez Stinky

Fuzzy Logic

The Art of Wag

Snow Furries

Bark to the Future

Howl at the Loon

The Good, the Bad, and the Pugly

The Treasure of the Hairy Cadre

The Luck of the Paw

Daydream Retriever

The Hound of Music

The Jennings & O'Shea Mysteries

Sensing Trouble

Sensing Secrets

Sensing Truth

Chapter 1

Inside & Outside

Jan Carpenter slowly drove her car along the pothole-laden gravel driveway, the rocks crunching under her tires. In the back seat, her black Labrador retriever Rosa ran back and forth from window to window. The dog stopped panting and looked surprised for a moment.

Jan looked over her shoulder at the dog. "Please Rosa, keep it inside. Please."

Rosa raised her eyebrows momentarily and then bent her head to throw up on the old, ugly bedspread Jan had placed across the back seat of the car.

Jan sighed and gazed at the dog's relieved expression in the rearview mirror. "You couldn't wait for two more minutes? We're almost there."

Rosa wagged enthusiastically and resumed her frantic back-and-forth routine, a small river of drool swaying from her lower jaw.

The trees opened up into a clearing with a log house surrounded by forest. Half of the metal roof was covered with a silvery gray tarp and a man was sitting on the peak of the steeply pitched structure having something to drink. Jan shuddered at the idea of the man rolling down the incline and landing with a splat on the ground in front of her. Because of how the house was set into the hillside, it was a long way down.

As Jan navigated the car toward the house, she took in the rustic, slightly run-down setting. *What was Cindy talking about? This place doesn't look like a boarding kennel.* Jan had enough to think about right now without worrying about Rosa, too. She parked the car under a tree off to the side of the driveway in front of the house and bent down to gather up Rosa's leash and other things from the floor of the passenger side of the car.

When she looked up, a petite woman with long, dark hair opened the door of the house and started down the steps. As she got out of the car, Jan grabbed the leash and raised her other hand to wave at the woman. "I'm not sure I'm in the right place. Is this a dog boarding kennel?"

"Not exactly. But we're working on it. I'm Kat Stevens. Cindy said you might be coming by with a dog who needs a place to stay."

The muscles in Jan's shoulders relaxed. She *was* in the right place. "That's a relief. I have to leave town and there's no one to take care of Rosa."

"We have an outbuilding with a kennel in it. I have five dogs here and I have to walk them every day, so Rosa will have lots of friends to play with." Kat peered over at the dog leaping around in the back of the car. "She does get along with other dogs, right?"

"Rosa may not be the smartest dog in the world, but she is the happiest dog you'll ever meet. She loves everybody."

"That's good to hear. Did you bring her vaccination records from the vet?"

"Yes, I've got them, all Rosa's favorite toys, and her leash." She waved the leash in the air. "Everything." Jan suddenly choked up at the idea of leaving Rosa. Why was she getting all weepy about vet records? She clutched the leash more tightly in her two hands. "I'm going to miss my girl. Thank you so much."

Kat nodded. "We're planning on building an official kennel in the spring, but Rosa should be fine. My dog Tessa stayed out there for a while, before it was fixed up."

"Let me get Rosa out of the car. She gets carsick, so she might...well...not smell good."

Kat smiled slightly. "I have experience with bad smells."

Jan turned back to her car to collect Rosa. A tall, lanky man was strolling up from behind the house, his long legs traversing the ground quickly. He was surrounded by a parade of three dogs cavorting around him. One dog was brown, incredibly hairy, and gigantic. The animal had to weigh 200 pounds. A small nervous tremor rose in Jan's stomach. At least the enormous dog looked friendly. As the group got closer, she recognized that the human was Joel Ross, Cindy's brother. Still holding the leash, she waved. "Hi Joel. Was that you up on the roof?"

Putting his arm around Kat's shoulders, he said. "Hi Jan. Yes, that was me. How are you doing?"

"I'm glad you didn't fall off. And well, I'd rather be at work than traveling like this. Cindy probably told you what's going on, right?"

"A little bit."

Kat turned her head and looked up at Joel. "Really?"

Joel squeezed Kat's shoulders slightly, but didn't say anything. He had to be almost a foot taller than Kat. Standing next to Joel, she seemed tiny.

Jan turned back to collect Rosa. She didn't want to talk about it all again and hoped they wouldn't ask a bunch of questions. Over time, Jan had learned from Cindy that Joel was somewhat reserved. His habit of "clamming up," as Cindy called it, drove his sister crazy, but meant Jan might be spared from yet another uncomfortable conversation about her mother.

Jan turned and opened the car door. She clipped the leash onto the dog's collar and said, "Time to get out of the car now, Rosa." The dog exited the car with a mighty leap, which caused her to pull her pudgy canine body around in a circle. "Easy girl. It's okay."

Rosa wagged so hard the entire rear half of her body flapped back and forth. The dog had a barrel-shaped torso and a smallish pointy head, which gave her an unfortunate resemblance to an oversized, hairy armadillo. Rosa jumped and yanked on the leash, trying to get closer to the other dogs. Jan struggled to retain her grasp, but smiled at the dog's exuberance. "Look, Rosa! You have lots of friends to play with while I'm gone."

Kat pointed at the three dogs surrounding Rosa, who were sniffing and wagging companionably. "The big, brown hairy dog is Linus. The smaller, brown collie mix is Lady and the black-and-white border collie is Lori. They're all very friendly."

Jan surveyed the group of wagging dogs. "I can see that. I feel better that Rosa will be among friends. I'm not really sure how long I'll be gone. I got an open-ended ticket, since sometimes events with my mother don't go as planned. But it should only be a few days."

Kat shrugged. "It's okay. We're not going anywhere. As you noticed, Joel is working on the roof, so we have to stay close to home."

Joel nodded. "Plus, Kat is working on a magazine article and has a deadline." He gave her a meaningful look. "Soon."

Kat moved out of his embrace and poked him in the ribs with her index finger. "I know. I know. I'm working on it."

Joel grinned at Kat and moved her hand away from his ticklish torso. "Every day I get more insight into the amazing procrastination abilities of writers." He bent to give her a peck on the lips. "I should return to the roof." He looked over at Jan. "It was nice seeing you again. Don't worry; we'll take good care of Rosa."

Jan cautioned him not to fall off the roof, and she and Kat watched as he ambled toward the back of the house. Jan envied the rapport Joel seemed to have found with Kat, particularly given that his last girlfriend had almost burned down his house when they broke up. His sister Cindy loved telling (and retelling) that story to pretty much anyone who would listen.

Jan could relate. There had been way too much drama in her life. And moving to Alpine Grove hadn't helped as much as she'd hoped, since everyone *still* seemed to know about it. Best not to dwell on that, though. Kat seemed to be mercifully clueless. Jan did a mental head shake and turned her attention back to Kat. "Is there anything else you need?"

Kat looked up and smiled. "No. I think we're set." She took Rosa's leash from Jan. "We'll go for a walk after you leave. I think Rosa will like the trail we have through the forest."

She reached down to stroke Rosa's sleek black head. "You'll have a good time, Rosa. Many new sniffies everywhere." Rosa wagged and panted, apparently eager to get on with the fun.

"Let's get your stuff and put it in the Tessa Hut."

"Tessa Hut?" Jan asked.

Kat strode with Rosa in tow toward the outbuilding and said over her shoulder, "Like I said, when I first came up here, my dog Tessa stayed out here. Ever since then, I think of it as the Tessa Hut."

Jan hurried to catch up. "Where is Tessa now?"

"She's in the house with Chelsey. They are buddies and like hanging out in the basement together. And Tessa is what you might call a high-energy dog, so she can be a little too excited about meeting new people." She pointed back toward the house. "Because the house is set into the hill, it's actually two stories. The log part is set on top of a daylight basement. The dogs hang out downstairs and spend a lot of quality time sleeping. Chelsey has a special spot under a table that she's claimed for her own. It's her favorite place to be."

Jan giggled. "So that's the Chelsey Hut?"

"Exactly."

After they got Rosa settled in her enclosure with food, water, and her toys, Jan turned to Kat. "Please take care of my girl. I'm dreading this trip, and I'm going to miss her."

Kat tilted her head and the flicker in her blue eyes made it seem like she wanted to inquire, but she said simply, "Rosa will be fine. Feel free to call and check in with me if you like. You have my number."

Jan crawled into her car and sat in morose silence as Kat walked back toward the enclosure to tend to Rosa. Closing her eyes, she took a deep breath and leaned her forehead on the steering wheel as she turned the key in the ignition. The next few days were going to be complicated.

~

As Jan's car clunked and rumbled away, Kat walked back to the Tessa Hut. She moved out of the sunshine into the darkness of the old building, and her eyes began to adjust to the light. Why was it so quiet in here? She bent down to peer through the chain-link enclosure. It was empty. Where was Rosa? Jan had been gone for all of two minutes and already Kat had misplaced the dog. She straightened, took a step backwards, and heard a yelp as her foot landed on Rosa's tail.

Leaping backward, Kat grabbed the chain-link fencing to keep from falling over on the dog. "Rosa, what are you doing there? You're supposed to be *inside* the kennel."

Kat was sure that when she and Jan had come in here with Rosa, she had closed the kennel gate. The latch was still in the locked position. As Rosa sat next to her and wagged, Kat flipped the latch up and down idly. How had the dog gotten out of the kennel without going through the gate? Kat walked into the enclosure and examined the fencing, looking for holes, while Rosa supervised.

Kat stopped and looked at the dog. "Okay Rosa, how did you get out? What did you do?"

Rosa continued to wag and pant. The dog seemed to have a slightly smug look on her face. Like any good magician, Rosa wasn't about to divulge her secrets. But she certainly looked pleased with herself.

Kat exited the kennel and led Rosa back inside. She stroked the smooth black fur on the dog's head. "Rosa, you are staying here. *Inside* the kennel. This is your bed while your mom is gone. You have to stay in it. Take a nap, and after lunch I'll take you for a walk. It will be fun."

Carefully securing the latch on the gate, Kat left the Tessa Hut and walked toward the house. She shaded her eyes and looked up at the roof where Joel was whacking something with a hammer. "Hey, could you come down here for a minute?"

Joel stood up and waved his okay. Even though he'd been working up there for a while without any problem, Kat still wasn't used to his ability to wander around on the steep roof. Having the person you love spending so much time two stories off the ground was stressful. Kat closed her eyes, acknowledging the twinge in her stomach, as he disappeared down the back side of the house. Hearing no crash, she opened her eyes again and smiled as he walked toward her. "I think there's a problem with the Tessa Hut."

Joel's gaze moved behind her. "I'd say you're right."

Kat turned to see what he was looking at. "Rosa!" She grabbed the dog's collar and started leading the dog back to the Tessa Hut. "What is wrong with you?"

Joel followed Kat as she led Rosa toward the outbuilding. "Did you lock the gate?"

"Twice. And yet here she is. I can't figure out how she's getting out. Tessa never got out." Hadn't Joel fixed the building? He said he had.

"Tessa doesn't focus well. Getting out would require an attention span longer than six microseconds."

Kat looked back and grinned at Joel. His tendency to make deadpan comments amused her. "Well, there is that. Maybe Rosa is smarter than Jan said. Or at least smarter than

Tessa. Could you look at the fencing? I can't figure out what she's doing. It looks secure to me."

Joel and Kat went inside the kennel and began examining the chain-link enclosure as Rosa looked on. Kat ran her hands down the fencing wires checking for any holes or broken areas. The outbuilding itself was old, dusty, and obviously not constructed by a skilled craftsman. The rough-hewn planks of the walls still exuded the scent of filthy antique straw. After he'd moved in with Kat, Joel had reinforced the building to keep it from falling down. But Kat didn't know if he'd looked at the chain-link enclosure inside the building. Tessa had been sleeping inside the house by that point, so he may not have bothered with it.

Kat crouched down to get a closer look at the bottom of the fence. Rosa leaped over and licked Kat's ear with her big pink tongue. Jerking her head away from the slimy feeling, Kat lost her balance and tipped over backward. As she went down, she grabbed the fabric on the leg of Joel's jeans with one hand, yanking him toward her. Twisting to try to grab her other hand, Joel slammed his foot into Rosa's water bowl, which flipped up and landed on Kat, covering her with dog-drool-infused water. Joel grabbed the fence and attempted to regain some equilibrium to avoid falling on top of her. Looking down at Kat's soaked flannel shirt and shocked demeanor, he smirked and said, "Mmm, doggie backwash. That's sexy."

Kat's expression clouded with fury and she blurted out, "Very funny. You were supposed to fix this! She's not supposed to be able to get out!"

Sensing trouble, Rosa stopped panting, furrowed her brow, and retreated to the farthest corner of the kennel.

Attempting to muster some small sense of dignity, Kat sat up, smoothed her hair, and glared up at Joel, who was still hanging over her, clutching the fencing. He straightened, reached out a hand to help her up, and said through tight lips, "I fixed the building; the chain link looked fine."

Kat had learned that when Joel used that particular low tone of voice, he wasn't happy. Maybe she shouldn't have snapped at him. She rubbed her left elbow, which had hit the floor hard. Pain made her cranky.

"But how is Rosa getting out? If something happens to her, Jan will kill me. And I'll feel horrible. So much for the whole idea of setting up a boarding kennel. Maybe this isn't going to work. I've only got one goofy black Lab here. What if I had more dogs?"

Joel took her other hand in his and looked down into her blue eyes. "This building wasn't designed to be a kennel in the first place. That's why we're planning to build something new this spring.

Kat nodded. "I suppose so."

"I'm not sure what Rosa is doing to get out. So far, she doesn't seem to want to go anywhere. She just sits next to you. Maybe she's lonely. Her owner has only been gone for a few minutes and she probably wonders where she is."

"Great. The first dog I board has abandonment issues. But she has to be getting out somehow. We've got *five* dogs in the house already; it's kind of crowded. I really want Rosa to stay out here like a dog that's being boarded is supposed to."

Deciding that the tense moment was over, Rosa jumped up from her corner and ran over to Kat to receive some affection. Kat obliged by stroking the dog's head. She sighed.

"Are you lonely, Rosa? Is that it? I guess taking care of you could be more difficult than I thought."

Rosa wagged and leaned her sleek black body onto Kat's thigh. Joel wrapped his arm around Kat and pulled her toward him. "At least she likes you."

Kat snuggled into his arms and looked down at the dog. "Oh Rosa, what are we going to do with you?"

Chapter 2

Odd Nuptials

Jan breathed a sigh of relief as she settled into seat 12F. It had been a long drive to the airport, and she was looking forward to some uninterrupted reading time during the flight. Considering that she was a librarian, she didn't seem to get much opportunity to read books. Finding, repairing, buying, and filing books, yes. Reading, no.

At the sound of a loud throat clearing, Jan looked up to find a large woman pointing to the seat next to her. "I'm in 12E."

Jan looked over at the man in 12D, who was disentangling himself from his seatbelt and moving into the aisle to let the woman get by him. He caught her gaze and frowned. Like him, Jan had hoped that the middle seat would remain unoccupied, but no such luck. She smiled in sympathy at Mr. 12D as the older woman rammed her luggage under the seat in front of her and settled her prodigious girth into the small space. Various body parts oozed over Jan's lap as the woman bent over, attempting to extract something from her suitcase at her feet. Jan cringed inwardly at the violation of personal space and the unspoken rules of air travel.

Having completed her luggage ministrations, the woman turned to Jan and thrust out her hand. "Hi! My name is Ethel and I'm going to visit my granddaughter in San Diego! But

I'm a little bit of a nervous flyer." Her eyes widened and she whispered, "Sometimes it affects my digestion."

Jan put her book down in her lap. So much for escaping into a good read. Clearly, she wasn't going to be able to make any headway on her novel. "I'm sure you'll be okay. It's not a very long flight." In the seat pocket, an airsick bag was placed within easy reach.

Ethel tilted her head, causing the ossified bluish curls on her head to shift in an unnatural way. "Why are you going to San Diego?"

Jan sighed a little too loudly. Maybe Ethel wouldn't notice. "My mother is getting married."

Ethel straightened in her seat and leaned closer to Jan. "That's wonderful! I love weddings. Who is the lucky man? What does he do? Are you excited? It's beautiful to see such an expression of love. Where are they getting married?"

It was apparent that Ethel had not been retrieving breath mints out of her suitcase. Jan replied slowly, "Well, they are getting married on the beach. The man was actually her next-door neighbor many years ago. I knew him when I was growing up." Jan shrugged. "I don't know if I'm excited exactly. But it will probably be interesting."

"Interesting? But weddings are so gorgeous. The flowers! The lovely food! How can you not just adore that?"

Jan twisted in her seat, leaning her back away toward the window. If she were any farther away from Ethel, she'd be outside the plane. Discussing anything related to her mother was never fun. "My mother tends to do things differently, I guess."

"What do you mean differently? It's a wedding! There are traditions. People say vows!"

"Well, I think for one thing, there will be a puppet show."

The woman looked slightly taken aback, but then smiled knowingly. "Oh, is it one of those sex-puppet shows? I've never seen that at a wedding. But it could be fun."

Jan didn't know what a sex-puppet show was. And she didn't want to know. She'd seen way too many puppet shows in her lifetime as it was. "No, no, nothing like that. My mother was on local children's television for a long time. She was the assistant to *The Farmer*, the kid's TV show in San Diego. She did the puppet shows with the sock-puppet farm animals."

"You mother is the *Farm Lady*? I loved her. My kids loved her. My grandkids love her in the reruns. Oh my goodness me, I can't believe I'm sitting next to the daughter of the Farm Lady. This is so exciting! Oh and the Farm Lady is getting married? How wonderful for her! Is she finally marrying the Farmer?"

After so many years, Jan was used to people knowing her mother as the Farm Lady with the sock puppets. And it never failed to embarrass her. Years of being teased at school by other kids making every possible form of revolting farm noise was hard to shake. The pig sounds were to the point that she still couldn't eat bacon. And what people didn't know was that the wholesome sweet TV persona was nothing like the real woman, Angie Carpenter. Responsible motherly farm matron, she certainly was not. "Maybe you didn't hear, but Bob Myers, the Farmer, died a few years ago and the show went off the air. The man my mother is marrying is in the plumbing business."

Ethel narrowed her eyes and gave Jan a knowing look, "Oh, plumbers make a lot of money. He must be a great catch. How did their love blossom? I'm sure there's a romantic story there."

"I don't know how romantic it is. Like I said, we were neighbors a long time ago, but he was on television, too. They met again recently on a retrospective special that featured stars from old TV shows and commercials. If you saw the ads for the Toilet King years ago, that's him."

Ethel clapped her hands together, "My heavens! The Farm Lady is marrying the Toilet King! I can't wait to tell all my friends. Does he still have purple hair and wear the blue jumpsuit? I just loved those commercials with the swirling and all that."

"I haven't seen him in a long time. I live in Alpine Grove now."

"That's a pretty little town. It's a lovely place, dear, but I can't believe you'd want to leave the glamour of show business. You must have had such an exciting childhood, being around all those TV people. Did you actually get to meet the Farmer? What about the Tool Man? Tim Allen is his name, right? I just love that *Home Improvement* show. He is so funny."

"No, *Home Improvement* is not filmed in San Diego. The show is set in a suburb of Detroit, but it's filmed at a Burbank studio, I believe. My mother only worked on local children's TV shows. But yes, I did meet Bob Myers, the Farmer." Jan didn't volunteer that he was also kind of a jerk. Over time, she had discovered that people didn't appreciate having their TV idols knocked off their pedestals.

A concerned look crossed Ethel's face and she looked over at Mr. 12D. "I think I need to use the little girl's room now. Excuse me!"

Jan closed her eyes. The row of seats moved as Ethel reached up, hauled on the back of 11E in front of her, and levered herself out of her seat. Seeing the woman's urgency, Mr. 12D quickly hopped out into the aisle to get out of Ethel's way.

Jan sat up straight and turned to peer down the aisle toward the back of the plane. What had Ethel said to the flight attendant to cause her to hustle toward the galley? Leaning back again, Jan closed her eyes and willed herself not to open them for any reason. Maybe Ethel would be gone long enough for her to feign sleep for the duration of the flight. It was worth a try.

～

Jan stood at the doorway of her mother's apartment. The bougainvillea plants were in bloom and magenta flowers cascaded down the stairway toward the unit below. Although the flowers were pretty, the generic apartment was a sharp contrast to the cute, funky bungalow in the little beach community where she and her mother had lived years ago. This apartment complex seemed sterile and plastic by comparison.

She raised her hand to knock on the door, but before her knuckles hit the wood, the door flew open and her mother stood in the doorway. "Janelle! You're here!" The tall, lithe woman was wearing a peacock-colored tie-dyed dress and had a ring of flowers in her purplish red hair. She reached out and grabbed Jan by the elbow, pulling her inside. Candles and incense were burning, and the smoke irritated Jan's lungs. "Hi Mom," she coughed as she stumbled alongside her mother into the dimly lit room.

"We're doing a cleansing of my space so I can be ready for what's next. Do you remember Skye? She's here to do a reading. I want to be better prepared this time. And Zoe over there is in charge of the smudge sticks, so we don't burn the place down. We don't want that to happen again, either."

Jan nodded her head in acknowledgment. From past events, she knew more firemen than she probably should. "Do you need any help with anything, Mom?"

"Could you take the suitcase? After we finish the reading here, we'll be ready to head over to the gardens for the ceremony."

Jan looked over at the suitcase that contained her mother's collection of sock puppets. She had spent a lot of time hauling that thing around, and she held a special animosity for the contents within. Intellectually, it was stupid to be jealous of a bunch of old socks, but they were more than just laundry, in this case.

"Okay, Mom. I'll meet you there." She turned to pick up the suitcase and with her free hand waved toward the other women. "Good luck! Make sure she doesn't forget anything important." When Angie had married Nick, she had forgotten the rings, and Jan was enlisted to run over to the local quick mart to get makeshift wedding bands from a gumball machine. Fifteen quarters later, the guy at the counter was starting to give her odd looks, but she finally had two rings and thirteen creepy molded-plastic animals. Yes, arriving the day of the wedding ceremony this time was cutting it close, but experience was a merciless teacher. The less time Jan spent with her mother, the better.

As she walked back down the stairs, Jan heard the sound of kids playing in the pool. Somehow she had managed to miss out on a lot of the fun of living in San Diego. When she was a kid, she never splashed around playing Marco Polo or hung out at the beach like everyone else. Maybe it was because she was too busy. When Mom was at work late taping shows, or out with her latest man, Jan was the one who had to walk to the grocery store or else there wouldn't be anything for dinner. Somebody had to do it. Between that and her schoolwork, it seemed like she hadn't had much free time.

She shook her head. Best not to dwell on the past. She should probably be more excited about the wedding. But since the Toilet King was about to become husband number six (or was it seven?), it was getting more difficult to muster up enthusiasm for the whole nuptial process. Given her mother's attire and the location, the theme of this wedding appeared to be reminiscent of wedding number three, which had sported a bit of a flower-child-hippie vibe.

Maybe Mom had run out of ideas, so it was time to start recycling old ones. Or maybe she just forgot. During the dreadful Richard phase, there was a lot of that kind of generalized distraction. And to make things even more confusing, right before the wedding Richard had changed his name to Wambleesha because it meant white eagle, which he thought was "most excellent." At the time, Jan had spent quite a bit of time in her room devising her own significantly less majestic definitions for the guy. But since Angie collected divorce papers like some people collect stamps, Richard/Wambleesha didn't last long.

At the gardens, Jan got out of the car and looked out past the lush tropical vegetation toward the crisp blue coastline of the Pacific Ocean beyond. Even if the wedding was a repeat performance, the gardens were still a beautiful location for the event. She spotted a large white tent across the lawn. Grabbing the suitcase from her rental car, Jan walked past the koi ponds and marveled at the well-tended oasis. It had to be an enormous amount of work to create and maintain such attractive manicured gardens.

In the distance, a small but extremely furry polar-bear-like animal was barreling toward her. Jan mentally chastised herself; polar bears were rarely seen in Southern California. But this one was moving at high speed right toward her. She dropped the suitcase and waved her arms in an attempt to suggest that the animal turn in a different direction, preferably away from her new dress.

As the hairy thing grew closer, it became obvious that it was a dog, not a bear. Its pink tongue was flapping in the wind, and it was smiling widely. Jan corrected herself again. Neither polar bears nor dogs are able to smile.

With a final burst of enthusiasm, the dog launched off the lawn onto Jan, slamming her to the ground and knocking the wind out of her. She squeezed her eyes shut as the dog stood on her chest licking her face and ears with unadulterated joyous abandon.

Jan was less joyful about the tongue bath. She flailed her arms and struggled to remove the whirling mass of white fur from her body. Finally, she was able to roll over and push the dog off, which resulted in the distinctive sound of tearing fabric as an errant claw caught on her dress. Still spinning and wagging, the dog gave her one last slurp before running off.

Jan looked down at the remains of her dress. What had been a pretty floral scoop-neck dress now was a torn and grass-stained wreck that was better suited for the rag bag than a wedding. Somehow even her stockings were shredded. All the time she had taken with her hair and makeup earlier was a total loss. She blew a lock of her curly, reddish-blonde hair out of her mouth. So much for that chignon. Tugging at the front of her dress, she made a feeble attempt to cover various tender body parts with fabric again. It was clear she wasn't going to be suitable for public viewing any time soon. She yanked at the remains of her hairstyle, pulling out the bobby pins and holding them in her mouth.

Hearing a panting sound above the noise of the ocean, she looked up from the sorry state of her wardrobe to find a man running toward her. He bent over in exhaustion, putting his hands on his knees. With a great exhale of breath, he asked, "Did you see a furry white dog go by here?"

Jan pulled the bobby pins out of her mouth. "Yes. I'm surveying the damage now. And I could have been seriously hurt."

"Sorry about that. She really likes to run. And she likes people. Sometimes those two things conflict."

"There's about to be a wedding here. You shouldn't have brought a dog. I don't think they are allowed at the gardens. Didn't you read the rules?"

"My dad is getting married, so they made an exception. My dog is participating in the wedding. Or she is supposed to be, if I can find her again."

"Don't you have a leash?" Jan shook her head. "I hate irresponsible pet owners. I could have been seriously hurt. And if I were afraid of dogs, I would have been terrified as well. In any case, my dress is completely ruined and the wedding starts in an hour."

The tall man crouched down to look at Jan more closely. His eyes widened in surprise. "Wait, don't I know you? You're Janelle, right?"

"I prefer Jan."

"I'm Michael. Remember? I lived in the house next door to you when we were little. My dad is marrying your mom."

He did look vaguely familiar, and she'd known he'd have to be here somewhere because of his father. But she had hoped to avoid him. A warm flush rose to her cheeks as Jan mentally connected the well-dressed man in front of her to the obnoxious skinny neighbor kid she'd known years ago.

Now instead of gangly limbs and tousled hair, he had broad shoulders and movie-star good looks. Not quite at the exceptional level of Cary Grant maybe, because of course Cary was the ultimate perfect male, but startling, nonetheless. The warm, amused sparkle in Michael's brown eyes was definitely exactly the same as it had been when he was a little boy. Jan nodded quickly. "Oh yes. I remember you."

The last time Jan had seen Michael, she'd been seven or eight years old. And naked. It was laundry day and she had just put all her clothes in the washer, including the ones she had been wearing. She walked back into her bedroom carrying her laundry basket and encountered ten-year-old Michael sitting on her bed, grinning at her. She'd thrown down the basket and run screaming from the room back to the basement. She had hoped she would never see him again. Fortunately, she and her mom had moved not long afterward, and it hadn't been too difficult to avoid the creepy kid next door.

Michael smirked and bestowed upon her the exact same sly grin she remembered from years ago, except that one of his front teeth now had a small chip in the corner. At least he wasn't totally physically perfect. With a discerning leer, he said, "It's been a while. You've filled out."

Jan looked down at her dress. Most of the top half of her body was still exposed. She yanked a shard of floral fabric across her breast, trying to cover up the pink lacy bra that Michael seemed to be studying intently. "Yes, it *has* been a while and apparently you are still rude. But not as rude as your dog."

Michael stood up and offered her his hand. To take it, Jan had to let go of the front of her dress, so the shredded piece of fabric flopped down listlessly to her waist. As she struggled to her feet, she looked up at him and was greeted with the same irritating leering look again.

Snatching her hand away from his, she grabbed her dress. Through clenched teeth, she said, "Thank you. I don't suppose you happen to have an extra dress handy, do you?"

Michael ran his fingers through his wavy brown hair. "I'm fresh out of dresses. Although I do have my jacket in my car. That might keep you from causing a scandal at the wedding. Could your mom lend you something? I really need to find my dog. I'm sorry she knocked you down, but my dad is going to kill me if my dog isn't there to do her routine."

Gripping the front of her dress more tightly, she locked her gaze with his. "That horrible, unruly animal is doing a 'routine' in the wedding? You have got to be kidding me." Why did good-looking men always have such amazing eyelashes? It was unfair. Particularly since at this point her mascara was probably on her chin by now.

With a smile he said, "Swoosie is a great dog. She's actually really easy to train, because she loves food."

Jan drew her brows together. "Swoosie? You have a dog named Swoosie?"

"Yeah, like the actress. Swoosie Kurtz."

"Oh yes, I think she was in *Dangerous Liaisons*, wasn't she?"

"I guess. I know her from TV. She's the kind of bitchy sister on that show *Sisters*. It reminded me of my dog. Independent. Kind of obnoxious. Swoosie is a Samoyed. They're like that."

"I've read about that breed. They were originally bred by the nomadic Samoyede tribes in Northeastern Siberia. But I definitely agree with the obnoxious part."

Michael shrugged and then turned his head to look around him. "I don't know about Siberia, but I'll buy into the nomadic thing. I've got to find her. We can go back to my car and get my jacket. Then maybe you can help me look for her."

Jan frowned. "I have a big problem with my dress, in case you haven't noticed. And my hair is a disaster. I can't go running around looking for your dog. But I'll take your jacket."

Michael turned and began walking back across the grass, "Fine. Let's go then."

Jan stumbled to follow him, tugging on her dress. This was shaping up to be a very long day.

～

After collecting the coat from the car, Jan and Michael headed across the lawn back toward the tent. Jan was still hauling her mother's suitcase full of puppets and Michael was shouting "Swwooooosie" repeatedly. To Jan, it sounded like he was calling for a hooker. She bent her head, hoping no one would notice her with this guy. Of course, since she was wearing an oversized man's jacket, it was hard to remain inconspicuous. Maybe everyone would think she was part of one of the wedding "routines," since whatever entertainment her mother had planned was likely to be odd. Jan did look a little like Red Skelton dressed this way. How mortifying.

A flash of white appeared amid the grove of eucalyptus trees up ahead, and Michael grabbed Jan's hand. "Let's go. You have to help me."

Reluctantly, Jan let herself be dragged across the lawn. At the trees, Michael released her hand and then reached into his pocket. "Give her this and say 'treat' in a sing-song voice. She can't resist it!"

Jan put down the suitcase and looked down at the stinky piece of desiccated meat in her hand. "That's revolting! What is it?"

"Dehydrated liver. Dogs love it." He turned toward the trees and called out, "Swoooooooosie. Come get your treat! It's right here. You know you want it."

A white muzzle peered around a tree, and Jan could tell Swoosie was wise to this ruse. If the dog fell for the old get-your-treat ploy, she'd be reattached to her leash and fun-time was over. Michael might have been a little optimistic about his dog's level of gluttony.

Undaunted, Michael kept calling the dog and holding out the treat as he approached the copse of trees. Swoosie moved slightly, but she didn't come toward him. As he drew closer, her body tensed and it looked like she might make a break for it. Jan was struck again by the fact that the dog appeared to be smiling mischievously. In fact, Swoosie looked downright amused by the whole situation. The dog's normally pointy ears were down against her head, so it looked like Michael was being taunted by an overly cheerful baby harp seal.

Jan had to admit that the fluffy white dog was cute. Even if she was a furry little twerp. Swoosie looked a bit like the stuffed white rabbit Jan had adored when she was little. Mr. Bunny had been her favorite toy and she'd carried him everywhere. Maybe the dog wasn't really so bad. Jan reached out her hand with the treat toward the dog. "Hi, Swoosie. I'm Jan. I have a treat for you. Come get your treat. It's really good."

Continuing to smile and wag, Swoosie took a few steps toward Jan. The dog's fluffy white tail curled up, so as she wagged the feathery tip of the tail dusted the middle of her back. Suddenly, the dog launched off her back feet into the air. Given Swoosie's earlier behavior, Jan put her hand over her head and ducked away from the flying white ball of fur, dropping the treat on the ground.

Swoosie pounced on the treat, gulped it down, and spun around on a back paw, heading back toward the sheltering eucalyptus.

Michael yelled, "What did you do that for? You almost had her!"

Jan straightened, put her arms at her sides and scowled at him. "Self preservation. I didn't want to get tackled again. I don't see a dog on the end of that leash you're holding. Whatever you're doing certainly isn't working, either."

Michael turned away toward the trees where Swoosie had disappeared, continuing to call her name and trying to lure her with food.

Jan was sick of trying to catch the wily animal. Clearly, Swoosie had no intention of doing what Michael asked. And Jan had bigger problems. Clutching the top of Michael's jacket to hold it closed over her chest, she picked up the loathsome suitcase again, turned back toward the parking lot, and sighed. She had to figure out how to fix her wardrobe situation before the wedding. Maybe she could run to a store in the next half hour. Who was she kidding? It had taken her three weeks of shopping angst to settle on her now-shredded dress.

Jan was disturbed from her thoughts by a howling "roo-roo-ROO!" and then happy yipping noises from the direction of the trees. A few seconds later, she heard Michael whoop, "HA! Gotcha!"

Michael emerged from the trees with Swoosie on her leash, walking sedately beside him. She looked like a model canine citizen. Jan turned and called out, "How did you do it?"

Michael grinned, "I never divulge my secrets. But with Swoosie, the key is to make her think whatever you want her to do was actually *her* idea."

Jan waved her hands in exasperation. "I've really got to go now. The wedding starts in a half an hour and like I said, I can't go looking like this. What would people think?"

"I have an idea. But I don't think you're going to like it."

"I don't have a lot of options. Right now, I'm wearing your jacket and I suspect you want it back."

"Yes. I have to wear it after my routine with Swoosie. If you agree to participate, I can get you some other clothing. But we have to move fast."

"Participate?"

"Yes, you'd have to be in our routine."

"In front of people?"

"Yes, that's usually the way a performance works."

"I don't like being the center of attention. That's always been my mother's thing. Not mine."

Michael surveyed her attire, "If you're in the routine, I can grab one of the costumes."

Jan mentally cringed. "Costumes? What kind of costume? This idea just gets worse and worse. People will think I'm some kind of nut case."

He tilted his head. "Look at it this way. If you're wearing a costume, people will think you're going to be in a show and the outfit is on purpose. Of course, if you aren't actually *in* the show, then they'll think you're weird or maybe just a cross-dresser. But worse than that, if you're half-naked in a torn dress, people will think you've got a major problem. Like one of those maybe–I-should-call-911 type of problems."

Jan sighed. "I suppose that's true. I didn't really think about it that way. And I look like a wreck. Or like I've been *in* a wreck. I guess all those years of suffering through my mother's shows has made avoiding them a reflex action. I'm not a performer, though. Just the idea of speaking in front of people is terrifying to me."

Michael smiled. "Don't worry. This will be fun. You won't have to say anything. I promise. All you have to do is follow my lead. Swoosie knows what to do. She's really cute when she does her thing and everyone will be looking at her, not at you. People love it!"

"You actually trained her to do something other than run away?"

"Ha, ha. Very funny. Like I said, Swoosie is extremely trainable when she has the right motivation. Let's go get the costumes. I need to get her suited up in her ruffles."

Jan looked at him quickly. "Ruffles?"

"Yes. Ruffles. You'll see."

⁓

Swoosie was looking remarkably composed now that she was all decked out in her costume. Michael hadn't been kidding about the ruffles. She had a little doggie skirt tied around her waist that was made up of bright red, black, and green ruffles. Meanwhile, Michael had changed into a silky green shirt so he looked like a burly mariachi dancer.

Michael glanced up from buttoning his shirt to assess Jan's appearance. "Hey, you look great! I guess the dress is a little small, but it accentuates your, ah, figure."

Jan looked down at the low-cut neckline and hoped all of her assets remained inside the dress. She could barely breathe, and because the top was backless, she had to go without her cute lacy bra, which was worrisome. Although the top was clearly way too small, the skirt was too large. It was like Goldilocks had had a major wardrobe failure. However, strategically placed safety pins were doing their part to keep the flowing flamenco skirt up around her waist. At the bottom, the skirt sported festive ruffles that matched the ones Swoosie was wearing. Jan wasn't entirely sure this outfit was any better than the shredded dress. Her stomach was doing back flips and her hands were shaking. It would be so humiliating if she actually fainted. Or threw up. She closed her eyes and tried to will her stomach to settle down.

Jan tugged on one of the shoulders of the blouse and then bent down to pet Swoosie's head. "Hi Swoosie. Nice outfit. You have to be good now."

Swoosie wagged and sat down expectantly. Michael was still fussing with a button and Jan asked, "So what am I supposed to do?"

"Just follow behind us. Put your hands over your head and clap to the beat of the music. Oh, and try to look happy. Like I said, everyone will be watching Swoosie, so it's easy. Hey, the intro music is starting up. That's our cue!"

The muscles in Jan's body clenched in fear. "But I'm not ready!"

"You are now. Come on Swoosie!" Michael waved a treat in Swoosie's direction and the dog followed him toward the entry to the garden area where wedding guests were gathering. Michael whistled loudly and the group parted to let him through. Swoosie sat down in front of him and he bent down and whispered something in the dog's ear.

Boisterous merengue music flooded the area and Swoosie hopped up on her hind legs. She took a few steps in front of Michael, her ruffles swaying merrily. He raised his hands over his head and clapped to the beat of the music, turning in front of Swoosie. Still on her hind legs, Swoosie followed him and when he moved forward, she stepped backward, so it looked like they were dancing. Michael looked over his shoulder at Jan, raised his eyebrows meaningfully, and waved slightly at her with one of his upraised hands.

Startled into motion, Jan tried not to think about all the eyes in the crowd and stepped out into the walkway to follow the dancing pair. She did as instructed and walked behind them clapping as the dog performed. It was remarkable that this was the same obnoxious animal that had played keep-away in the trees. The little white dog was being so cute. And as Michael had predicted, the audience adored her.

Swoosie sat, presumably to rest her legs, and Michael put his hand on her head and danced around the dog in a circle. Then Swoosie got up on her hind feet again and Michael took one of her front paws, spinning around her. The routine went on with more spinning and dancing as the audience clapped and cheered them on all the way down the aisle.

For the big finish, Swoosie hopped behind Michael up to the floral awning where the ceremony was to be held. Michael pulled a little bag that contained the wedding rings out of his pocket with a flourish. He hung the bag around Swoosie's neck and the dog sat quietly next to him, panting and smiling as the music faded. The wedding crowd was still cheering and Michael motioned to Swoosie, who stood up and then stretched deeply, bowing to her legion of adoring fans. Jan sidled up next to the pair and took a deep breath. It was over at last. And apparently she was now part of the wedding party.

Michael grinned at her and whispered, "See, that wasn't so bad, was it?"

Jan shrugged, hoping the panicky feeling in her chest would go away soon. Her mother probably wouldn't appreciate it if she had a heart attack in the middle of the ceremony. "At least my dress didn't fall off. But Swoosie was amazing. I can't believe you taught her to do that."

Michael wiggled his eyebrows. "I have hidden talents."

"You mean other than being an irresponsible pet owner and leering at little girls?"

Michael made a mock serious face and put both hands over his heart as if he were being stabbed, "You're killing me here. I'm not really that bad once you get to know me."

~

Swoosie's wasn't the only performance at the wedding. The canine dance routine was just the beginning. Jan suffered through her mother's sock puppet show for perhaps the 7,000th time and a skit parodying one of the old Toilet King ads. After all of the acts were over, she patiently stood next to Michael and Swoosie and watched as her mother promised to love yet another person for the rest of her life. On a positive note, the Toilet King had opted against wearing his blue jumpsuit and his hair was a distinguished salt-and-pepper, rather than purple spikes. He looked downright normal and even somewhat handsome in his jacket and tie.

After the bride and groom scuttled down the aisle, Jan followed Michael toward the tent where the reception was being held. Her heart had finally stopped racing and she was starting to feel almost normal again. At least it was over and no clothes had fallen off. Maybe she should thank Michael for getting her the costume, but she really wanted to get out of it so she could breathe again. The idea of eating and then having even less room in her precariously tight blouse didn't hold much appeal.

The tent was filled with people milling around talking. The guests all seemed to know each other, except for Jan. That was the downside of moving around so much when she was young. Even though she had lived in San Diego for quite a while when her mother was doing local TV, they never stayed in one place for long, so she didn't know anyone at the wedding.

Michael didn't seem to be having the same problem. He had an infectious smile and as Jan followed him through the crowd, it seemed like everyone knew him and wanted to say hello. He stopped at the buffet table and was laughing with someone who appeared to be a long-lost friend. Swoosie was standing next to him also enjoying herself, surveying the vast array of food displayed on the table. As a waiter walked by, Swoosie followed his movements, her white muzzle pointed directly at the tray of prime rib he was carrying, much like a compass homing in on due north.

Michael turned away from his conversation to look back at her. "Jan, come meet my old buddy Bob."

Bob was a slightly balding man with short legs. He looked like a former linebacker who had been tackled a few too many times. His hazel eyes were fixating on Jan's blouse, never moving from her cleavage as she walked over to join them. Jan looked down hurriedly to verify that all of her body parts were still inside her blouse.

She reached out her hand to introduce herself. "Hi Bob. My name is Jan."

"I liked the dance you did. So are you a stripper or something?"

Jan shook her head. It seemed Bob had already discovered the open bar and spent some serious time there. "No. I wasn't really dancing. Just walking and clapping my hands. Swoosie and Michael were doing the dancing. It was a modified version of the merengue in fact, which is a type of music and dance from the Dominican Republic. Professionally speaking, I'm a librarian."

"Wow, that's a great shtick. Do you wear big horn-rimmed glasses and then take them off and let down your hair? I have fantasies like that all the time. Brainy chicks wearing glasses are hot."

Jan pulled her hand away from his clammy grip. "No. I mean I really am a librarian. I have a master's degree in library science and I work at the library in Alpine Grove. And I don't wear glasses."

Bob expression fell as his illusions of scantily clad librarians were shattered for the moment. Jan looked down at her ruffles. Did this guy ever actually look at the face of any woman, or was it just this outfit that made her bust line uniquely intriguing?

Bob looked over at Michael. "Hey man, I'm heading back to the bar. Do you want anything?"

Michael looked up from handing Swoosie a potato chip. "No thanks, Bob. It was good to see you again."

He turned to Jan. "I didn't know you were a librarian. That's interesting. I mean what little kid thinks, 'Hey, I wanna grow up to be a librarian'?"

Jan's lips tightened. "I did. When I was in junior high school, my mom was married to a guy named Tony for a while. I didn't like him and there was a library that I could walk to from our house. There was an ad on the bulletin board that said they were looking for people to shelve books, but you had to be fourteen. I was there almost every day anyway, and on my fourteenth birthday I asked about the job. Because of child labor laws, I could only work a certain number of hours per week, but I loved being there. It was much better than being at home."

Michael shrugged and popped a potato chip into his mouth. "I guess I was out playing sports when I was that age. I don't really remember anymore." He looked around. "So are we supposed to be getting a dinner here or just the buffet? I'm hungry."

Although Michael was certainly nice to look at, eye candy didn't make up for the fact that he obviously had the sensitivity of a tree stump. Why had she even bothered explaining anything to him? It was well past time to be rid of him and his obnoxious dog whose nose was perilously close to the buffet tabletop. As Jan looked on, Swoosie silently and carefully slipped a piece of bread off a tray with her tongue and snuffled it down. It was hard to believe a dog could eat so quickly and quietly. Jan turned back to Michael. "I think I'll skip the food. Do you know where my dress is?"

"Didn't you leave it with your mom's suitcase in the dressing area? I was watching Swoosie, so I wasn't paying attention to what you were doing. But thanks for being in the routine. Bob sure liked it."

"Yes, Bob is charming. How do you know him?"

"He was one of the kids I played sports with in junior high. In high school he was a football star, but we didn't really hang out. After that, we lost track of each other."

"What a shame."

At her tone, Michael glanced up from his chip and the bowl of dip. "Hey, he's a good guy. Or he was, anyway. He was there during some tough times."

"I'm sure he is a fine human being. By the way, you might want to keep a closer eye on Swoosie. I think she has inhaled most of this side of the buffet table."

Michael looked at the empty platters on the buffet and then down at the dog, who was sitting and slowly wagging her tail in a feeble attempt to look innocent. "Swoosie! We've talked about this. Counter surfing is bad. You're a bad, bad girl!" He stepped away from the table, pulling the dog with him. "Thanks for letting me know. I wonder what was on those trays." A look of concern crossed his face. "There wasn't anything bad she could have eaten, was there?"

Jan shrugged. "I don't know. I was entertaining Bob, remember? I do know chocolate is bad for dogs. But I don't think this is the dessert section of the buffet."

Michael sighed. "I know my veterinarian way too well. Swoosie eats everything. It's better now that she's older, but she's eaten towels, a coffee table, part of a door, and any food she can get at. I can't leave anything out in my kitchen at all. When a, um, friend brought me dinner one time, we put it on top of the refrigerator and somehow Swoosie got up there, knocked it down, and ate a bunch of it. Including some of the glass casserole dish. That was a bad one. She had surgery and everything." He bent down and stroked the white fur on the dog's head. "Are you okay, girl? I really can't take you anywhere, can I?"

Swoosie looked pleased that Michael wasn't angry at her anymore, then her brow furrowed and her expression changed to one of distress. She stood up quickly.

Michael jumped back, "Uh-oh. I know that look. Let's go Swoosie!" Gathering up the leash, he ran away from the buffet table with Swoosie dragging behind him trying to stop. Her body was twisting and she finally was able to gain purchase and dig her paws into the grass, forcing Michael to a halt. The dog's back arched as she retched. Jan and most of the other wedding guests looked on in wonder. It was hard to believe such a small animal could make so much noise while expelling the contents of its stomach.

Michael waved weakly back at the crowd, "Sorry! I think she ate something that disagreed with her."

Jan shook her head. She'd had enough of this guy and this place. Any time she had anything to do with her mother, it was always filled with endless embarrassing scenes, drama, and mayhem. Why should today be any different than the legendary fire of 1977 when the lava lamp exploded? Or the various scandals that littered the newspaper and gossip rags in the 80s? It wasn't like her mother didn't have a bedroom. But no. Mom had to have her romantic interludes outside in odd places. Savvy photographers had learned to follow her around, leading to years of mortifying media coverage with headlines like, "Farm Lady and friend found in the buff on a bluff."

Jan shook her head. Getting a scholarship and leaving San Diego had been the best thing that had ever happened to her. This place was filled with bad memories. And today, because of the open bar, the tone of the reception was likely to go even further downhill. Time to find her clothes and get out of here.

The library had always been her refuge and she was looking forward to returning to her books and her sweet dog Rosa, who didn't eat things she wasn't supposed to. The rotund black dog mostly just spent her day lazily sleeping on the floor of the library office. Jan turned away from the crowd and walked toward the head table to say goodbye to her mother.

After returning to her motel room and packing, Jan called to set up her return flight. She was pleased she'd planned ahead and left her schedule flexible, even if it was more expensive. It wasn't the first time she'd wanted to escape an uncomfortable family situation, after all. Calling Kat was a little more worrisome, since she'd be picking Rosa up earlier than expected and it could be an inconvenience. Although Kat had seemed surprised about the change in plans, she didn't seem to mind and said Jan could pick up Rosa that afternoon.

Chapter 3

Rumors

Back in Alpine Grove, Jan drove out Forest Avenue to the outskirts of town where she lived. As her cheerful little yellow cottage came into view, she breathed a sigh of relief. She always felt a sense of calm when she returned to her tidy little house. The leaves on the huge tree out front were starting to change color, and although the summer flowers in her mini-garden were beginning to fade, the lawn hadn't turned brown yet. Apparently there hadn't been a frost, but she made a mental note to get out the rake this weekend and clean up some of those leaves.

Jan stopped by the bright kelly-green mailbox out front and collected her mail. Then she went inside and dropped her luggage in the hallway. It was odd not to have Rosa there to greet her or see Rosa's wide body snoring away on the old multicolored rag rug in the living room.

Although it was good to be home after all the weirdness and travel, Jan couldn't relax. The library was always a good antidote for anxiety, so she might as well go to work until it was time to pick up Rosa. After grabbing a snack, she locked the door and headed back into town.

The Alpine Grove library wasn't particularly large, but it was crammed full of books. Years before, it had been the town post office, so it wasn't ideally designed, but after many creative modifications, it was now a nice quiet space for people to enjoy reading and research time. Jan greeted a few regular patrons and noted that the other librarian, Jill, was helping an older man find a book back in the woodworking and crafts section. Jill was about twenty years older than Jan and had gray hair that she pulled back into a long braid that fell down to the middle of her back. Periodically, Jill complained about how much work it was to deal with her long hair and that she wanted to cut it. But Jan couldn't imagine her actually doing it; the long braid was part of Jill's identity.

Jill walked up to the desk and leaned forward, putting her elbows on the counter. "What are you doing here?"

Jan picked up a pencil and put it into the cup holder with the others. "I decided to leave early."

"You're not exactly Miss Spontaneity. You had this trip planned for weeks. What happened? And where's Rosa? It was strange to not be tripping over her in the office."

Jan smiled. Jill loved Rosa, but refused to admit it. "I'm picking up Rosa this afternoon. She's staying with a friend of a friend."

"And? Why aren't you in San Diego? Did you ditch your mom's wedding?"

"No, you know I would never do that. But I didn't have a good time." Jan waved her hand in the general direction of Southern California. "The whole thing was strange and stressful and awful. I was tackled by a dog and met a rude man. Oh, and that pretty dress I bought is completely destroyed. I loved that dress."

"So was the rude man cute?" Any mention of a man and Jill wanted to know. No matter how many times Jan told her that she was engaged to her boyfriend Steve, Jill kept trying to find her another man. It was annoying.

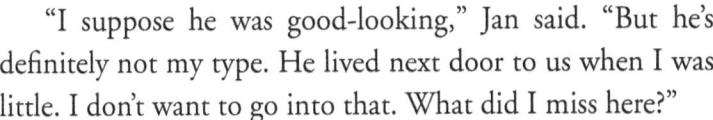

"I suppose he was good-looking," Jan said. "But he's definitely not my type. He lived next door to us when I was little. I don't want to go into that. What did I miss here?"

"Well, I thought Steve was going with you to the wedding, but then I saw him here. Do you want to know more?" Jill made no secret of the fact that she was not a big fan of Steve and delighted in sharing her low opinion of him at every opportunity. It had become a touchy subject between them, but Jan knew that Jill meant well in a kind of over-protective-mother type of way.

"I'm sure it wasn't him." Jan said as she picked up a stack of books. "He had to cancel at the last minute to go on a business trip. It was for a major client. I talked to him before I left."

Jill gave her a knowing look. "That's so typical. I know it was him, all right. Yesterday I had to write a letter to the book distributor. So I used that infernal machine."

"It's called a computer."

"Whatever. I used it, okay? I know it's 1995 and we're all supposed to be 'embracing technology,' but I still hate it. And of course, something happened and then the screen was blank and my letter was gone. I don't know where it went. That never happened with my typewriter, you know. It was the end of the day and I was fed up with it all. So I turned the stupid machine off and locked up. I was so angry that I decided to go for a walk to enjoy the pretty fall weather before I dared get in my car. I needed to clear my head, and it was so beautiful outside. I walked by the H12 and saw Steve come out of one of the rooms with a very blonde woman."

The H12 was a low-budget motel that had earned its moniker because it had 12 rooms. Those rooms were in dire need of restoration and it was not the type of place anyone would go to impress a date.

"The H12? That's not a very nice place. I wonder why he would be meeting a client there."

"Honey, that woman was no client." Jill cleared her throat. "Unless he's selling something more than just drywall. Or maybe *she* was selling something, given how she was dressed."

"You're just saying this because you don't like Steve. He'd never cheat on me."

"I hate to be the one to tell you this, but they looked pretty cozy." Jill crossed her arms. "I'm serious, Jan. I've heard rumors about him before, but I didn't want to pass on anything that was just idle small-town gossip. This time I saw him with my own eyes." She reached out and put her hand on Jan's shoulder and looked into her eyes. "You really need to talk to him, honey."

Jan shook her head. "I'm sure it's all just a misunderstanding. I'll give him a call after I pick up Rosa. Everything will be fine." But the slightly sick feeling she had in her stomach suggested that it might not be.

~

After the conversation about Steve, the rest of the afternoon at the library with Jill was awkward. Jan asked a couple of questions, but Jill kept repeating that she "knew what she saw." Jan decided to leave a little early to pick up Rosa and let Jill lock up. As her car bumped along the driveway toward Kat's house, she replayed the conversation with Jill over in her mind. But she kept coming back to the same place. Steve would never cheat on her. He just wouldn't. They'd been together too long. Maybe sometimes he got angry or didn't understand what she was saying. But after all these years, she knew him. He wasn't a bad person. Sure, he spent a lot of time on the road for work, but Steve always said she was the best thing that had ever happened to him. Jill just didn't get it. Jan was the woman Steve wanted to marry and he would never jeopardize his future with her.

Jan got out of the car and went over to the Tessa Hut straightaway so she could say hello to Rosa. A flash of panic went through her chest at the sight of the empty cage. Where was Rosa? She heard noises outside and peeked out the door. Kat was walking over from the house surrounded by three of her dogs and Rosa on a leash. Jan exhaled with relief. Her black dog was obviously happy to be part of the pack trotting toward her.

Jan waved. "I wondered where Rosa was for a second."

"Yes, she's with me. And everyone else. They all got along well, although I think Rosa may have some issues with cats. The cats took the safe approach and opted to hide while she was here."

"Wasn't she out here in the kennel?"

Kat looked toward the Tessa Hut. "Not exactly. I wanted to ask you about that. Has she ever been in a kennel before?"

"I'm not sure. She was my mother's dog, and my mother is not particularly good about caring for, well, much of anything. I guess you'd say Mom doesn't have a very long attention span. She got Rosa, kept her for a little while, and then gave her to me when taking care of a dog wasn't fun anymore. At first I was angry about it, but Rosa is so sweet, I couldn't just give her away.

"I know that feeling." Kat smiled. "I inherited all of my Great-Aunt Abigail's dogs and cats. And Joel's dog, too."

"You get to work here, where you can take care of your pets. The problem for me was that I have to work all day at the library, and I wasn't sure what to do about Rosa. I talked to Jill, the other librarian, and she was okay with Rosa being our office dog as long as she didn't disturb the patrons or cause any trouble. And she doesn't. She's really good. Sometimes Rosa hangs out with the kids at story time, too. They love her."

Kat nodded. "I guess that makes sense. It's funny; I've been to the library many times and never seen a dog there."

"Rosa mostly sleeps back in the office. Jill complains about how she's in the way all the time, but she really loves her." Jan looked over Kat's shoulder. Joel was walking toward them from the house. "Hi, Joel."

"Hi. Sorry about the problem we had with Rosa."

Jan looked from Joel to Kat. "Problem?"

"More of a mystery, I guess." Joel looked over at Kat. "Didn't you tell her?"

"I was getting to it."

Jan bent down to pet Rosa. "Is she okay? She seems okay. What happened? She didn't get sick or anything, did she?"

Kat shook her head. "No. But she kept getting out of her kennel in the Tessa Hut. We couldn't figure out how she was doing it. I'd put her inside, go to do something, and then I'd turn around and she'd be sitting next to me. It kind of freaked me out, to be honest. We've checked the chain link, the latch—everything. I have no clue what she's doing."

Jan stroked the dog's head. "Wow, Rosa. I didn't know you were so creative."

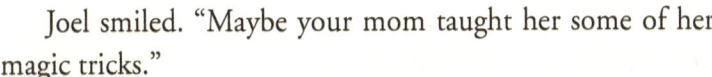

Joel smiled. "Maybe your mom taught her some of her magic tricks."

Kat gave him a blank look. "Magic tricks?"

Jan scowled at the mention of her mother; it was always about her. "That would be her style, I suppose. Anyway, I should get Rosa home. It sounds like everything worked out." Jan pulled her wallet out of her purse and opened it. "How much do I owe you?"

Joel and Kat exchanged a glance and Kat looked down at the photo in Jan's wallet. She pointed at the photo.

"Hey, do you know that guy?"

The picture was a photograph that a Japanese tourist had taken of Jan and Steve in front of a waterfall when they'd been on vacation in Maui many years ago. "Yes, that's my boyfriend Steve."

"Oh. Oops. Sorry to be nosy."

Joel put his hand on Kat's shoulder. "She gets like that."

"I know. I can't help it." Kat said. "It's just that the other day in the parking lot at the grocery store, I saw that guy with a woman and she seriously smacked my car door with a shopping cart. Then she yelled at the guy to be careful of the wine bottle. My poor Toyota has enough problems. It hasn't recovered from moving here. Now it's got another dent. I think the woman was really pissed off and she took it out on my car."

Jan frowned. "What did the woman look like?"

"She was a tall blonde woman wearing a red dress and heels. I don't think I've seen her before. But like I said, I don't know many people like everybody else does in this town. Isn't Cindy your friend? She might know."

Joel nodded. "That's true. Cindy makes it her business to know everybody else's business."

As the implications of what Kat had seen sank in, a sick feeling settled in Jan's stomach. She tried to smile. "I agree. Cindy does know everything. But we're actually not that close. I see her at story time with her son almost every week at the library, and she does love to talk. I told her about my situation with Rosa and she said she knew a solution. I'm glad she led me to you. Rosa looks happy."

Kat reached out to touch her arm. "Are you okay? I'm really sorry we couldn't keep Rosa confined. We talked about it and you don't have to pay us anything. It was such a short time—only a couple of days. It's okay."

Jan sniffed and shook her head. "That's very nice of you, but I'll pay you." She yanked some bills out of her wallet, and thrust them toward Kat. "Is this enough?"

Kat took the money quietly and looked up at Joel questioningly. His eyes widened slightly, but he didn't say anything. Kat turned to Jan again. "That's more than enough. I'm sorry. Did I say something wrong? Sometimes I speak before thinking."

A tear slid down Jan's cheek and she blurted out, "I think Steve is seeing someone behind my back!" Wait. Did she really think that? It was impossible. And even if it were true, why was she telling this to people she hardly knew? She grabbed her purse more tightly, digging her fingernails into the leather. "I know this isn't your problem and I'm so sorry to fall apart like this in the middle of your front yard. It's just it's been a long couple of days with the wedding and travel... and everything. Steve and I have been engaged since I got out of college. We've just been waiting for things to settle down before we get married."

Kat squinted slightly. "I know I haven't lived here long, but Alpine Grove is not exactly a hotbed of activity. I don't think you can get more settled than this, can you?"

Joel gave Kat a long look and turned back to Jan. "I think what Kat wants to say is that maybe you should talk to him."

Jan opened her purse, pulled out a tissue, and wiped her nose. "This is so embarrassing. It's just a big surprise. I really should go. I appreciate your kindness and for taking care of Rosa."

Kat nodded. "No problem. Any time. Like you said, she's a sweet dog. And apparently because of her magical abilities, when she's here she receives the ultra-red-carpet treatment and gets to stay in the house."

Jan smiled weakly and took Rosa's leash from Kat. "Yes, I'll talk to her about that, but I doubt she'll reveal her secrets."

Kat grinned. "Great magicians never do."

～

Jan opened the door to her cottage and Rosa rushed past her into the living room, flopping down on her dog bed with a furry flourish. Jan bent down to stroke the sleek fur on Rosa's head. Somebody was sure glad to be home. Although it was good to be back in her cozy space, Jan was anxious about whatever may or may not be going on with Steve. Maybe it was nothing. But Joel was right; she should call and ask Steve a few questions. He'd probably have a reasonable explanation and everything would be fine. It had to be.

Steve lived in the city because of his job, but he often drove up to Alpine Grove and spent the weekend with Jan.

They'd settled into a routine where he'd arrive on Saturday, they'd go out to dinner or she'd make him dinner. They'd take Rosa for a walk around the neighborhood and go to bed. Then he'd leave early Sunday morning. Because he traveled a lot on business, she usually didn't see him more than one weekend every month.

Last weekend she'd been in San Diego for the wedding, so obviously she hadn't seen him then. But why had he been in Alpine Grove? She had tried to be reasonable and understanding when he'd backed out of attending the wedding at the last minute. Unfortunately, Jill was right about that. It certainly wasn't the first time he had canceled plans with her. And it had been uncomfortable explaining why he wasn't there to her mother.

Jan was tired of her own spinning thoughts. She could go around and around making up stories, or she could just call Steve and find out why he had been here in town. Or she could make dinner, since he probably wasn't home yet anyway. Smiling, she turned to Rosa. "What do you think about dinner?" Rosa jumped up at the mention of the magical word "dinner." As her waistline indicated, feeding time was Rosa's favorite time of day.

After Jan fed Rosa and herself and then ever-so-slowly cleaned up the kitchen, she could no longer think of any decent excuse to put off calling Steve.

"Hi Steve."

"Hey babe, how are you? I guess you made it back okay?"

"Yes. Then I picked up Rosa."

"How's my fuzzy little girl? I miss that sweet dog. Tell her I'll bring her an extra-special treat when I see her."

"Rosa is fine, although I think she's glad to be home."

"Yeah, I wasn't sure about that place you took her."

"They were really nice and Rosa seemed to like the owner. I think it was fine. Actually, I called because I want to ask you something."

Steve sighed and Jan could imagine the long-suffering pained expression on his face. "What now? Do you have something scheduled that I have to do? Sometimes your super-organized Type A thing is annoying."

"No. I have nothing scheduled for you or with you. And, by the way, my mother asked why you weren't at her wedding. I made excuses and apologized for you. But that's not why I want to talk to you. I heard from Jill that you were here in Alpine Grove this weekend. And then someone else said they saw you, too. At the store. With a woman. Who definitely wasn't me."

"Oh, you know I entertain clients all the time."

Jan looped the phone cord around her index finger. "The last I heard you didn't have any clients in this 'backwoods town,' as you like to call it. And most people buying drywall aren't dressed in heels and a slinky red dress, either."

"Oh come on, babe. What? You think I was cheating on you with someone there? That would be stupid."

"So are you saying you're cheating on me when you're at home as well?"

"No. Jeez, that's not what I meant. Don't put words in my mouth, Jan. I just had to meet the daughter of a client. She was visiting Alpine Grove, and I told the guy that I spend a lot of time up there, so I could show her around. You weren't there, so it wasn't my fault I had some free time."

Tears were running down her cheeks and Jan choked back a sob. This had to be the worst pack of lies she'd ever heard. Sure, Steve was a rotten liar, but this was pathetic. How stupid did he think she was? "Entertaining this woman here in Alpine Grove was your *business trip*? The reason you missed my mothers wedding? I'm guessing your client, if there is one, didn't ask you to show the woman the inside of the H12 or how to buy wine at the grocery store."

"Aw come on, Jan; you know me. I wouldn't do anything like that. We've been together for a long time and little Rosie is my favorite dog in the whole world. I'd never do anything to hurt either of you."

Jan wiped her eyes and said stiffly. "Do I know that you wouldn't do that? Do I really? I'm not so sure anymore. Maybe you've just been lying to me all this time. At this point, one thing I do think is that you like Rosa better than you like me. Maybe that's appropriate. I know for certain that I like her better than I like you right now."

"Hey, that's not true. You know how I feel about you. I'll tell you what. I'll make a special trip up to see you this weekend. We can go to the fancy restaurant. You don't have to cook. I'll take you out to dinner. You know we always have a good time. We'll talk about everything. I'll stay over and it will all be fine."

Even though the idea of a potentially conflict-laden scene made her anxious, she did want to see him again. It seemed only fair. In small towns, people gossiped. Maybe it wasn't really his fault. "Okay. I'll give you a chance to explain. And it will be nice to see you again."

"Yeah, it's been a while. That sounds good. I've gotta go now. A client is coming in for a meeting and I need to prep for it. Talk to you later. Love ya."

Jan sank back into her chair, leaned down, and put her face in her hands. She had been complacent about her relationship with Steve for a long time. When they'd met in college, he'd been so romantic and charming, taking her out on dates to restaurants and bringing her flowers. And it didn't hurt that she found his Scandinavian blonde hair and athletic build so attractive. Plus she got along great with his family. He had a big family and holidays were such fun. She'd help his mother cook fantastic meals. Jean was one of her favorite women in the world. On the walks Jan took with Steve and Rosa around the neighborhood after dinner, they used to joke that they were like an old married couple, settled into a comfortable routine.

They'd been together for so long that until now it never even occurred to her that he might be seeing other women. The security of having a steady boyfriend was convenient. Was she just taking it for granted now? Was he? Jan never had to worry about having a date for Valentine's Day or a wonderful extended family to visit during the holidays.

But as she mentally went back over the conversations she'd had with Steve recently, some of the business trips seemed suspicious. He usually called her on Wednesday nights. But what if he wasn't calling from his home? Steve had always said that she was exactly the type of girl he wanted to marry. That made her feel cared for and happy, but he never mentioned an actual date for them to get married. Of course, given her mother's track record, Jan had never pushed to set a date for the wedding, either. Maybe she should have. Now, after all this time, maybe Steve was looking for more excitement. And finding it somewhere else.

Rosa got up, came over to Jan's chair, and placed her muzzle on Jan's thigh. Jan sat up again in the chair and stroked the dog's head. "Thanks for the sympathy, Rosa. I needed that. At least I always have you."

~

After a few bouts of berating herself and some time crying on Rosa's shoulder, Jan decided that there was only one solution to this problem: ice cream. She washed her face, changed her clothes, and set out on a mission to the store to acquire some frozen goodness. Healthful things like soup could work as comfort food for small stresses, but for a relationship implosion like this one, it was time for some serious caloric intake.

Jan stared down into the ice cream case pondering her options. She picked up a carton with a smiling cow on it. In this instance, it might be necessary to go all out and get the obscenely expensive designer-style Rocky Road made with pristine cream from only the happiest of bovines.

The sound of off-key singing came from the back of the store, and Jan looked away from her ice cream label. Near an end cap stacked with cans of chocolate syrup, Kat was grinning at another woman with a big mop of curly hair who was doing the cha-cha down the ice cream aisle toward Jan. Kat waved at Jan, smiled, and shrugged slightly.

Kat pushed her cart up to Jan and introduced the other woman. "Hi Jan. This is my friend Maria. We used to work together. Now she comes up here to tell me stories of Corporate America to ensure I never lose my mind and consider returning."

Maria was wearing a very tight leopard-print dress that showed off her shapely form. Jan was impressed she could dance so well in the stiletto heels she was wearing.

Jan put out her hand. "Hi. I'm Jan."

Maria shook her hand and said, "I'm thinking you're having a relationship situation. Your hand is cold and you've been fondling that ice cream. Women don't stand in front of the ice cream case deliberating like that unless they've got a man problem."

Jan glared at Kat. "Did you *tell* her? Are you spreading my business all around town?"

Kat shook her head. "No. My lips are sealed. Maria is gifted in the relationship and food departments. If it involves men or junk food, she has a wealth of insights."

Maria put her hand on her hip. "You betcha. I'm like a sleuth. I can spot a bad man situation anywhere. Here's what I know. Your eyes are red. You were crying, right? That means your man...okay, maybe your woman...I'm cool with that, too. But whatever. Your 'significant other' has done you wrong. Do you have a POSSLQ? Did he just move out? Okay, maybe not that. But it's something bad. I don't even know you, but I can tell you're just way, way too close to that over-priced Rocky Road right there."

Jan's eyes widened. "What's a possle-que?"

Maria smiled. "Aw, come on. Everyone knows that. It's an acronym. Person of Opposite Sex Sharing Living Quarters. So do you have one? Did he move out? Or she. Sorry. But then it would be a person of the *same* sex, or PSSSLQ, but that just sounds like hissing in the middle because of that extra S, so it's hard to say without sounding creepy."

Jan straightened. "No, my boyfriend is not my POSSLQ. He lives in the city, but I see him on weekends quite a bit."

Kat said, "But he's your fiancé, right?"

"Yes."

Maria nodded knowingly. "Okay, there you go. He's your man, even if you aren't living together. Now what did he do? Because I know he did something."

Jan stammered, "I'm not sure exactly. I don't think I want to talk about it. I should just get my ice cream and go home."

Kat reached out to touch Jan's hand. "Maria and I are having a Wine and Whine event tonight. Would you like to come?"

"Wine and what?"

Maria pushed a chunk of unruly hair back behind her ear. "A Wine and Whine. We drink wine and we whine about whatever we want to whine about. Stupid bosses. Bad boyfriends. Uncomfortable shoes. Whatever is on your mind. We are equal-opportunity whiners."

Kat leaned on her cart. "What she means is that it's kind of a free-for-all. Talk about what you want. Or nothing. You can listen to us gripe about people you don't know. But the wine will flow. You might feel better if you have a little company. I've spent some time sitting in an empty house with a bunch of dogs feeling sorry for myself, so I know what I'm talking about here. If you're gonna have a pity party, sometimes it's better not to be alone. More people can help."

"And more wine," Maria added.

Kat said, "Think of it as a 'girls' night' or something, if that makes it sound better to you. We'll be at my house and Joel is off doing something nerdy, so he won't be around, either. Just my dogs and cats. You can even bring Rosa. Everyone likes her."

Maria bent over the counter and looked down at the colorful cartons of ice cream. She turned to Kat. "I think we need some of that Rocky Road. So what's in Rocky Road, anyway? Do we know what makes it rocky? It's all frozen. They could have put anything in there. Rocks, even."

Jan said, "Originally Rocky Road was just chocolate ice cream, but now it usually has chocolate chips, almonds, and marshmallows. It was invented by William Dreyer in 1929."

Maria gave Jan a blank stare and then turned to Kat. "Wow. How does anyone even know that?"

"She's a librarian," Kat replied.

Jan blushed slightly. "I'm sorry. Steve hates it when I spout off facts like that. I tend to remember little tidbits of information. He says my brain is wired funny."

Maria squinted slightly at Jan. "Hmm. We need to talk about this Steve guy. Time to cha-cha back to the wine aisle! We're gonna need the extra-big bottle for tonight." Maria started to move forward, saying, "One-two-cha-cha-cha!" as she sashayed down the aisle.

Kat turned to Jan. "She's taking dancing lessons."

"I see."

"I need to catch up with Maria. Will we see you later?"

Jan nodded. "Sure. Okay. Do you want me to bring anything?"

"No, Maria has only just begun to shop. She's a power grocery shopper. Joel and I will be eating slightly odd food for the rest of the week. I just need to try to keep her away from the Twinkie display. See you later!"

"Okay."

Kat looked over her shoulder as she hustled down the aisle with the cart after Maria, "And don't forget Rosa!"

~

Jan scowled at herself in the mirror as she reapplied her face. She hated her freckles and unmanageable wavy hair, so she spent a lot of time trying to get both of them under control. When applying cover-up, there was a fine line between "flawless-and-fresh" and "zombie-pancake." Given that today was clearly a bad hair day, she gave up and yanked her hair into a ponytail. She twisted her wavy hair up into the standard knot she usually wore to work and jammed in a few bobby pins for good measure. It would have to do.

She looked down at Rosa, who was sleeping next to the bathroom door. "Okay Rosa, it's a good thing you ate earlier because we're going for a car ride."

Rosa lifted her head, looking concerned.

"Don't worry. You will eat again. I've never missed giving you a meal, have I?"

Apparently accepting the idea that she would get food someday, Rosa put her head back down on her paws and sighed heavily.

Jan leaned toward the mirror and dabbed a tissue on her lower lid, trying to remove the extraneous mascara around her hazel eyes. She jammed the mascara wand back into the tube and threw it into the drawer. "Okay, I give up. Let's go."

It seemed that Rosa's dinner had enough time to settle and would not be making a return visit all over the back seat of the car. As Jan slowly drove down the bumpy driveway toward Kat's house, Rosa was just quietly sitting and staring out the window, not racing back and forth anxiously like she had last time. Good girl!

Jan pulled into a spot under a tree. Kat, Maria, and several dogs were starting down the front steps of the house, looking like they were on a mission. What were they doing?

Jan got out of the car, clipped the leash on Rosa, and grabbed the bag with the food and the little hostess gift she'd brought. The dog hurled her body out of the car, obviously excited to be back with her canine buddies. Jan waved at the two women. "Hi, I made it!"

Kat smiled and waved back. "We're heading over to the Tessa Hut. Maybe you can help solve the mystery."

Jan and Rosa followed the parade to the outbuilding and crowded inside with the others. Jan decided she probably had overdressed for the Wine and Whine, not realizing that it would include standing around in a dusty kennel. On the other hand, Maria was wearing a tight black dress that wrapped around her shapely form like a wet suit. It was remarkable that she could move her legs at all. Jan's flowery print skirt and jacket were dowdy by comparison.

Kat opened the gate and said, "Okay folks. I need suggestions. How does a dog get out of a locked kennel? Dogs don't have opposable thumbs. Joel is annoyed with me because I said he didn't fix the kennel. According to him, there's nothing to fix. But according to Rosa, it's not escape-proof."

Jan looked down at Rosa. "So? How did you do it?" Rosa ignored the question and wagged enthusiastically.

Maria ran a hand across the kennel fencing. "That's one tricky dog you have. My sleuthing abilities don't extend to chain link. I think we need to think like a dog. Kat, get down to Rosa's level."

"What?" Kat said, "Why me?"

"You don't really think I'm gonna get down on that floor in this dress do you? A) I might not be able to get back up without ripping something and B) Ick. I know there's dog snot down there."

"Fine. You are such a girl about stuff like this." Kat said as she got down on all fours and was immediately crowded by the dogs, who thought what she was doing was unique, amazing, and extremely worthy of investigation. She pushed Lori's nose away from her face. "Lori, eww, stop that."

Maria nodded. "I'm girlie and proud of it. If you insist on wearing those ugly blue jeans all the time, you're gonna get nominated for tasks like this. So what do you see?"

Kat turned her head to look around her. "Well, mostly dogs." She shoved Linus, the huge hairy dog, over toward the doorway. "Listen Big Guy, you are just going to have to move. You don't fit in here." Looking dejected, Linus lumbered out through the gate, turned, and glared at her.

Outside the kennel, Jan crouched down to dog level. "I don't think she could dig out. There's no evidence of claw marks, either."

"Nope. We checked." Kat said. "And we've checked the wood on the building too. It's fine. No holes."

Maria looked down at Rosa. "Not to be rude, but that's one full-figured dog. I don't think she is much of an athlete, is she? I'm thinking jumping and climbing isn't an option for her. She's not like one of those agility dogs that can scale walls and jump through tires and stuff."

"Definitely not," Jan said. "At home and at the library, mostly she naps."

Maria said to Kat, "Okay, crawl around and then jump up on the gate like a fat dog."

Kat glared at Maria as she reached up to close the gate. "You're enjoying this a little too much." But she complied, crawling and shoving furry canine bodies out of her way. Then she got on her knees and leaned up with her hands on the gate. "Happy now?"

Maria stared at the gate. "I got nothing here."

Lori, the black-and-white border collie, was still inside the kennel with Kat. The dog was having a good time, since all this human crawling activity was a lot of fun. Lori jumped on the gate and stood on her hind legs next to Kat, giving her cheek a slurp, just to be social. Kat wiped her face with the back of her hand. "Thanks, Lori. You're being really helpful here."

"I think I know what Rosa did," Jan said. "See where Lori is located in relation to the gate? She could poke her nose in that gap and push up the latch. Rosa has a kind of pointy nose too, particularly for a Lab."

Maria said, "Yeah, that's what gives her that kinda pinhead look."

"Well, I guess she's not the prettiest Lab," Jan said. "But she could get her nose in there, push up the latch, open the gate, and get out."

Kat sat back on her haunches and put her hands on her knees. "And then she did the same thing again to close the gate behind her? What dog does that?"

Jan said, "Well maybe if she did it quickly the door would swing closed and the latch would fall back down?"

Maria flipped the latch up and down. "Good enough for me. It's better than any other theory we have. Who knew that a dog could be so sneaky? I think we need to celebrate with some wine."

Kat stood up and looked at the latch. "It's got a hole. I could put a leash clip in the hole, and then she couldn't push it up. Problem solved! Jan, you're a genius. I agree; let's go have wine. It's getting cold out here."

Jan followed the women and dogs up the stairs into the house. She entered the house and noticed the aroma of aged wood as she crossed from the entryway into the kitchen. It made sense that a log house would smell a little like a tree. Although the house was old, it was obvious that Kat and Joel (probably mostly Joel) had been working on the place. Various areas of wood trim had the shiny white, clean look of new, unfinished lumber, which contrasted with the old, seasoned look of the logs.

Maria made a beeline for the box of wine on the counter and grabbed a glass from the cabinet. "I'm pouring. Who's in?"

Jan reached into her bag and said, "You can save this for later, but I brought a bottle as a thank-you for inviting me."

"Hey, that looks way better than the box," Maria said. "It has a pretty horse on the label and even a cork. Stylish. Let's go with that. Thanks!"

Kat opened the pantry and stared into it. She looked over her shoulder at Jan. "Please sit down. Relax while I figure out what we're going to eat. I've got the drink and be merry part, but the eat part of the equation is still in question."

Maria said, "You could make pasta."

Kat sighed. "I really need to learn how to cook. It's time to break out of my pasta habit. But most of the time Joel cooks, so that has made it easy to avoid the issue."

Jan walked over to the pantry and looked over Kat's shoulder at the contents within. "That's quite an eclectic combination of foodstuffs."

Maria looked up from pouring the wine. "Foodstuffs?"

Kat said, "I told you that shopping with Maria is an adventure. Joel always manages to use up the more unusual things eventually, but it takes a while."

Jan turned to the refrigerator. "Do you mind if I take a look?"

"Go for it," Kat said.

Jan surveyed the contents of the fridge. "Well, you have milk and flour and vegetables. You could make fettuccine Alfredo or a cream soup. All you need to do is cook the veggies and create a roux for a béchamel sauce."

Kat frowned. "I think you've overestimated my cooking abilities."

"I'm *sure* you have," Maria said.

"Don't you have any cookbooks?" Jan said. "If you want some, we have many selections at the library. They are in the 641 section. In fact, 641.51 is cooking for beginners. You should start there."

Maria leaned back on the counter and raised her glass toward Jan. "That's impressive. I guess you can take the librarian out of the library, but it looks like you can't take the library out of the librarian. Your brain must be full."

Jan laughed. "I don't think anyone has ever put it that way. But if you'd shelved as many cookbooks as I have, you'd know where they go, too."

Maria handed Jan a glass of wine. "I hope this wine goes with whatever sauce you were talking about. But if it doesn't, that's fine too."

Jan handed the wine over to Kat. "I don't drink. But technically, since it's a red, no, it's not supposed to be consumed with a béchamel sauce. But you're not having it with dinner, either. It's an aperitif."

Kat took a sip from her glass of wine. "Works for me."

~

Jan spent an enjoyable few hours showing Kat how to cook dinner and watching the two women enthusiastically eat and drink wine. It had been years since she had just hung out with friends cooking and talking. After she graduated, Jan and her friends had drifted apart as they started new lives at libraries in various locations around the country.

After feeding themselves and the dogs, the women gathered in the living room on the old sofas, which were covered with sheets and old blankets to repel the copious quantities of dog hair. Lori leaped up next to Kat and curled up in a corner for a post-dinner nap. The big dog Linus was snoring loudly on the floor, looking a lot like a bear rug.

Maria leaned back and slumped down in the sofa. "That was some fantastic food. Larry would swoon. It's better than that Italian place he used to take me to."

"Who is Larry?" Jan asked.

"Larry was my man, but we broke up. It was fun for a while because he liked to take me out, and I like to go out. But he's such a lawyer. I couldn't deal with all the motions and appeals. Plus, I think he's got the hots for the hostess lady at that Italian restaurant. But she's never gonna give him the time of day. He's just lucky someone as fabulous as I am was willing to date him. He's got no prayer with her."

Kat giggled. "Motions and appeals? Gross. That's just way too much information."

"Get your mind out of the gutter, girlfriend," Maria said. "I meant he talks about all that legal stuff all the time. It's a good sleep aid, but sometimes I want to be awake, you know what I mean?"

Jan snickered. "Oh wait, you mean Lawrence Lowell, the lawyer? You went out with *him*?"

Maria turned to face Jan. "Yes, I did. And it was good for a while. But that's done now. You're the one with the man problems, right? Isn't that why you went on that trip?"

"No, that was my mother's wedding," Jan said. "And there was an obnoxious man there, too. It was horrible. I think I'm having a string of bad luck."

Kat peered over her wine glass. "So was he cute?"

"Why does everyone ask me that? Yes, okay. He was extremely good-looking. Tall with dark wavy hair and brown eyes. But he's not my type."

Maria said, "Do you seriously think a lawyer is my type? That doesn't matter. I don't believe in the whole concept of types. It's outdated. This is the mid-90s, ladies. We need to be free to date out of type if we want to."

"But I don't *want* to date him," Jan said. "He was unpleasant and his dog was even worse. Steve is my fiancé. We've been together for a long time and I thought we were happy. But now I'm not sure he's happy."

Kat said, "So did you talk to him?"

Maria waved her glass, sloshing a few drops of wine on the sofa cover. "Forget talking. Did you dump him? Because he sounded like he needed some serious dumping. If you go waltzing around town with a bimbo, you need to get dumped."

"Yes, I did talk to him. I kept putting it off," Jan said. "But I finally did make myself call him. It was all okay. I think it's just a misunderstanding. He's taking me out to dinner this weekend."

Maria tipped the top of her wine glass toward Jan. "Did he cop to screwing around on you or not? Because I'm sorry; I've seen that place and nobody is going to the H12 for the ambiance."

"No. I suppose he didn't really admit to anything per se. He said we could talk about things."

"Per se? What does that mean? I don't like where this is going," Maria said. "When men get weasel-like and wishy-washy, you just can't trust anything they say."

"I didn't know the trip was for your mother's wedding," Kat said. "I guess you didn't have a good time? What happened?"

Jan closed her eyes and leaned back on the couch. It was nice that Kat had obviously made an effort to change the subject, but this subject wasn't much better. "What *didn't* happen? Anything having to do with my mother is always strange." She exhaled loudly and then explained who her mother was and whom she was marrying.

After Jan had described the Toilet King's commercials, Kat started giggling quietly. By the time Jan had finished relating the entire tale of the torn dress, lost dog, the merengue, puppet shows, Bob the drunk guy, and Swoosie's digestive indiscretions, they were all laughing uncontrollably. In retrospect, the whole situation was funny, even to Jan.

Maria had rolled off her chair and was lying on the floor next to Linus. "Oh man, my stomach hurts. That's the best wedding story ever. I want to be invited to your mom's next one."

Jan snickered and said, "Don't worry; I'm sure there will be another one. I just can't believe Michael got me to do the merengue in front of people. I never do that kind of thing. In fact, I hate even the idea of performing anything. I practically flunked English in tenth grade because I refused to do the oral report. At the wedding, when the music started I thought I was going to throw up. But after it was over I felt exhilarated in a way. Maybe because it was so scary. And I really did it."

"That sounds intense," Kat said. "But wait...a librarian who almost flunked English? No way." She stared thoughtfully at her wine as she swirled it around in the glass. "Hey, if you put a cowboy hat on this Michael guy, it sounds like he looks like a younger, hotter version of the Marlboro man."

"And he can dance!" Maria said. "That's gonna get my attention every time. He can even dance with hairy white dogs. Impressive."

"Yes, well, I'll probably never see him again," Jan said. "I don't even know where he lives. He was too busy trying to find his annoying dog or talking to his friends to have much of a conversation with me."

Maria glanced at Kat and then turned to Jan. "I'm noticing that you don't get that animated about this Steve guy. Do you even like him? If you're planning to marry Steve, you should at least like him. I'm a romantic you know, and personally, I prefer to hold out for true love. But even if you're not like me and you're gonna settle for this guy, you gotta at least start out with some 'like' happening, anyway."

"Of course I do," Jan said, sitting up on the sofa again. "We have a comfortable relationship. Maybe it's not rip-roaring hilarity all the time, but it's easy being with him. There's not a lot of stress like there is being around my mother and all her drama. It's a relief, really."

Maria widened her eyes. "Sounds boring. I sure hope he isn't that dull in bed."

The color rose on Jan's cheeks, "I, ah, well…"

Kat stood up quickly, and all of the dogs leapt up after her as she started collecting the glasses and various snack foods strewn around the living room. Jan helped her clean up, but kept replaying what Maria had said in her mind. Boring? Was it possible her relationship with Steve had become so routine and humdrum that she hadn't noticed she didn't even like him anymore? And after so much time, obviously they weren't teenagers anymore groping at each other all the time. But it wasn't that bad. Was it?

~

After Jan left and Maria had retired to the downstairs bedroom, aka Kat's office, Kat curled up on the couch with a novel and Lori, who was enjoying having her fuzzy ears scritched while Kat read. Now that it was quiet, Tessa the golden retriever, and Chelsey the small brown-and-white dog, had ventured up to the living room from their lair in the downstairs hallway. They were curled up on the floor with Linus, who was lying flat on his side snoring audibly. Tripod the three-legged cat was ensconced in Kat's lap. All the fur and snoring around her had a soporific effect and Kat was startled awake when Tripod shot off her lap. All four dogs launched toward the door, barking furiously.

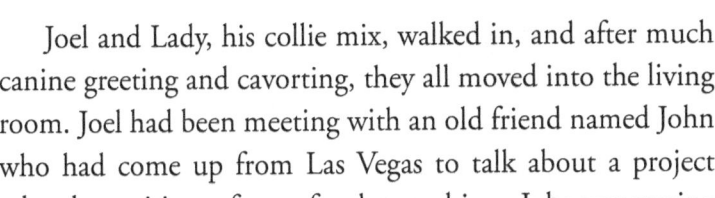

Joel and Lady, his collie mix, walked in, and after much canine greeting and cavorting, they all moved into the living room. Joel had been meeting with an old friend named John who had come up from Las Vegas to talk about a project related to writing software for slot machines. John was staying in Joel's small cabin, affectionately known as The Shack.

Kat unfolded her legs from under her and wrapped her arms around her knees to try to discourage Tripod from returning to her lap. As Joel walked toward her across the room, Kat enjoyed the delicious fluttery thrill she always got when she saw him. "Hi. How was the meeting? Does John like The Shack?"

Joel sat down on the sofa next to Kat, wrapped his arms around her, and gave her a quick kiss hello. "It was good. John is settling in okay. I think he's having trouble adjusting to the quiet. Being in the middle of a forest is different from the bright lights of Vegas. At least The Shack smells better now. I think the burnt smell is finally mostly gone now."

Kat nodded. "Well that's an improvement, anyway. He probably wasn't happy when he found out that Allison threw your TV out the window before she tried to set The Shack on fire. I think there are football games on, aren't there?"

"It's fall. There are always football games on. I gave him a book about database theory, which will help him sleep. How was your evening? Is Maria still here somewhere?"

Kat moved closer to Joel, snuggling up next to him and nudging Tripod aside. "She has retired to my office. I think she may have indulged in a little too much in the liquid aspect of the Wine and Whine. She didn't really do much whining herself, but I think she may have stressed out Jan."

"I'm not finding this particularly difficult to imagine."

"She said that Jan's relationship with her fiancé was boring. I think Jan had never really thought of it that way. Maria calls us boring all the time and it doesn't bother me."

Joel raised an eyebrow suggestively and smiled. He traced the outline of her jaw with his fingertips. "That's because you know we're not always boring."

Trying not to let him distract her from the point, Kat said, "Well, yes. I do know that. But I felt bad for Jan, since I invited her. She really seemed surprised and upset. But the good news is that I think she figured out the Rosa mystery. Or maybe Lori did."

"I know border collies are smart, but Lori isn't that smart."

Lori raised her head at the sound of her name and Kat reached over to stroke the dog's soft fur. "Aw, now you'll give Lori a complex. Actually, she jumped up on the kennel gate and Jan noticed that Lori's pointy little snout was right near the latch. The current theory is that Rosa pushed the latch up with her nose, went out, and the latch fell back into place. Or she went out and closed the latch."

Joel shook his head. "I'm not sure I'm buying into this idea."

"It's a working theory. And the solution is simple. I can just put a little clip on the latch to keep her in."

"It's worth a try. And it's a cheap fix, which is good. I did some more calculations on the costs for building the kennel and it's going to be more than we thought. Concrete work is expensive."

"Well, I still have money from the inheritance."

"But you'll want to have something to live on until you get things going."

"It's no big deal. Something will work out."

Joel released her from his embrace and looked into her blue eyes. "I'm serious. Not having any money in Alpine Grove is a problem. You can't just go and get another job, unless you plan to become a logger. Having a financial buffer gives you some security."

"No. I'm not going to go chop down trees for a living," Kat said. "Chain saws disturb me. But I do have some freelance-writing money. And the house is paid for." She grinned. "Plus, I'm hoping you'll feed me if I start to starve."

Joel leaned back away from her on the couch. "You're kidding, right?"

Kat picked some dog hair off her jeans and threw it on the floor. What was this about? "Have I ever asked you for money? Let me answer for you. No, I haven't."

Joel crossed his arms across his chest. "Of course you haven't, because you just inherited money. Why would you?"

Sensing dissent, Tessa stood up and put her golden snout on Kat's thigh. Kat rubbed the velvety fur. "It's okay, Tessa. We're talking about money." She turned to Joel. "And it seems Joel is going to be weird about it."

"I don't think it's weird to say that you should have savings. In case things don't work out."

"What things do you mean, exactly?"

"Well, the dog-boarding business. Or writing. Things. You've only boarded one dog so far. What if you hate owning a kennel?"

"Don't you think I've thought about that? I boarded one dog and she immediately escaped. So far my track record is not good." As if she weren't already insecure enough about starting a business, she'd been bested by a fat Labrador retriever. How pathetic.

The hard glint in Joel's green eyes softened and he leaned over to kiss her gently. "I'm not saying you can't do it. Just that it's good to have a back-up plan. And that requires money. When I lost my job, it was a good thing I had some money saved up and that I'd paid for The Shack in cash, so I'd have a place to live."

Kat tilted her head. "So how much money *do* you have? Are you secretly a gazillionaire?"

"Hardly. But I have savings."

"You're not going to tell me, are you?"

Joel narrowed his eyes and leaned away from her again. "So do you want to look at my bank statements?"

Kat shook her head and raised both hands in surrender. "No. I'm not suggesting anything. You brought it up. I'm not some gold digger trying to get into your wallet. It's your money."

"Okay."

Kat got up off the couch and the dogs all stood up expectantly. "Okay." But she was pretty sure it wasn't okay.

⌒

In bed, curled up with a book and her black-and-white cat Murphee, Kat listened to the sound of feline snoring and tried to get into the plot of her novel. It wasn't working, because she kept reliving the conversation with Joel in her mind.

Because he spent daylight hours working on repairing the house, Joel usually spent a few hours at night working on various projects on his computer downstairs. He was a night owl and whatever he did was something nerdy related to programming circuit boards. Kat wasn't entirely sure. The geek factor was way too high for her to even want to know.

Was he feeling like she was taking advantage of him? After his money? What money? His last girlfriend had been a super model. She didn't need money. Since Kat had gotten her inheritance from her Great-Aunt Abigail, she now had money, too. Not super-model-level money, but some money. Maybe his negative reaction to her joke about money was a male ego thing. Being the breadwinner? Maybe underneath it all he was a complete cheapskate. But it didn't seem like he was most of the time. She loved Joel, but he could be pretty close-mouthed about a lot of things. Annoying herself with her endless circular thoughts, Kat sighed and flopped over onto her back. Murphee squalled loudly, expressing her displeasure at being squished.

"Sorry Murph. You could move, you know." The cat stood up, stretched, and walked across Kat's stomach to find a warm spot. Kat closed her eyes and tried to will her brain to shut up.

She stirred when Joel crawled into bed. He wrapped his arms around her and pushed her long wavy hair aside so he could nuzzle her neck. Kat turned her head to look at him. "I guess you're not mad at me anymore."

"I wasn't mad. And you're all warm. I'm not really thinking about that anymore."

"So it seems. But I am."

Joel lifted his head from her neck, looked at her face, and sighed. "Oh."

"Maria keeps leaving her *Cosmo* magazines here and I read an article about how most couples break up because of fights about money. Didn't we just have a money fight? It seems like we did."

Joel propped himself up on his elbows and looked down at her face in the moonlight. "I think we had a discussion about money. Not a fight."

"Shouldn't we talk about it? I don't know why you reacted the way you did. And I don't want to break up."

"I think you may be reading a lot more into one conversation than you should."

Kat sat up and wrapped her arms around her knees. "I don't know. Are you an investor if you help build the kennel? Should we have contracts and legal stuff? For the business? Should I set up an LLC? I'm not sure what LLC even stands for. I guess it's a type of corporation, right?"

Joel sat up next to her and put his arm around her. "Okay, now you're really over-thinking this. I said maybe you should have savings. Not that you have to become the Donald Trump of the dog-boarding world. And you know I'll help. By the way, before you mention it again or worry about it—no, I definitely don't want to break up." He leaned over to kiss her for emphasis.

Kat poked him gently in the ribs. "So does that mean you are just a cheapskate then? Because when I was kidding around about feeding me, you got all weird."

He tilted his head slightly. "I suppose maybe I was a little weird. I spent a lot of years taking care of my sister. Figuring out how to feed her was on my mind a lot back then."

Kat ran her hand through his dark blonde hair and gazed into his eyes. "I didn't think about that. Okay. I get it."

He smiled. "But I still might be kind of a cheapskate, too. I had to be frugal for a long time."

Kat smiled in return. She had an over-active imagination sometimes and Joel's unflappable, rational nature often had a way of calming her down. It was a relief to understand what he was thinking. Like a dark cloud had lifted. "Being frugal is great if you're calculating how to save money on fixing the house and building the kennel. But when it comes to my birthday, you can feel free to splurge."

Joel gathered her up in his arms and kissed her. "I'll keep that in mind."

Chapter 4

Research

The next day at the library, Jan sat at the front desk entering book data into the computer. In a way, the mindless data-entry work was soothing. It was a good thing she hadn't drunk any wine last night. Maria had looked somewhat shredded by the time she disappeared down the stairs. But she didn't have to return to work the next day, so presumably she could sleep it off.

The front door of the library opened and Jan glanced up from her monitor. Michael was walking toward the desk. What was he doing here? Her heart raced and she sat up straight in her chair. She'd hoped she'd never see this guy again. So much for that idea. She hadn't been exaggerating to Kat and Maria. He definitely was as good-looking as she remembered. Today, he was even wearing a cowboy hat, so he really *did* look like the Marlboro man. Maria would have had a heart attack.

Jan smiled at the thought. "Hello, Michael. What brings you to the Alpine Grove library?"

With an amused glint in his brown eyes, he said. "You weren't kidding, huh? You really are the librarian here."

"I have no reason to lie." She fidgeted with a pencil in her hands. He hadn't answered her question. What *was* he doing here?

"Oh, come on. People lie at weddings. They're like high-school reunions. You think, 'hey, I'll never see these people again and they'll never know I'm really a janitor in Petaluma.'"

"I never asked you what you do. Are you a janitor in Petaluma?"

Michael grinned. "Actually, no. I work in advertising. That's why I'm here. My agency is shooting a commercial and I need to look something up."

"What kind of commercial? I didn't know Hollywood was interested in Alpine Grove." Cowboy hat aside, he certainly didn't seem like the type of person to be hanging out in a small town.

He lounged casually against the desk. "I don't think Hollywood is interested. But we're saving money by driving out here to the sticks because we need some pine trees in the background. The ad is for men's cologne and we needed a more outdoorsy, Wild-West look than we can get in San Diego."

Jan inclined her head slightly toward his. "I guess that explains the cowboy hat."

Michael took the hat off his head and turned it around in his hands. "We all have them. The client gave them to us. Actually, Ron, the actor doing the commercial, has a much cooler one. No real cowboy would be caught dead in these things. Mine is already falling apart. But it works to keep the sun off my face."

"Skin cancer is always a risk. Particularly if you were badly sunburned when you were a child."

Michael placed his elbows on the desk and leaned over the counter toward her. "I know you weren't sunburned. Anywhere."

Jan leaned back on her stool. She could feel the flush rising in her cheeks and she crossed her arms in front of her. "That was when I was eight. I have seen sunlight in the intervening years. So again, why exactly are you here?"

Michael widened his eyes and stretched his body over the counter so his face was close to hers. Jan noticed again how long and thick his eyelashes were. Giving her a penetrating look, he said, "Maybe I just missed you."

Jan shook her head. "I doubt that." It was a good thing she took her job seriously. He had the most gorgeous eyes. Up close, she could see that chocolate-brown color was flecked with tiny specks of gold.

Michael stood up straight again and placed his palms on the counter. "I told you. I need to look something up. Ron is having a meltdown and says he can't do the commercial. He needs to understand his motivation. So I need information about the Wild West and cowboys. Can I borrow some books?"

Taken aback by his sudden return to business, Jan picked up her pencil again and attempted to look businesslike. "This is a library. That's what we do. But you do need to have a library card. Please fill out this form."

He frowned. "Oh come on. Really? I don't live here. Do I really have to fill out a bunch of bureaucratic forms just to get a book on cowboys?"

"If you want to check them out, yes. However, if you prefer, you can go to the history section over there and see if you can find what you need. Try 978—that section has the history of the western states in North America. Bring the books to the desk here and I can make copies of the pages with the information you need. But each copy does cost ten cents."

Michael glanced up at the clock on the wall behind the desk. "How long will that take? I'm in a rush. I need this now. Yesterday, even. Every minute Ron is whining about his motivational angst is costing the agency a lot of money."

Jan looked at her watch. "Do you take a break for lunch? Maybe you can distract him with some sandwiches. It's not very busy here today. If you give me an hour or so, I can look up some information for you while the actor eats. There's a deli just around the corner."

The muscles around Michael's lips relaxed and he smiled widely. "Would you do that? He reached across the desk and grabbed her shoulders. "I could just kiss you! You have no idea how much this helps me out."

Jan jerked back, away from him, and put her hands up in front of her. "That's not necessary. I do research for people all the time. In fact, I enjoy it. Are there any specific questions that the actor wants answered?"

Michael paused for a moment and said, "Well, Ron is worried that his clothes don't look authentic and he wants to understand why his character is there. I told him that he's selling cologne and that's why he's there, but he's not buying it. He says he wants a better understanding of why he's standing around with his horse in the trees. I can't believe this guy. Do you know how expensive it is to hire a trained horse to stand around in trees? It's killing me!"

Jan nodded. "I'll see what I can do."

Michael raised his hat in the air with a flourish and yelled "Yee-HAW!" At the outburst, several people quietly reading magazines in the row of chairs along the wall looked up and glared. A gray-haired woman glowered at Michael and hissed "Shhhh!" in his direction.

Glancing at the woman across the room, Michael said in a stage whisper, "Oops. Sorry. But thank you! I'll be back in an hour."

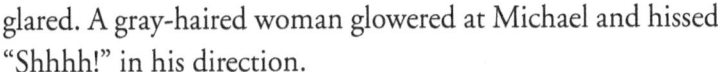

Jan adored doing research and she had a lot of fun researching cowboy locations, activities, and motivations. It was like a treasure hunt or mystery story trying to find out why a cowboy might be standing around in a copse of trees. Pleased with her finds, she made copies of relevant pages, highlighted important information, and placed the stack of papers on the desk. When Michael walked through the door of the library, she waved at him.

At the desk, Michael looked down at the stack of paper. "Did you find anything? Please tell me you did and that big pile of dead trees is mine. The sandwich distraction only took me so far. Ron is getting antsy again."

Jan was eager to share what she'd learned. "It was so interesting. Cowboys led a fascinating life."

Michael was nodding as he riffled through the papers. "That's great. What do I owe you for all these copies? I have to get back right now before Ron blows a gasket. The guy is so temperamental. Even the potato chips weren't right. Sheesh. Dealing with actors drives me nuts."

"Don't you want to know what I learned?"

"Not right now. I'll read it. I've really got to go." He poked around in his wallet and proffered a bill at Jan. "Here's a twenty. I'll come back for the change later. I've really got to run. This shoot is going to blow my budget and my boss is freaking out. Thank you, though. I'll be back later."

Disappointed that she wouldn't get to explain more about cowboy life, Jan took the money and smiled. "Oh, this is more than enough. I'll have your change waiting for you when you return."

Michael leaned across the desk and wrapped Jan in a bear hug. "You are amazing. Thank you!" He gave her a loud smacking kiss on the cheek.

Startled by the impact of the sudden embrace, Jan squeezed her eyes shut. "You're welcome," she said weakly.

Michael's body was yanked away from Jan's, and she opened her eyes to find Steve standing in front of the desk with one of his beefy fists clutching Michael's shoulder.

"What are you doing making out with my girlfriend?" Steve said.

Michael turned his head to look at Jan. "I take it you know this gentleman?"

Jan nodded. "Yes. He's my fiancé, actually."

Steve narrowed his eyes at Michael. "So why are you messing with her?"

Michael shook his shoulder out of Steve's grip. "Unhand me, you brute."

Jan giggled. Michael didn't seem to find Steve particularly threatening and she hadn't heard a reference from old Popeye cartoons in a long time.

Steve's face reddened. "Are you making fun of me? Who are you, anyway?"

"I am a patron of the library," Michael said slowly, as if he were explaining something to a sleepy three-year old. "And

I'm an old friend of Jan's. I was her neighbor a long time ago. And then I saw her last weekend at her mother's wedding."

Steve whipped his head around toward Jan. "You didn't tell me about this guy. Are you running around on me? And here you were accusing me the other night. You've got a lot of nerve."

Jan waved her hands at the two men and whispered, "You both need to calm down. And for heaven's sake, be quiet. This is a library. You're making a scene. Steve, Michael really is here at the library for research. This pile of papers is for him. He was just picking them up. And yes, I saw him at the wedding last weekend, but that's because his father was marrying my mother. Which you would know if you'd been there."

Michael smirked. "But I have seen her naked."

Steve's fist whirled around. Michael ducked to the side, and the momentum of his swing caused Steve to half-fall across the desk so the punch glanced across Jan's cheek with a great smacking noise. She shrieked and her hands flew to her face.

The two men stood in shocked silence for a second and then Michael ran around to the other side of the desk and tried to pull Jan's hands away from her face. "Are you okay? Let me see."

Jan shook her head. Hot tears were streaming down her face, fueling her anger. "What is wrong with you? This is a library, not a bar."

Michael looked into her eyes and smoothed her hair back from her face. "I'm sorry. I shouldn't taunt someone like that. But I couldn't help myself."

Jan snuffled. "Someone like what? He's my fiancé."

Michael gently ran his fingers across the red mark that was developing on her cheek. "I'm sorry about that, too. Are you going to be okay?"

"I think so. I need to go get some ice from the refrigerator. And call Jill and ask her to come in. I'm the only one here."

Steve leaned over from the other side of the desk and said, "Listen buddy, I told you before. Don't touch my girlfriend."

Michael lifted his hands from Jan and backed away from her with his palms facing outward. "Okay, not touching anymore." He walked back around to the front of the desk and leaned his face close to Steve's. "For the record, I'm not your buddy. And maybe you should check and see if your *girlfriend* is okay."

Jan could feel her mascara running down her cheeks and wiped her eyes hurriedly. She probably looked like a demented raccoon at this point. "I think you both should leave now." She handed Michael the pile of papers. "I hope this is what you need."

Steve grabbed Michael's shirt collar. "I don't want to see you in here again, pretty boy. Stay away from her. I mean it."

Jan took her hand away from her cheek and smacked the counter with the palms of her hands. The row of readers all jumped at the noise and glared at her in unison. Jan didn't care. She was sick of these two testosterone-laced morons. "Steve, stop it. Both of you. Get. Out. *Now.*"

Clutching his papers tightly in his fist, Michael glared at Steve. "Let's go."

The two men walked out the door and Jan exhaled the breath she didn't realize she'd been holding. She could feel the bruise blooming under her skin. Her cheek hurt and she wanted to cry not just from the pain, but also from

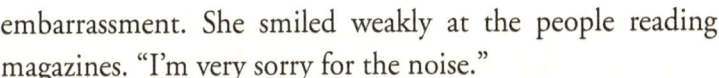

embarrassment. She smiled weakly at the people reading magazines. "I'm very sorry for the noise."

With her hand pressed to her cheek, she walked over to the phone to call Jill. What kind of Neanderthals have a fight in a *library*? This was supposed to be her place of refuge. Quiet. Peaceful. But every time Michael appeared, something horrible happened. She hoped she never saw him again.

Jill arrived at the library and fussed over the bruise on Jan's face. Although it was nice the older woman cared, Jan was ready to leave. "Jill, I'm fine. Michael said he's coming back to get his change for the copies later and I don't want to be here. Every time I see him, there's some disaster. I have a note on the desk that says how much we owe him in change."

"Okay, honey, I understand." Jill hugged her with finality. "You go on home. I might give him a talking-to while I'm at it."

"Please don't. It wasn't his fault. Steve is the one who accidentally hit me. But I think Michael is one of those people like my mother who just attracts drama wherever he goes. I don't want to be near anything or anyone like that anymore. I just want to go home."

Jill looked unconvinced, but bent down to give Rosa a farewell pat. "I think Rosa's ready. Have a good evening."

"Thanks Jill. I owe you one."

Jan loaded Rosa into the car and drove out Forest Avenue to her house. Her little yellow cottage came into view and Steve's car was parked out front. Jan took her foot off the accelerator and let her car coast to a stop next to the curb. She wasn't ready to talk to him yet. Rosa poked her nose up from the backseat. The car was stopped, but they weren't getting out. The dog stood up on the backseat and wagged her tail. Jan could see her in the rearview mirror staring out the window toward the house. "Hi Rosa. Sorry for the delay. I need to think for a second." What was she going to say to him?

Rosa jumped down to the floor of the backseat and put her front paws up on the center console. She looked up at Jan and licked her hand. Jan stroked the dog's head. "Thanks for the support, sweetie. I'm trying to get it together." Talking to Steve right now was not what she'd had in mind. Normally in a situation like this, she'd try to escape somewhere. Probably to the library. But there was no way she was running away from her own house. She had to face him.

Jan straightened in her seat and put the car into gear. She was going to have to deal with Steve sooner or later. Apparently, he had found time in his busy schedule to drive up here, so she may as well get it over with now. After parking her car in the driveway, she got out, clipped the leash on Rosa, and walked to Steve's car. He had told her at least 10,000 times that the IROC-Z was the best Camaro ever made. Jan had been allowed to drive the car exactly once, and she wasn't impressed. The handling was sloppy on the winding road she'd driven it on. Of course, she hadn't volunteered that information to Steve, since he loved that car more than life itself and had special-ordered it from the factory.

Steve was fiddling with the complicated controls on the radio in the car. He glanced up and when he saw Jan, he rolled down the window. "Hey babe. I just stopped by to say hi to Rosa and see if you're okay."

"I'm fine. So is Rosa. But she isn't going to have to buy ten gallons of makeup to cover up the fact that her fiancé smacked her at her place of employment."

Steve's eyes widened and he moved to get out the car. "Hey, I didn't do that on purpose. I was trying to belt the pretty boy. He said he saw you naked."

As the anger welled up in her, Jan tried not to shout. "When I was EIGHT!"

"What?"

"I told you. Michael lived next door to me when I was little. He was trying to make you angry. He taunted you and you fell for it. Maybe we should talk about this inside. I'd really rather not have the entire neighborhood hear our business."

Steve shrugged his shoulders and locked up his car. "You were eight?"

Jan walked to the house and opened the front door. Rosa rushed inside and flopped down on her dog bed, and Jan turned to face Steve. "Yes. I was eight. It was laundry day. But I'd really rather not go into it."

"Whatever," Steve said as he sat down on the sofa. "I thought you were cheating on me." He patted the sofa next to him and said, "Hey Rosa, you wanna sit next to me?"

Rosa looked up from her dog bed and appeared to ponder the option, but stayed put.

"Hey, how come Rosa doesn't like me anymore? Come on, Rosa. We always hang out on the sofa."

Jan put her bag on the table. "Maybe because you *hit* me."

"Oh come on. I told you that was an accident."

"I believe you. But this isn't the first time you've been angry and jealous. It's been a problem for a long time. When we first met, you weren't irritable all the time like you are now. You weren't always this way. I don't know what changed, but I can't seem to get you to talk about it. And as far as I know, you've never done anything to deal with whatever is bothering you. I've been thinking about that and the fact that you were seen with a woman at the H12."

"I told you about that too! She's a client."

Jan leaned back on the counter and faced the living room again. She took a deep breath to try to bolster her courage and collect her thoughts. "Here's the problem. We either trust each other or we don't. You've accused me of cheating before. And I never have. But you're going to *think* I've done something wrong whether I have or not. So we end up with situations like today, when you're trying to beat up some guy I barely know at the library."

Steve clenched his fists. "But he deserved it. I thought he was messing around with you. I was defending your honor."

"My honor was fine, which you would know if you had simply asked. I think you're missing the point. The point is, you don't trust me. And I realized yesterday that I don't trust you, either. If you'd given me a ring, right now I'd give it back."

Steve looked shocked for a second. "Are you still harping on the whole ring thing? You're unbelievable."

"I think we should stop seeing each other. I'm not sure either of us ever truly believed we'd get married anyway."

Steve's face clouded with anger. "You're kidding, right? You're breaking up with *me*? You're the type of woman who wants to get married. And my mother thinks you walk on water. I know you want that whole white picket fence thing and all that. You'll never get that now if you break up with me."

"No. I'm not kidding." Jan clasped her hands in front of her in an effort to retain her composure. But she could still feel them shaking. What if she was making a terrible mistake? She straightened her shoulders. "I'll miss her, but your mother is going to have to get over it. I'm going to miss you, too. I thought I loved you for so long, I guess I didn't notice that I don't anymore until people started talking about seeing you with another woman. I was upset. Really upset. But after talking to some people, it occurred to me that I was mostly just confused and embarrassed. Not hurt like I would be if I were truly in love with you. After a lot of reflection, I've come to the conclusion that I don't trust you and I'd be happier if you were no longer a part of my life." There. She said it. The words were out there. Maybe he'd argue. Try to change her mind and win her back.

Steve stood up from the couch, knocking some pillows onto the floor. He shook his finger at her. "You'll regret losing me. I'm the best thing that has ever happened to you or that *will* ever happen to you."

Jan bowed her head and looked down at her hands. His reaction made it clear she was definitely not making a mistake. She looked up at him again. "I'm willing to take that risk."

"You're not getting any younger or prettier, you know. You're getting to the point that it's gonna be more likely that you'll get attacked by a terrorist than find a man and get married."

Jan was tired of hearing that old statistic. Her heart was pounding in her chest as her sadness twisted back to anger again. "It was one article in *Newsweek* a decade ago. Get over it. And in case you haven't noticed, I'm also not over 40. The study was flawed and even if it weren't, I was not born in the mid-1950s. I'm willing to take my chances."

Steve turned toward the door and then paused. "Hey Rosa, I have to go. Don't you want to say goodbye?" He patted his knees to encourage her to come to him.

Rosa sat in her bed and didn't move. She didn't even wag her tail.

Steve stood up straight. "Fine. Be that way. You both can be old spinsters together." He walked out and slammed the door behind him.

Jan walked over and bent down to pet Rosa's glossy black fur. "Good girl. Even though it doesn't feel that way right now, I think we're better off without him."

Rosa thumped her tail, stood up, and shook her body vigorously, rippling her fur from head to tail.

Although tears were streaming down her face, Jan smiled and ruffled Rosa's ears. "Exactly!"

~

After such a long, traumatic day, some comfort food was in order. Jan ordered a pizza and she and Rosa shared an enjoyable junk-food extravaganza. Rosa sat with her head on Jan's thigh, hoping for some pizza crusts to be directed her way. Jan obliged. She was such a soft touch. No wonder Rosa looked like a bowling ball.

"Okay Rosa, after this, I think we need to go on a health kick. With the over-indulgence at Kat's place, and all the ice cream and pizza, I'm not going to fit into my clothes anymore. And you won't be able to keep up with Kat's dogs the next time you have to stay there. Maybe we can take up jogging."

Rosa licked her chops, still focused on potential pizza crusts.

"I know. Who am I kidding? I hate jogging. But I promise I'll buy more nutritious food the next time I go shopping." A tear slid down her cheek and she reached down to wrap her arms around Rosa's neck. "It's been a long day, sweetie. How about if we go hang out on the couch and watch a total chick flick that Steve would hate? I'm thinking a little *Princess Bride* with Westley, Buttercup and 'wuv, tru wuv' is in order. What do you think?"

Detecting that mealtime was over, Rosa wagged her tail, ran over to the sofa, jumped up, and spun around a few times before settling into a corner.

Jan grabbed a comforter and smiled. "As you wish, Rosa."

Later, Jan was startled from the travails of the fire swamp and rodents of unusual size by the sound of the phone ringing. She reached over Rosa to grab the receiver.

"Hello. Wait. Hold on a second." She dug around the sofa, discovering the remote under Rosa's ample hind end, and muted the sound on the movie.

"Sorry. This is Jan."

"Hi Jan. It's Michael. I'm just calling to see how you are doing."

Jan closed her eyes. Not again. She *so* didn't want to talk to Michael. Why didn't she get an unlisted number? It was far too easy to find anyone in the one-eighth-inch-thick Alpine Grove phone book. Trying to keep the annoyance out of her voice, she said, "I'm fine. Rosa and I are just watching a movie. Actually, I'm watching. She's sleeping."

Michael laughed. "Sounds like another big night in Alpine Grove. Are you sure you're okay? I feel bad about what happened. I hope your friend is taking care of you. You seemed pretty angry and upset."

"Yes, you and Steve embarrassed me. But I don't think there's any permanent physical damage. I put some ice on my cheek and that helped. Rosa is my dog, by the way. And she's been very supportive."

"I'm glad you're feeling better. I went back to the library to get the change from the copies and that other librarian said you'd gone home. She had some choice words for me, too. I don't think she likes me."

Jan smiled. "I'm pretty sure she doesn't. If it helps, I asked her not to say anything. But sometimes Jill is a bit protective of me, I think. It's really sweet, but I keep telling her it's not necessary."

Michael cleared his throat. "She suggested that I apologize to you. And she's right. So, I'm sorry. I shouldn't have let your boyfriend get to me. It's probably a guy thing. But the way he was talking to you pissed me off."

Jan didn't know what to say. This was a surprising development. Steve certainly hadn't apologized. "Well, ah, Steve isn't my boyfriend anymore."

"Really? That was fast."

Jan took a deep breath in an effort to keep the tears from starting up again. She said quickly, "I am surprised that I'm even thinking this, much less telling you, but it may have been a good thing. Steve has had anger issues for a while. I've tried to ignore it—and a lot of other things, too. So I think everything will work out for the best."

"I hope you're right." Michael paused. "So since you're feeling better, I was wondering if you'd like to have some coffee. I'll be here for the next few days. Thanks to your research, Ron is on track again and we might finish shooting this commercial before my boss has a heart attack. The screaming and level of crazy was over the top."

"The actor was screaming? It's just a commercial, right?"

"No, Ron is nit-picky and annoying, but he doesn't scream. I meant my boss. The client is kind of nuts. They say one thing one minute and then change their minds. I guess they think we're psychic. I think my boss may be melting down a little under all the money and deadline pressures. He's a good guy, but he's been in ad-land for a long time. It can get to you."

"That level of stress sounds terribly toxic. I don't think I could handle that." Nor would she want to. Advertising certainly sounded like a horrid way to earn a living.

"I think you either thrive on the stress or you get out. I love it. Every day is different. Sometimes you get ten people in a room all bouncing ideas off each other. The creative flow is incredible. There's nothing like it."

Jan examined her fingernails. She needed a manicure. "I'll take your word for it."

"Hey, you didn't answer me about coffee. I'd like to see you before I go back to San Diego so I can verify for myself that you're healing up okay. And to thank you for the research. You really saved me."

Jan didn't want to see him again, but he was being so conciliatory and friendly at the moment, it seemed mean to shoot him down. Plus she couldn't think of any reasonable excuse to get out of it. What the heck. It was just coffee. "I guess I can do that. I hate to think how awful this bruise will look by then, though."

"I'm sure it will be fine. You always look great. How about tomorrow? I guess the library closes at five, right? How about if I meet you there."

"Yes. That will work."

"I'll see you then!"

Jan's shoulders slumped as she hung up the phone. She leaned over on the sofa, putting her forehead on Rosa's back. "Oh Rosa, what is wrong with me? Why didn't I just say no?"

Rosa wagged the tip of her tail in sympathy.

"Yeah, I know, that would be inconceivable. I'm such a wimp."

～

At ten after five, Jan was sitting at the desk entering book data into the computer again. It was a never-ending marathon project and Jill wanted nothing to do with it. Whenever a new order of books came in, they needed to be entered into the system. The process was excruciatingly dull, but the end result was worth it. Being able to search for any book by just typing in text was so much easier than dealing with the old card catalogs.

She looked up at the knock on the front door, which she had locked at five. If Michael wanted to score points with her, being late certainly wasn't the way to do it. Waving toward the back of the building, she indicated that she and Rosa would be going out the back door.

Michael was standing outside waiting when Jan and Rosa exited the building. "I'm sorry I'm so late," he said.

Locking the door behind her, Jan turned to him. "It's fine. Rosa got in a little more nap time."

Michael bent down to pet the dog. "So this is Rosa, huh? I've heard a lot about you." Rosa wagged her tail. Michael reached into his pocket and held a dog treat in front of her nose. "I'm guessing you know what this is. Do you know how to sit?" Rosa sat down proudly and then snorfled the treat with enthusiasm.

Jan giggled. "Yes. She definitely knows about t-r-e-a-t-s. The other night, someone called Rosa 'full-figured' and I decided that's a more polite way to describe her. We try not to use polarizing terms like overweight or fat."

"Certainly not," Michael said. "No one wants their dog to have body-image issues. I saw that the coffee shop is just around the corner. Do you want to walk?"

"Sure. I look for any excuse to give Rosa some exercise."

Michael smiled and turned toward her. "Wait a minute." He reached over and gently cupped her chin with his hand, turning her cheek toward him. "Not bad. It looks like macho man only grazed you."

A guilty little tremor of excitement flooded Jan's body at his touch. She smiled. "Thank goodness for the magic of Cover Girl. And it looks like I won't get a black eye, which is a relief."

He let his fingertips skim her jaw line as he released her chin. "Good thing he wasn't wearing a gigantic Super Bowl ring. He could have really done some damage."

"He was a football player in college, but he never made it to the pros." Jan had been subjected to that story at least 400 times. Now she'd probably never hear it again.

Michael took her hand in his. "I suspected as much. Because of all those years of playing sports, I can spot a football player at fifty yards."

"Maybe you should just avoid football players from now on. They don't seem to like you."

"It was just the one. Normally, I play nice with jocks. And he started it."

"Oh please. You realize you sound like a ten-year old when you say that, right?"

Michael swung her hand back and forth and began skipping. "I'm embracing my inner child. Some people find it endearing."

"Are they ten-year olds?" Jan said breathlessly, trying to keep up. She *was* out of shape. And what was she doing walking—or skipping—hand-in-hand with a man who wasn't Steve? It seemed so wrong and even worse, she looked like an idiot. What if someone she knew saw them? She looked quickly over at Michael, who seemed unconcerned about the contact, apparently enjoying capering through town among all the fall colors. It was a gorgeous sunny day and the maples along the side of the street were putting on a fantastic show of red, orange, and yellow leaves. Rosa's paws crunched through the fallen leaves scattered on the ground. The dog was panting heavily as she trotted alongside them.

Michael looked over at Rosa and slowed back to a leisurely walk. "Sorry. All this fresh air is invigorating. I think your dog might have a heart attack, though."

"Rosa and I might need to embark on a new physical-fitness regimen." Not to mention cut back on the number of pizza nights.

At the outdoor patio of the coffee shop, they settled into chairs and sat sipping large mugs of coffee with Rosa snoring quietly under the table. Jan held her mug with both hands, enjoying the warmth. "Did you finish your commercial?"

"Almost. We have a half-day of shooting tomorrow. Then it's back to San Diego for me."

"Your dog probably misses you. Well, assuming she's still there."

Michael smiled. "Very funny. Swoosie is at her favorite boarding kennel. I refer to it as 'doggie boot camp.' It's kind of a drive, since it's out in East County, but the place is huge and they tire her out. They have people who volunteer to come in and go jogging or running with the dogs. Swoosie tends to sleep for a few days after she comes home."

"It's hard for me to imagine that dog tired."

"You might not have seen her at her finest moment."

Jan paused before taking another sip of coffee. "Which one? There were multiple disastrous moments."

Ignoring the disparaging comment about his dog, Michael leaned back in his chair and surveyed the people walking down the street near the coffee shop. "Check out this guy. The way he's walking, I think he's an undercover cop. See how he's looking right and left. Shifty. Maybe a private detective."

Jan looked over her shoulder. "What are you talking about? That's Ralph. He works at the grocery store."

"Maybe that's his cover. Are you absolutely *sure* he's just a bag boy? Maybe there's more to him than that. Everybody has secrets."

"I suppose that's true," Jan said. "And they probably want to keep them secret."

Michael leaned forward, put his elbows on the table, and looked into her face. "Where's the fun in that? Everyone has a story. Don't you ever look at people and wonder?"

Jan fiddled with the handle of her mug. "That's their business. I guess sometimes I wonder what they're thinking, though."

"Exactly!" Michael said. "What's going through Ralph's mind right now? He looks like he's on a mission. Where's he going? What's he doing?"

The corners of Jan's mouth twitched with amusement. "If you met Ralph, you might not be so curious."

"Okay, maybe not him." Michael turned in his chair. "How about that woman over there? She's busy trying to ride herd on that little boy. Maybe she's taking him to the doctor and he doesn't want to go."

Jan put down her mug. "Do you usually make up stories about people while you're having coffee?"

"All the time. And when I'm waiting in line to do my bank deposits. Wherever. It passes the time. Like Shakespeare said, 'all the world's a stage.' I'm just here watching it play out."

"Wow. Quoting the Bard?" Jan said with a smile. "I never would have guessed it of you."

Michael arched an eyebrow in mock surprise. "Hey, I'm a complex guy."

"I'll take your word for it. At this point, I'm waiting for the next disaster to befall me."

Michael threw an arm over the back of his chair. "You're really not much of an optimist, are you?"

"So far, I've experienced extreme wardrobe destruction and violence when I've been around you." Jan said. "I think that should be cause for concern." Although to be fair, she was enjoying herself now. He was entertaining. And, of course, not exactly hard to look at, either. Things could be worse.

Michael grinned and Jan noticed his chipped tooth again. Why hadn't he ever gotten it fixed? He stretched his long legs out under the table and folded his hands across his stomach. "Well, you better get used to it, because I just thought of something. I'm now your step-brother! We'll probably be spending holidays together. It will be like the Brady Bunch."

"I wouldn't get too attached to that idea," Jan said. "I'm guessing you haven't spent much time with my mother, have you? Over the years, I've seen quite a few step-siblings come and go." That was an understatement.

"Speaking of which, I always wondered why Greg and Marcia didn't ever get it on," Michael said. "They weren't related, after all. They were steps. And they were what, 16 or 17? With all those hormones? Get real. They would have been trying out Carol and Mike's water bed the first chance they got."

"Well, if you believe the gossip rags, the actors actually did have some type of relationship. So did Keith and Lori Partridge, supposedly."

Michael leaned forward and wrapped his large hands around his coffee mug. "I see your reading extends beyond Shakespeare."

"It's an occupational hazard. I read everything."

"So can I be amused for a second that your name is Jan? Oh—and now thanks to me, you can have middle-child syndrome. How cool is that?"

"Unless you have a younger sibling I don't know about, I'm not a middle child. And this may come as a surprise, but you're not the first person to point out the Brady Bunch connection. If you ask me to say, 'Marcia, Marcia, Marcia,' in a whiny voice I'm leaving."

Michael laughed. "Aww, you're no fun."

~

That evening, Jan was washing up the dishes from dinner when the phone rang. A sinful little glimmer of hope skittered through her when she considered the possibility that it could be Michael. It was inappropriate, given that she had just broken up with Steve, but she'd had fun drinking coffee with him. Was it a date? Did he think it was a date? She shouldn't be dating anyone right after a break-up. That would be insane. And he was leaving town soon, anyway.

All thoughts of Michael vaporized when Jan heard her mother's voice on the other end of the line.

"Hello, Janelle darling! How are you?"

"I'm fine, Mom. But I'm surprised that you're calling all the way from Hawaii. Aren't you still on your honeymoon? I thought it was a two-week trip."

"The islands are a fantastically spiritual place. You can feel the ancient mystical energies throughout your body. The ocean and the tropical air create such a beautiful harmony and it permeates my soul. We spent some time at the beach and then I found a shaman who gave me a crystal that aligned my chakra centers. I felt so balanced. It was beautiful."

"I'm glad you're having such a good time. I'm sure Hawaii would be a wonderful place to spend a honeymoon." She had hoped to go back to Maui with Steve, in fact. Someday.

"Yes, it was lovely. But then the vibrations shifted."

Jan tightened her grip on the receiver. "What shifted? Is everything okay?"

"I had to go home. It was meant to be this way. Crystals only work on the vibrations of light and love. Bruce didn't understand. I needed to fill my being with love. My consciousness needed to be free."

Jan sighed. Since her mother had discovered New Age teachings, she was even more difficult to decipher than she used to be when she spent all her time with six-year olds and sock puppets. "Wait. What are you saying?"

"I had to be surrounded by authentic love and free of Bruce."

"You mean you dumped the Toilet King...I mean Bruce... *already*? On your *honeymoon*? I think this is a new record, Mom, even for you."

"No, we are still together as one. I'm trying to tell you I was sick. It was my heart. I had to go home."

Jan shook her head. "I'm confused. Did you dump him or not? Or are you actually sick? Are you okay? I mean physically okay?"

"Well, I'm back in San Diego. Right now, I'm at the hospital with Zoe."

A twinge of panic shot through Jan's chest. "What? Is something really wrong with you? Have they done tests?"

"My heart is sick. I'm feeling a range of emotions and surges of energy. Zoe says there's a disturbance in my aura."

Jan readjusted the receiver on her ear. "Have you talked to a doctor? A *real* doctor?"

"Yes, there have been several here. I am trying to remain attuned to their truths."

"Okay, now you're scaring me, Mom. Do you need me there? Should I come down? I have some vacation time at work. I can call Jill to cover for me at the library. I can do it right now."

"I'd love to see you darling. Of course, I need you. I'll always need you. You are a part of me. But don't worry about me. Bodies get sick and they break. It's a disruption in my energy field."

Jan tried to keep the tremor out of her voice. "How sick are you?"

"The shaman in Hawaii told me not to worry, Jan. He said that my body is not what is truly me. My consciousness will heal. My aura has a memory of everything that has ever happened to me. My heart is just a part of my body. I am merely an observer in this thing called life. My soul cannot be touched by the complexities of the world. The pain in my heart is not permanent."

Jan twisted the phone cord, "I'll be on the soonest flight I can get. I just need to make some calls now and see if I can get someone to take care of Rosa."

"It will be delightful to see you. We didn't get to spend much time together before the wedding."

"Will you be at the hospital?"

"No. I'll be at home."

"So you're recovering?"

"Yes, I am. My spirit is mending. We are all of us healing. All the time."

"Please take care of yourself, Mom. I'll be there soon."

Jan's hand was shaking as she hung up the phone. Her mother had seemed so invincible and had been such a force in her life for so long, it was strange to imagine her having some type of heart problem.

She looked down at Rosa, who was dozing in her bed. "I guess you get to see Auntie Kat again. Here's hoping she's still willing to take you, after last time."

Chapter 5

Smells & Dances

Jan drove her car down the pothole-filled driveway toward Kat's house again. She'd stopped by the travel agency and the plane tickets were in her purse. Once again, Rosa was running back and forth across the back seat. Although the dog could handle the short trip to the library without any problem, getting out here to Kat's house in the sticks was apparently farther than Rosa's sensitive digestion was willing to tolerate.

"We're almost there, Rosa. Only a few more minutes. You can make it."

Rosa paused in her frantic pacing for a moment. Jan looked up at her rearview mirror and watched the all-too-familiar motions of Rosa losing her breakfast all over the back of the car. After sitting for a week at the airport while Jan visited her mom, this poor car would be outrageously ripe. Best not to dwell on the reality of that olfactory scenario.

As Kat walked down the front steps of the house, Jan had an unrelenting sense of déjà-vu. The last time she was here, she was going to San Diego for happier reasons, even if she hadn't been particularly happy about it at the time. Now that her mother was sick, she felt guilty for not being more enthusiastic about her latest marriage.

Jan extracted Rosa's stinky black body from the back of the car, wishing again that she had remembered not to feed Rosa this morning. Waving at Kat, she said, "She doesn't smell particularly good. Again. Except I think it's worse this time. I forgot we were coming here and I wasn't thinking, so I fed her breakfast. Twice. Then I think she rolled off the seat into it. Sorry."

Kat bent down to pet the small area on Rosa's head that did not appear to be coated with used dog food. "Wow Rosa, that's nasty. How do you feel about baths?"

"Actually, she doesn't mind. I guess it's because she's a Labrador retriever and they're water dogs. She usually just stands in the tub quietly and lets you scrub," Jan said.

"I think we have a plan for the afternoon, then."

Jan handed the leash to Kat. "I appreciate you taking her on such short notice. My mom's call was a surprise last night. I'm just glad I could get a seat on the flight. And that I have the money. Flying last-minute is so expensive. I did book a round-trip, so at least you know when I'm coming back this time."

"I'm really sorry to hear about your mother. I hope she's okay."

"With her, it's hard to tell. I think she actually may have dumped her new husband already, which given her history doesn't come as a huge surprise." Jan shrugged, "But then she kept talking about something being wrong with her heart. And that she was in the hospital. That can't be good. I thought she was in Hawaii."

Kat nodded. "If I were on my honeymoon, I think I'd be frolicking on tropical beaches for as long as I possibly could before I had to return to the real world."

Jan fidgeted with the leather handle of her purse. "I guess I'll find out what happened soon enough." It was awful to think about something being really wrong. She hadn't been able to sleep much at all last night.

"I heard about the whole thing with your boyfriend in the library, too."

Jan groaned. "This is such a small town. How did you find out?" People had warned her that living here would be like living in a fishbowl, but she'd never been the target of gossip until now.

"Cindy called Joel to ask him to help her with something. When she calls she also likes to report on the latest Alpine Grove happenings. The fight in the library made the cut, I guess. Joel told me, because almost every time he talks to his sister, he needs to vent about it afterward."

"Yes, usually when I talk to Cindy, she's venting about him. I guess they don't get along very well?" That was a nice way of putting it.

Kat shook her head. "That would be a major no."

"He seems like such a quiet and sedate person, though." Or cryptic and geeky, to hear Cindy tell it.

Waving the end of the leash toward the house, Kat said. "He has his not-so-mellow moments."

Jan looked at her watch and said, "Okay, I really should go now. I don't want to miss my flight. Please take good care of Rosa. I'm going to miss her and I feel terrible dumping her on you again so soon."

Kat smiled. "It's no problem. We'll take good care of her. And with any luck, she'll smell better by the time you return."

~

As Jan's car rumbled down the driveway, Kat walked Rosa toward the house. "Alright Rosa, before we test out your magical ability to escape from the Tessa Hut, I'm cleaning you up. This is a truly horrible smell you have going on here. I know I have referred to this place as Chez Stinky, but you really didn't have to participate. The house was doing so well too until you got here. It's time to lower your stink factor."

Rosa wagged, content to let Kat continue to chastise her about the offensive stench as they walked along.

When Kat entered the kitchen, she encountered Joel making one of his surreptitious half-sandwiches. Although he never would admit to snacking, food tended to vanish at a startling rate. She nodded at the sandwich, "Lunch time?"

He looked up from his task. "No. This is to tide me over until lunch. Being on the roof makes me hungry."

"You weren't on the roof. You were doing geeky things on your computer."

Joel waved his sandwich at her, "Well, I will be on the roof soon. I'm getting ready to go up there." He looked down at Rosa and wrinkled his nose. "Yuck. What is wrong with that dog? She smells like six-week-old decomposing salmon."

"Jan forgot to skip Rosa's breakfast and there was an incident in the back of her car on the way here. We are going to see how Rosa likes baths now."

Joel hurriedly gathered up his napkin and sandwich and moved toward the door, "'Bye."

"Wait. Could you help me? It would be a lot easier with two people."

"No thanks. We have a division of labor. I deal with power tools and you handle dog-related matters."

"I suppose keeping me away from the power tools is probably wise."

"That's well-documented. Good luck with the stink dawg."

The bathroom in the house was extremely small and Kat was not looking forward to being locked in such a tiny space with such a bad smell. She led Rosa into the room and closed the door behind her. Turning to face the dog, she said, "Okay Rosa, this is the bathtub. Jan tells me you know about baths. So do you know how to hop in? Nothing personal, but I really don't want to touch you. It would be great if you could just jump in." She waved both arms in the direction of the tub and patted the white porcelain side. "Come on. Let's go. Get in the tub, Rosa."

Rosa sat and stared blankly at Kat. A chunk of well-masticated dog food fell off her front leg and landed on the tile. Kat straightened. This process might be more difficult than she anticipated. "I guess you're not going to make this easy are you? I need to ask Jan what is in that dog food you eat. I mean, *gross*—what *is* she feeding you? I may never get this smell out of my nostrils. Not to mention my clothing. Eww. I definitely don't want my clothes touching you." Kat stripped off her clothes and jammed them into the tiny linen cabinet next to the sink. She stood naked in front of the dog. Rosa wagged and looked expectantly up at her.

"Okay Rosa, we've got to do this. No matter how much I don't want to." Kat gingerly reached around Rosa's slimy body to hoist the dog's considerable girth over the side of the tub. Viscous ooze squeezed through her fingers. *Gross.*

"You're definitely not a lightweight, are you? It would be helpful if you could try and cooperate here."

Rosa pushed against the side of the bathtub with her front paws, but Kat leaned on the dog and Rosa's front feet slipped forward and landed in the tub with a resounding thud. The dog's rear feet were still outside, so she was stuck with her torso spanning the edge of the tub. High-centered like an off-road vehicle stuck on a rock, the dog was unable to go forward or backward. Kat let go of the dog's body and Rosa attempted to throw all paws into reverse, scraping and flailing on the porcelain. "No Rosa! You're going IN the tub."

Kat reached around Rosa's hind end, lifting and shoving to try to get all four of the black dog's paws into the tub. Jumping into the front of the bathtub, Kat pulled and dragged until all parts of Rosa were inside the tub with her. "Okay dog, this is how it's going to go. I'm turning on the water now and you are getting a bath."

Continuing to grip Rosa's collar, Kat turned and reached behind her to spin one of the knobs for the bathtub spigot. Freezing cold water spewed out of the tap onto her back and both she and Rosa began flailing to get away from the frigid spray. The dog lurched forward against Kat, ramming the small of her back into the faucet. Shrieking in pain, Kat lost her grip on the dog's collar, and Rosa leaped out of the bathtub back onto the tile, hurtling herself around in a spastic circle.

After turning off the arctic water, Kat sat in the bathtub with her legs stretched out in front of her. She rubbed her back where she'd hit the faucet and groaned. "I think this bathroom is out to get me." This wasn't the first time she'd fallen in here. Wasn't slipping in the bathtub a common way to die? Or was it an old wives' tale? Jan probably could recite the yearly statistics for home accidents. She turned and looked over at Rosa who was sitting in the corner looking unhappy. "We're not even close to being done here, you know. New plan. I'm turning on the water first. Then you go in."

Kat got out of the tub and started the water again. "Look, warm water, Rosa. Nice water. You're a Lab. You're supposed to like water, remember?"

Rosa was unconvinced and turned to paw at the bottom of the bathroom door, her claws clacking on the tile.

Kat maneuvered around the dog to collect the soap and some old towels from the cabinet. Clearly this was not going to be a simple exercise where the dog stood sedately while being washed. Jan was either lying or had an odd idea of what "standing quietly in the tub" meant. Kat's next sortie was going to have to be significantly more strategic. She turned off the water, laid the towels on the edge of the sink, and placed the soap and a plastic cup where she could get at them easily from within the tub. She grabbed the dog around the torso again and said, "Okay, Rosa, one more time. We're doing this thing."

Kat used all of the body weight she could muster to lift and haul the front half of the dog into the tub again. Rosa thrashed her front paws in the water, creating a reverse waterfall that shot up into the air drenching Kat, the bathroom walls, and the towels on the sink. Kat readjusted her grip and shoved the dog's rear end up and over the side of the tub. Rosa splashed in and began to try to stage an exit, but Kat quickly leaped in next to her and leaned on the side of the tub, half sitting on the dog. "HA! We're in." She grabbed the bar of soap and the cup and began frantically dumping water on the dog and lathering her up. "Die, stink, die!"

Rosa seemed to enjoy the soaping-up process more than the initial getting-wet process and Kat started to relax slightly. She bent over the dog, scrubbing particularly putrid areas on Rosa's legs and underside. In the distance, the phone rang and a cat yowled, but Kat remained focused on her task. The noises seemed to rouse Rosa from her lull and with a mighty grunt, she lurched into the air, throwing Kat off her back and into the water. Leaping over the side of the bathtub, Rosa slid across the tile and slammed her body into the door, which popped open. Cursing the lousy antique latches on the doors in the house, Kat sat up in the tub and heard Rosa thundering down the stairs. Was the doggie door in the basement open?

Kat splashed out of the tub and slipped and slid over to the stair landing and ran down the stairs after the soapy dog. She skittered across the downstairs hallway Linoleum past the dogs, who had all stood up and were looking interested in all the excitement. Chelsey and Tessa were secured behind a baby gate in Kat's office, but the dog door was unlatched. Uh-oh.

Kat opened the back door and ran outside followed by Linus, Lori, and Lady, who leapt around in glee, thrilled with the new fun follow-the-naked-human game. Linus slurped a big glob of soap off Kat's thigh and then jerked his tongue in and out in disgust. Soap was not quite as tasty as it might look. Kat shooed his head away from her leg. "Yuck Linus. Stop that. Everyone please focus. We have a problem here. Where did Rosa go? We need to find her."

Joel stood up on the roof and waved down at Kat. "Hey, this is a good look for you."

A fall chill was in the air and Kat crossed her arms across her chest, suddenly feeling extremely exposed. And cold. "Did you see which way Rosa went?"

"No. I'm guessing the bath didn't go well?"

Kat scowled. "What do you think? I'm freezing here. Could you come down and help me look for her? I need to put on some clothes before I get hypothermia and die. I'll be right back."

After putting on an over-sized thick wool sweater and her jeans, Kat returned outside to find Joel crouched next to a shivering Rosa, surrounded by the other dogs.

With a firm grip on Rosa's collar, Joel straightened. "Way to bundle up. I think Rosa is cold, too."

"Forgive me if I'm not feeling particularly sympathetic to her plight at the moment," Kat said through chattering teeth. "Let's go inside. I still have to deal with the rinse cycle. She's a soapy mess."

Joel smiled. "At least she smells a little better. But now I think you might need a bath."

"Gee, thanks."

"I'd be willing to help with that."

Kat glanced up, saw the amused lascivious look on his face, and her expression softened. "You have been known to be pretty helpful sometimes. Maybe this day won't be a total loss, after all."

～

Joel helped Kat rinse the remaining soap off Rosa and lived up to his promise to help her wash dog stench off herself as well. Later they collapsed on the sofa, surrounded by the other dogs, who had exhausted themselves with all the excitement.

Rosa was curled up in a tight clammy ball, sulking as she worked to generate a soggy spot on the rug.

Kat leaned back on Joel's chest and closed her eyes. "I hope I never have to wash a dog again. That was horrible." She sat up and turned to him. "What if I had to wash Linus? There's no way I can get a 200-pound dog into the bathroom, much less into the bathtub. It's a good thing I'm not a very large person or I wouldn't even have been able to wash Rosa."

Joel wrapped his arms around her carefully. "True. But your petite body is looking a little battered after the experience. Does your back still hurt?"

"Yes. I'm glad I can't see what it looks like."

"It's colorful."

"Great," Kat said with a sigh. "If there are a lot of carsick dogs like Rosa, we're going to have to add a grooming area to this whole boarding kennel thing. Or just board Chihuahuas that fit in our itty-bitty bathroom."

"Maybe you should add grooming services into your business plan and see if it will work out financially. You never know—maybe you could make a profit with it. But in addition to the extra plumbing for a bath in the kennel, you'd probably also need to hire a groomer. How is the plan going, anyway?"

Kat shifted in his arms. "It's a work in progress. I've been busy."

"Have you started it?"

"I loaded that spreadsheet software on my computer. And then I opened it."

Joel raised one eyebrow. "And?"

"And then I closed it." Kat turned and laid her cheek on his chest, listening to the beat of his heart. "You're the numbers guy. When I look at a blank spreadsheet, my brain shuts down and I think of something else I'd rather do." *Like get a root canal.*

"Even if you don't deal with the money stuff yet, you can still do the other parts of the plan. Like how you'll get customers and market the place. You got a bunch of books about writing business plans, right?"

"Yes. I read some of it." *Three paragraphs is some.*

"Great! I got some more numbers on the building costs, so we can start there. You can put them into your spreadsheet."

Kat squeezed her eyes closed and hugged Joel more tightly. "Do I have to?"

"Yes, you have to."

Kat turned to face him. "I know. It just all seems like a whole bunch of guessing. There's all this stuff about finding your ideal clients and positioning statements. I don't even know what that means. What if I do it wrong? And how many dogs even live in Alpine Grove? I have no clue. Plus, how can I possibly know how much money I'm going to make in five years? Realistically, five months ago I wouldn't have expected to be sitting here in my aunt's old house with you. I didn't even know who you were. The whole thing just makes me feel tired. Or maybe I just am tired. Rosa wore me out."

"If you don't know about the business, who does?"

"Marketing people. I was a technical writer, remember? We editorial types always tried to give those marketing people a wide berth."

Joel stroked her cheek. "I hate to tell you this, but until you make enough money to get yourself a marketing department, I think the department is you."

Kat kissed him and put her head on his chest again. "I know. That's what scares me."

～

Jan stood on the steps to her mother's condo and knocked on the door. It had been a long flight full of delays and airport annoyances. Flying last-minute meant she got the worst seat on the plane, so she got to enjoy some special time next to the lavatory in a seat that didn't recline. Jan now knew more than she wanted to know about the toilet habits and digestive issues of her fellow passengers. It was good to be on the ground again.

The door opened and her mother stood in the doorway wearing a magenta caftan and holding a glass filled with a gelatinous moss-green concoction.

"Hi Mom. I made it."

"Hello darling. It's good to see you. Come in."

Jan hauled her suitcase through the doorway and was pleased to find that today the condo was not full of incense. The psychic scrubbing and purification must have been successful.

"How are you feeling?" Jan said. "Did you find out anything from the doctors?"

"I'm fine."

"Did they do tests?"

Her mother clasped the glass with both hands. "Tests for what, dear?"

"The tests on your heart. You said you had a problem with your heart and you were listening to the doctors."

"They were talking to Zoe. I was providing emotional and spiritual support."

Jan looked around the room. "What? Why?"

"Well, because she was in the hospital, of course."

Jan sat down on the sofa next to her mother. "I thought *you* were in the hospital."

"I was there with Zoe, helping her clear her energy blockage. She had a fall and sprained her ankle."

"What's wrong with your heart then? You said there was something wrong."

"My heart is sick."

"Yes, you told me that. What's wrong with it?"

"Well, you know I'm a Leo. I take everything to heart and I am a passionate person. I tried to work with Bruce and have him lift his consciousness beyond his usual mundane life. He has not resolved some issues and he can't move forward if he reacts the same way he always has. He must find new approaches, and address the reality of his situation. I am trying to give him my love and tolerance, but I also must listen to the guidance of my inner voice. My heart is sick about it."

"You're sick *about* it?" Jan slumped back on the sofa and put her face in her hands. She was such an idiot. "You're saying you're heartsick. Not that your heart is sick."

"What did you think I meant? I am trying to manifest love with Bruce, but it just isn't working and I'm encountering energetic resistance. You are always so literal about everything."

"I'm sorry Mom, but it's easy to be confused. Here's a question: how are you supposed to 'manifest love' with Bruce when he isn't even here? Aren't you supposed to be moving in with him? Last time I was here, I saw boxes. Did you already move? Or bail out? Again?"

"I'm feeling negativity in your tone. I'm going through a transformation right now and it's complicated. I am trying to trust myself and let life flow."

Jan looked into her mother's face. "You really did dump him, didn't you?" She waved her arms in exasperation. "I can't believe it. You ditched him after what, less than a week? Half the wedding guests probably haven't even made it home yet. This is unreal. Have you even tried to talk to him or work it out?"

"I tried to talk to him and harmonize our conversation in a fulfilling and enriching manner. But he didn't understand. He was very negative. So I came back here to uplift my spirits."

"I don't know Bruce," Jan said. "And this is just a guess, but I suspect that most men don't take being dumped on their honeymoon particularly well."

Her mother's eyes brightened. "Speaking of which, how is Steve? He is such a sweet man. I loved how kind he always was about carrying my suitcase with JoJo in it. He was strong and patient, helping me with all those shows. I've been looking forward to your wedding for a long time. Have you set a date yet?"

Jan sighed. "No. I know you like weddings, but that one isn't going to happen. Actually, we broke up."

"Oh no! What happened?"

"Over time, he changed. I didn't want to believe it, but I think I actually fell out of love with him. Or maybe I never really loved him in the first place. I'm not sure, but I don't like who he is now."

Her mother looked crestfallen and genuinely sympathetic. She put her hands over her heart. "Oh honey, I'm so sorry. I didn't know. You need to redirect your energy to the future instead of focusing on what has gone by. As time passes, it's too easy to accumulate more and more baggage. Believe me, I know! I'm so glad you are moving forward and focusing on your own new path and the lessons learned from the experience."

Jan enjoyed a maternal hug for a moment and then said, "Thanks, Mom. I'm sad and I miss him, but I think it was time for us to call it off." She looked toward the window and noticed a huge purple crystal hanging from the curtain rod. "Wait. Don't change the subject on me! You really need to talk to Bruce. It's not fair to him to just run away like this. If he loved you enough to marry you, he deserves more than a halfhearted try at talking. Talk about baggage. You and I both know you've run out on a lot of men. Maybe it's time to give this marriage a real try. I flew all the way down here because I thought you were dying. If you think it would help, I can go with you when you talk to him."

"Would you do that? There were words. Unkind words that I am not proud of saying. I thought of asking Zoe to come with me to try to smooth things over with Bruce, but she is not really up to doing much walking yet. I don't want to tax her vitality."

"I can go with you if you want. Why don't you call him and set up a time to meet?"

"All right, darling. My horoscope says that I need to have courage. Perhaps this is what it meant. I must remind myself that anything is possible and I can create whatever I hope to achieve."

Jan shrugged and passed the phone to her mother. "That sounds good, I guess."

~

Jan stood with her mother in front of the row of beach cottages and marveled at how little the old neighborhood had changed in twenty years.

"Wow, Mom, it looks the same."

"Yes, except now it's extremely expensive to live here. It's a shame I rented and couldn't buy the place next door to Bruce's where we lived. Bruce has owned his little house forever and it is now worth a fortune. But the time wasn't right on my life journey."

Jan touched her mother's shoulder. "Are you ready?"

"Yes. Thank you for coming with me, dear. I'm trying to hold a vision of how I want things to be."

Jan knocked and Bruce opened the door quickly. It was startling how large the man was. He had to be six-foot-five. Seeing him in normal clothes was odd after watching him cavort around commercials in the blue jumpsuit for so many years. He was actually a handsome man, trim and athletic with distinguished salt-and-pepper hair. Mom always went for the good-looking ones, so that wasn't a huge surprise.

"Hi, um, Bruce. I know I didn't get a chance to talk to you at the wedding, but I'm Jan. I lived next door a long time ago."

Bruce grabbed her and wrapped her in a big bear hug. "Jan! I've heard so much about you! Come on in." The Toilet King was just as exuberant in person as he was on TV.

Jan extricated herself from his grasp and walked through the doorway into the house, followed by her mother. The place had the exact same floor plan as the house they'd lived in next door. Slippery beach sand crunched under her heels.

Maybe Bruce didn't have a housekeeper. Or a vacuum cleaner. Or a broom. The house was filled with lived-in furniture that appeared to date from the late seventies. Bright orange and harvest gold permeated the decor. It was like stepping back in time.

Michael was sprawled out on an orange sofa in the living room, wearing shorts and a shredded t-shirt with a surfboard logo on it. He was flipping through a magazine. One leg was hooked over the wooden arm of the sofa and a plastic flip-flop dangled lazily from his foot. Swoosie the Samoyed was curled up next to him on the sofa, panting. Looking up from the magazine, he said, "Hey Jan. How's it going?"

Jan's jaw dropped. She couldn't get away from this guy. "What are you doing here?" The surfer attire really showed off the well-defined muscles he had...everywhere. She tried not to stare. But wow. The half-naked version of the Marlboro man was even more impressive than the fully clothed edition.

Michael peered over the top of his magazine at her. "Isn't your beloved step-brother allowed to visit his dad?"

Jan crossed her arms in front of her chest. "I'm just surprised to see you, that's all. You look like you're about to go surfing."

"No surfing today. Just running. Swoosie and I came up from my place in Del Mar to say hi to Dad and see how he's doing."

"Well my mother and Bruce need to talk," Jan said as she turned to look at her mother. "Right, Mom?"

Bruce reached out his hand. "Angie, it's good to see you again. I've missed you. And you look lovely today."

Angie took his hand. "That is a reflection of my inner happiness at seeing you, too."

"That sounds promising." Bruce said, "Why don't we go sit down and talk."

Michael jumped up off the couch, followed by Swoosie. "Okay, it sounds like you have some stuff to work out. Jan, why don't you come for a walk with me and Swoosie?"

"I'm not sure. I promised my mom I'd stay." And ensure Mom didn't make a break for it. Again.

Her mother turned from Bruce to look at her. "It's fine, Jan. I wish life were more certain, but I'm putting my faith in my higher power that all of this will work out. You and Michael can go. Enjoy the power of the sea and embrace the healing miracle of nature."

Michael gave Jan a questioning look. "I think it's okay, then."

"I guess," Jan said shrugging her shoulders.

"Cool. I need to get Swoosie's leash. Then we can go embrace some nature."

Michael attached Swoosie's leash to a harness and waved back at Bruce and Angie, who were now deep in conversation. "We're leaving now. Good luck!"

Jan followed Michael and his dog out the door. After he shut the door behind them, she said, "I'm not sure about this. My mom was really worried about talking to him. I guess they had a big fight or something."

"Hey, they're grown-ups, right? They can figure it out."

"I think your dad may be more of a grown-up than my mom."

Michael smiled and glanced over at her. "I won't argue with that."

"You probably already know this, but Bruce is husband number seven. Well, I think it's seven. Maybe it's six. I keep forgetting."

"You? Forget? I thought your brain was chock full of facts like that."

Jan scowled. "Ha. Ha. You're terribly funny."

Michael stopped as Swoosie started walking back and forth across a particularly special piece of grass. "Oops, looks like the poop dance is about to happen."

"The poop dance? Only you would have a name for this activity."

"It's good to know when the poop dance is going to happen. You don't want to be caught unaware. Swoosie has a particular way of stopping and circling. And then there's this happy serene look she gets, so you know it's not just another boring sniff fest. She means it."

"You spend a lot of time walking your dog, don't you?"

"I have to clean up after her, so it's good to know when to be at the ready. And yes, here it is, the moment we've all been waiting for: poop tail! A Samoyed's tail flips backwards when the dog is doing the deed."

Jan shook her head. "I can't believe I'm having this conversation. Shouldn't we be talking about our parents? That's more important." Although by now, her mother had probably fled the scene.

Michael yanked a plastic bag out of a pocket in his shorts and bent down to clean up. He looked over at Jan. "Well, this is important to Swoosie. It's a big moment in her day."

"You're making me glad I live in a place where I don't have to get quite so up-close-and-personal with my dog's excrement. I just let Rosa out and she does her thing." Of course, that was also why Rosa was starting to resemble a hairy beach ball.

"Don't you ever take her for walks?"

"Well, sometimes. There are acres upon acres of forest where we can walk. My feeling is that if the wildlife can go there, so can Rosa."

Michael dropped the bag into a garbage can. "Here no one likes it when dog owners turn a beach neighborhood or the beach itself into a giant litter box. I always imagine some little kid joyfully playing in the sand. He finds a fantastic new toy and runs up to the beach blanket, clutching his exciting brown discovery. He proudly shows it to his mom, but she screams and tells him to put it down. Mayhem ensues. They pack up their coolers and vow never to return to Litter Box Beach ever again. It's all just nasty. Not to mention bad for tourism."

Jan studied his profile as they walked. "You have quite a vivid imagination. I thought dogs weren't allowed on the beach."

"They're allowed on a couple of them like Dog Beach, which isn't too far from my place. And in some cases, people just ignore the 'no dogs' signs, particularly in the winter."

"I think I'll watch my step the next time I go to the beach." Jan looked down at the ground, surveying the general area just in case.

Michael grinned. "Now I've freaked you out. It's like the movie with the Baby Ruth in the pool...DOODIE!"

She looked back at him. "That was *Caddyshack* with Chevy Chase and Bill Murray. It was directed by Harold Ramis and filmed in late 1979. The Doodie scene was actually based on a real event."

"I know you're a librarian, but how do you remember all these things? I have trouble remembering where I left my sunglasses."

"I'm not sure," Jan said. "It's just the way my mind works. Steve used to say my brain was filled with UBI."

"UBI?"

"Useless Bits of Information. He said it drove him nuts. That I was trying to card-catalog the world."

Michael narrowed his eyes. "That's a little harsh, don't you think? If you ever want a career in advertising, let me know. You're like a one-woman research department."

"I'm afraid you have made the world of advertising sound unpleasant." Jan shook her head. "No thanks. Your description of the stress and deadlines makes it seem like a horrible way to earn a living. I'll stick with the library. At least it's quiet. No temperamental actors or yelling bosses."

"I suppose that was not one of my best days."

"You certainly look a lot more relaxed today. I almost didn't recognize you dressed like a surfer."

Michael surveyed her attire. "You may want to dress down a little while you're here. Aren't you hot? You look a little flushed. And those shoes have to be painful."

Jan *was* feeling a little overheated. Perhaps the suit and heels hadn't been an ideal choice. "I thought I'd be sitting around in a cottage mediating my mother's marriage, not walking through the old neighborhood with you."

"Let's find a place to sit down and get something to drink. If you get heat stroke, your mother will kill me."

"Maybe. But these days she'd do it in a very heart-centered and loving way."

Michael laughed. "Hey, I don't want any bad karma. Let's stick to good vibrations. Gotta keep those lovin' ones happening."

"Are you referencing the Beach Boys song?"

"I suppose you know when it was released?"

Jan smiled. "October of 1966, actually. It was composed by Brian Wilson and the lyrics are by Mike Love."

~

Jan waited on the outside patio with Swoosie while Michael got some drinks. The little cafe had a row of festive green umbrellas out front and Jan settled into her chair, relieved to have some shade. Opting for a more casual wardrobe would have some advantages. Maybe she should head to the mall this afternoon.

Michael returned with two tall glasses of iced tea. "Here you go."

"Thanks. By the way, what did you do to your dog? She's being really good, just lying here like a model canine citizen. I can't believe this is the same animal that terrorized the wedding."

"It's all those walks. Or runs, really. Most weekends when I don't have to work, Swoosie and I jog from my place in Del Mar up here. It's about six or eight miles. We do it in the morning before it gets hot. I like to check in on my dad and we usually have breakfast together. All that exercise is good for Swoosie and Dad loves her."

Jan looked down at Michael's muscular legs. He was obviously in extremely good shape. "I'm guessing you don't run in flip-flops."

"No, I'm not that much of a beach bum. I do have running shoes. But I take them off when I get there. Dad's house has enough sand in it already. It's getting so he could build castles in there."

Jan giggled. "I'm glad I'm not the only one who noticed that. The floor feels kind of gritty when you walk around."

"He's got the money for a housekeeper." Michael trailed his index finger on the glass, making swirly designs in the condensation. "He just doesn't want to deal with it. And sometimes he complains that he doesn't want someone going through his stuff. Most of his stuff is from 1974, so I'm not sure who'd want it."

Michael looked oddly melancholy about this topic. Now she was curious. "So when did you find out that your dad was marrying my mom?" Jan jiggled the straw around in her glass, poking at the ice cubes. "The whole wedding thing came out of nowhere for me. But I don't live nearby and my mother and I have a sort of...difficult...relationship."

Michael leaned back in his chair and crossed his legs at the ankles. "I met her at Dad's house one Saturday a couple of months ago. I hadn't seen her in years. Way back when, she was the hot neighbor mom. Then all of a sudden, I find the woman from my boyhood fantasies standing there in my father's kitchen making pancakes. They looked really cozy. And frankly, when it comes to my dad, that's just not something I want to think about. I walked in the door with Swoosie like I always do and there she was in a long shirt and nothing else. It kind of freaked me out, if you really want to know."

Jan smiled. "Look at the bright side. At least she was wearing clothes. You missed the nudist phase."

"Yikes." Michael leaned forward in the chair and put his elbows on the table. "Thanks for that image. Now I'm gonna have nightmares. The thing I can't figure out is how they pulled off such a huge wedding so fast. I'm no expert, but aren't wedding places booked up years in advance?"

"My mother has had lots of practice. One of her best friends, Skye, is a wedding planner. I think Mom has her on speed-dial. Skye might have figured Mom was due for another marriage and reserved a place just in case."

Michael smirked. "Now you're just messing with me."

"Maybe a little," Jan said with a half-smile. "But she does have a friend who is a wedding planner. Skye loves to plan and my mother loves weddings. She definitely loves weddings more than the actual being married part."

"It is a great excuse for a party, I'll give her that. And you looked great in your flamenco outfit. Speaking of little-boy fantasies...that's the stuff dreams are made of. Even when your mom was young, she didn't compare to you in those ruffles."

Jan blushed and looked down at her iced tea. "Oh please. Spare me."

"After you left, a few people asked where the cute chick with the ruffles went."

"They were probably talking about Swoosie."

"I'll grant you Swoosie is completely adorable in her ruffles," Michael said as he patted the dog on the head, "but her ruffles weren't snug in all the right places like yours were."

Jan looked into his face to see if he was serious. It appeared he was. She smiled. "Thank you. I think." She looked across the street at the passersby and noticed that a tall blonde woman in a bikini top was making faces at them.

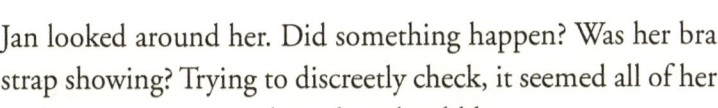

Jan looked around her. Did something happen? Was her bra strap showing? Trying to discreetly check, it seemed all of her undergarments were where they should be.

Michael frowned. "Is something wrong?"

Jan leaned toward him across the table. "That woman is making faces at us. Do I have something in my teeth?"

Michael looked around and smiled. "Do you want to pet her?"

The woman waved and ran across the street, rushing to their table. "Oh yes! That is just the cutest dog I've ever seen. Look at how furry she is!"

The woman crouched down and put both her hands into Swoosie's deep fur coat. "She's soooooo soft! What kind of dog is she? Or he?"

"Her name is Swoosie," Michael said. "She's a Samoyed."

"Sam-oy-ed? I've never heard of that. What beautiful fur. How do you keep her clean?"

Michael smiled. "Well, it does take some work. I have to brush her. But in general, dirt mostly just falls out of her coat. I call it magic fur."

Enjoying all the attention, Swoosie rolled over on her back for a tummy rub. Her tail wagged slowly along the ground.

After giving Swoosie's tummy the required rubbing, the woman stood up again. "Thank you so much! My name is Tammy, by the way."

"I'm Michael. And this is my sister Jan."

Jan nodded. "Step-sister actually."

Tammy pressed her hands together and squealed. "Wow, like the Brady Bunch! I used to watch that show all the time."

"I think everybody did," Michael said.

"Yes, that's true," Jan said. "Thanks to the power of syndication, I'm doomed to be compared to Jan Brady forever. The show has never been off the air since it was canceled in 1974."

Tammy's shoulders drooped and she looked bewildered for a moment. "Well, thanks again." She waved half-heartedly at Jan and Michael and then crouched down to cuddle Swoosie. "Bye, my little oogie–woogie-snuggle-doggie."

After Tammy crossed the street, Michael looked at Jan. "I think you lost her with the word syndication."

"It does have a lot of syllables," Jan said. "So does that happen a lot?"

"What?"

"Women running over to pet your dog like that?"

"Yes. Everybody loves Swoosie. Well, except you."

"I'm assuming your dog doesn't shred the clothing of most of the women you meet. She certainly must be a boon to your social life, though."

Michael gave her a mock leer. "How do you know I didn't teach her that little disrobing trick? But yes, you're right; she's a chick magnet of the highest order. It's even worse with little girls. Every little kid under the age of ten thinks she's a stuffed animal and wants to pet her. Not that I'm trying to attract little girls or anything like that old guy in the book by Nabokov."

"Eww. Now, you're just being creepy. Or making a reference to a song by the Police. It's hard to tell with you."

Michael laughed. "Hey, brothers are supposed to creep out their sisters, right? I have to make up for lost time."

"Speaking of which, we should probably go back and see if our parents are still speaking to each other." She'd lay odds her mother had disappeared by now.

Michael pushed back his chair and Swoosie stood up and stretched. He ruffled the dog's ears. "Okay. If we must."

"Sorry. No more adoring bikini-clad women for you today."

"We'll see. The day is young."

Chapter 6

The Great Sandini

Michael and Jan returned to the house and found Angie and Bruce sitting on the sofa in silence. At least Angie was still there, anyway. Michael unclipped Swoosie's leash and the dog ran over to the sofa, jumped up, and settled in between the couple. Bruce looked down at the dog and reached over to pet her back. "Hi Swoosie. Did you have a good walk?" Swoosie wagged her tail in response.

"That is a truly beautiful animal," Angie said as she reached over to stroke Swoosie's ears. "Look at how the light makes her fur sparkle. And she is so soft. She obviously is a compassionate creature. What a soothing spirit."

Swoosie smiled and panted cheerfully, obviously enjoying the compliments. Jan looked at Michael. "Obviously, my mother hasn't spent as much time with Swoosie as I have. She hasn't seen the dark side."

"Never underestimate the power of the dark side," Michael replied. "Strong Swoosie is in the ways of the Force."

Angie looked up. "What are you two talking about? You seem to have developed an interesting form of communication."

Jan sighed. "Oh Mom, come on. He's referring to *Star Wars*. Yoda? Darth Vader?"

Angie furrowed her brow. "It's true. We are all trying to be in alignment with the stars."

"So does that mean you and Bruce have worked things out now?" Jan said. "Remember, you are married, after all. You made a commitment."

Angie folded her hands in her lap. "We have resolved some matters that have pained me for a while. Bruce has helped me come to terms with some issues from my past."

"So are you going to move in here? Or is Bruce moving to your place?" Jan said. "I'm here for a week, so I could help. I'm sure Michael would, too."

Michael looked over at Jan quickly. "I might be able to do that, depending on the timing. But I do have to work."

"I don't feel completely aligned in this space," Angie said. "I will need to bring Skye over for a cleansing."

Bruce shifted his position on the sofa. "You're not going to mess with my stuff, are you?"

"The house needs to be clean," Angie said. "There is a feeling that pervades this space that I can't live with. I don't feel grounded here."

"There is a little too much ground here. Mostly all over the floor." Jan volunteered. "Maybe we could sweep up some of the sand to start? I could even hire someone to help." At least, cleaning was something constructive and real. All these vague answers from her mother were slowly driving her insane.

"I don't want a stranger messing with my stuff," Bruce said. "They might steal something."

"Dad, we've talked about this," Michael said. "No one *wants* your stuff. It's old and most of it is covered with a layer of sand. Cleaning this place would be a good way to kick off your new life with Angie. Have you actually cleaned this house since Mom died?"

Bruce shook his head slowly. "Not really. I do dishes and little things, but I haven't ever done a real thorough cleaning. I was afraid I'd do it wrong and she wouldn't approve."

Michael sat on the arm of the sofa and put his hand on his father's shoulder. "You never told me that. All this time, I thought you were just a slob. It's been long enough and you've remarried. I think you need to let go."

Jan turned to her mother. "If the house is thoroughly cleaned, will you be willing to move in?"

"It must have a spiritual cleansing as well. I'd like to have Skye come over with her smudge sticks and herbs."

"Whatever works," Jan said. "Is that okay with you, Bruce?"

Bruce shrugged his shoulders. "I guess so."

Jan stood up. "Great! We have a plan. I'll make arrangements to get a cleaning crew out here. Bruce, I'll supervise and make sure no one takes anything or does anything with your stuff that you don't approve of. Will that work?"

Bruce nodded and turned to Angie. "So you'll really stay here if I do that?"

Angie nodded. She leaned over Swoosie and tentatively embraced Bruce. Swoosie decided she'd had enough togetherness and leaped off the couch.

Michael hooked Swoosie back onto her leash. "Okay, I need to check in with work, so I'm going to head home."

"Mom, can Bruce give you a ride home? I need to go to the mall and get some different clothes if I'm going to be working on cleaning." It was great to finally feel useful.

Angie was still holding Bruce's hand. She smiled. "Yes dear. That would be lovely. Thank you for helping us. We'll stay here and talk some more."

Jan turned to Michael. "Do you and Swoosie want a lift? Or does she need more running?"

Michael smiled. "A ride would be great. I'd like to see what's up at work sooner, rather than later. Swoosie has been a pretty good girl today, so I'll give her a break." He handed Jan the leash. "Let me go grab my running shoes and then we can head out."

Jan gave her mother a hug. "Mom, I'll set everything up as far as the cleaning. I really want you to try to make this marriage work this time. Bruce deserves it. And you deserve it, too."

Michael took the leash back from Jan. "Let's go make the jump to hyperspace, baby."

Jan rolled her eyes. "It will take a few minutes to get the coordinates from the nav computer. I don't know how to get to your place."

They walked out and Michael closed the door behind him. "No problem. I'll direct you. And we're outta here! Here we go, Swoosie. Strap yourself in; it's time to hit light speed!"

Jan opened the rear door of the car for Swoosie and grinned at Michael. "Fixing your parents' marriage ain't like dusting crops, that's for sure."

"Don't get cocky, kid. That marriage ain't fixed yet."

He was probably right. But at least for now, they had a plan.

Jan dropped Michael off at his house, which was a cute bungalow located two blocks from the beach in Del Mar. Before he went inside, they exchanged phone numbers, so they could coordinate what they now referred to as The Great Sandini project.

After a stop by the mall for shorts and t-shirts, Jan went to work trying to find a cleaning company that would work on a large, sandy project on short notice. Her mother would be looking for any excuse to escape this marriage. The current state of the house was something Jan could actually do something about and she was determined to make sure it was clean by the time she returned to Alpine Grove.

The following day at Bruce's house, Jan met Michael as well as Evette, of The Maison Maid. Evette was a stout gray-haired woman wearing a classic black-and-white French maid's uniform that looked decidedly uncomfortable.

"Evette, thank you for coming today," Michael said. "This is my father Bruce. It's his house."

Evette waved her hand toward her vacuum cleaner, "Monsieur, I can tell you are not familiar with the exciting world of vacuums. I am thinking yours must be an inferior model. But this machine I have here is the finest machine. It uses a water-filter system to keep the particles out of the air."

Jan bent to look at the famous vacuum. "Is running sand through this going to be a problem?"

Evette shook her head. "Nonsense. It will work on the most difficult dirt. Wet dirt cannot fly! It will even pick up sand, which can ruin your carpet, you know. The sharp edges of the petite crystals cut the carpet fibers, so when you run the vacuum across it, you are picking up pieces of the rug instead. That is why you have a worn traffic area. It is because that is where the carpet is now missing! My machine is one that picks up sand. So you will not have to buy new carpet! I can give you more information, since I also sell this fine machine. I love to show it off."

Michael looked at Jan, then back at Evette. "Thanks Evette, but I think we'll see how this goes first. New carpet wouldn't be such a bad thing. The green shag is looking a little tired."

"Hey, I bought that carpet!" Bruce said. "It was expensive."

"In 1979," Michael said. "Why don't you take off, Dad? Aren't you meeting Joey and Dave at the cafe?"

Bruce nodded. "Okay. Fine. I'll leave you to it. Make sure nothing happens here."

Michael patted his father on the back, "No worries, Dad. We've got it covered."

Jan turned to Evette. "Where would you like to start?"

Evette swiveled her head, looking around the living room. "I think here would be good."

"Okay. Michael and I are going to deal with the kitchen, then."

Michael raised his eyebrows. "We are?"

"Yes. We are."

Evette started unpacking a wide range of complicated vacuum attachments from a case, and Michael followed Jan into the kitchen. Jan pointed at the stove. "So I'm curious. How many kitchen fires have happened in here?"

Michael peered at the blackened stove hood. "I lost count."

"My mother isn't good with fire, either. Maybe we should give them a six-pack of smoke alarms as a belated wedding present."

"Good idea. I'd be happy to go off to the hardware store and get some."

"Nice try," Jan said. "See that green stuff on the wall and the ceiling? That's your first project."

Michael leaned toward the wall to examine the offending green spots. "I think this dates from Dad's kale smoothie phase. He had blender issues."

Jan stood on tiptoe to get a closer look. "I'm guessing the brown spots are peanut butter?"

"Yeah, that was the protein shake era. Maybe late 80s?"

"That's disgusting. It's all yours."

Michael turned his palms upward. "Why me? What are you doing?"

Jan opened the cabinet under the sink and pointed at the dark space. "This. I don't know what that yellow slime is under there, but I bought industrial-strength rubber gloves especially to deal with it."

"I think Mr. Clean is rolling over in his grave."

"Mr. Clean is not dead," Jan said. "He's concentrated. Now he's Ultra Mr. Clean. Did you know that his first name is Veritably?"

Michael paused in his vigorous wall-scrubbing. "Oh come on. You've got to be kidding me."

"In the sixties, there was a contest to give him a first name."

"They had a contest to name the bald guy?"

Jan smiled, sat back on her heels, and wiped her forehead with her wrist. "I don't make these things up. Truth is stranger than fiction."

A screeching noise came from the living room. Evette shouted, "*Merde! Mon Dieu!*" and then a long string of unintelligible French phrases.

Michael dropped his sponge into the bucket and looked at Jan. "That didn't sound good."

They both went into the living room and found Evette crouched over her vacuum cleaner, looking distressed. "I think there was a sand dune here in the living room. And it has hurt the motor of my fine machine. I must go take it to the shop and have it fixed *tout de suite!*"

"What about cleaning the rest of the house?" Jan asked. The sand level appeared to be unchanged.

Evette stood up and put her fists at her sides. "I cannot risk any further damage to the machine! This is *très horrible!*"

Jan looked down at the machine, which was apparently no longer fine. "I'm sorry. You said you could do it and the machine was up to the task."

Without another word, Evette gathered up her many implements and left, slamming the door behind her.

Michael turned to Jan. "That went well. Now what?"

Jan bent down to examine the edge of the carpet. "I think your Dad used a staple gun to put down this carpet. It's coming up here at the edge."

"Dad has never been much for home improvement." Crouching next to Jan, Michael grabbed the edge of the carpet with both hands and yanked upward. A flurry of dust and sand flew into the air when the carpet released from the floor. Michael dropped the carpet as they both started coughing.

Pausing to gasp for air, Jan bent over and peered at the floor underneath the carpet. "Look at that! There are wood floors under there."

Michael crouched down again. "I think it's quarter-sawn hardwood. Wow. I forgot that's what the floors used to look like before the shag arrived."

Jan turned to him. "Those floors are gorgeous and this carpet has gotta go. Evette and her fine machine have proven that the green shag won't ever get clean, so there's no great loss. Start pulling."

"I think my dad is going to consider this messing with his stuff."

"But my mom loves hardwood floors."

Michael shrugged. "Okay. But only if it means I don't have to clean peanut butter off the ceiling anymore."

"Fine. I'll deal with the kitchen. Apparently choosy dads choose Jif, too."

Michael laughed as he ripped up another section of carpet. "Apparently."

~

A few hours later, Jan walked into Michael's old bedroom and held up her hands at him. Each finger had a plastic tape dispenser looped on it. "How many rolls of tape does one man need?"

Michael shook his head and pointed to the large black garbage bag in front of him. "Chuck the dead ones. Tape that doesn't stick anymore has gone beyond its useful lifespan."

"Judging from the packaging, I'd say cellophane tape lasts about ten years. That's good to know. It looks like you're making progress in here." He was sitting on the floor surrounded by piles of yellowing papers. The soles of his bare feet were sandy and blackened with dirt.

"Yeah, when I moved out, Dad just pretty much just closed the door to this room," Michael said, picking up a book and moving off the floor to sit on the bed. "Here's the book I was reading. It was still sitting on this shelf next to my bed."

Jan leaned over him to look at the cover. "*The Two Towers*? Tolkien?"

"Yeah, I could never get through it, although I tried for almost a year. I set it aside and put it on that shelf. And there it has stayed."

"So you never found out how the *Lord of the Rings* ends? That's sad." How could anyone not finish a book?

"I was okay with it. No book should be that boring."

Jan sat down heavily on the bed next to him, holding her dusting rag in her lap. "I appreciate you taking off work to deal with this mess. It's a lot easier with both of us, since you know more about your dad's important stuff than I do."

"It's okay. Something is going on at the agency. They told everyone to take a couple of days off because there's some type of audit. I haven't taken a vacation in a long time. It feels strange to *not* be at the office." He smiled at her. "Not that this feels like a vacation, by the way."

Jan chuckled. "Oh come on. There's a lot of nostalgia here."

"Yeah, it's just one big trip down amnesia lane."

"Wow, quoting *Dead Poets Society*? With Robin Williams and Robert Sean Leonard? I loved that movie."

Michael turned and looked into Jan's eyes. "It amazes me how you get every pop-culture reference. I have never met anyone like you."

Jan giggled nervously. "I know. I'm unusual." The gold flecks in his brown eyes glinted in the afternoon sun streaming in through the window.

He leaned over and kissed her on the lips. A jolt of surprise and desire shot through Jan's body. She had kissed Steve countless times, but the feel of Michael's lips on hers wasn't like anything she'd ever experienced. Shouldn't she feel guilty? This was wrong for so many reasons. Yet she placed her hands on his broad shoulders, closed her eyes, and reveled in the sensations anyway.

Michael pulled away first and they stared at each other for a long second. "Well, that certainly wasn't a chaste sisterly kiss."

"You started it." And he was really good at it.

"I suppose I did," Michael laughed. "But now who sounds like a ten-year old?" He stood up and the book fell off the bed onto the floor. As he put the book back on the shelf, he said. "I guess we should get back to work."

Several hours of cleaning later, Jan collapsed on the living room sofa. "I'm done. I can't clean anything else. Or move."

"Just one more thing," Michael said. "We need to move the shag carpet out of the front yard. Dad may be a slob, but he does have a few standards."

Jan groaned as she levered herself up off the couch. "All right. But that's it."

"Hey, I think we really deserve a treat after this long sandy day of grime. How about I take you out to dinner tonight? There's a great Indian restaurant not too far from here."

Jan looked down at herself. "I'd need to go back to my mom's place and shower and change. I can't let anyone see me looking like this."

"I suppose you have looked better," Michael said, looking at her appraisingly. "Maybe we can do that another time and just get a pizza instead. That might be easier."

"Yes. Pizza." Jan closed her eyes and leaned her head back on the sofa. "Mmm. Pizza."

"Let's move the carpet. Then I'll call in the pizza, go get Swoosie, pick it up, and come back here. It would be good if you could stay here in case my dad comes back. He may freak out when he sees that the carpet is gone."

"That would be an awkward conversation, particularly since I barely know him. You need to hurry back, so I don't have to go through that explanation. But I suppose maybe he won't notice, either."

"Believe me, he's going to notice. Come on, get up."

"Fine," Jan said as she used both hands to push her body up off the sofa. "Let's get this over with."

Later, Jan and Michael were eating pizza at the newly cleared-off dining room table. Swoosie was resting her muzzle on Michael's thigh, supervising the consumption and hoping for a handout. He slipped her a small piece of crust. The dog wagged her tail as she snuffled it down.

They all looked up from the meal when Bruce walked in the door. Swoosie ran over to Bruce to say hello. Bruce looked around in confusion as he stooped down to pet the dog. "What happened?"

Michael stood up. "Hi Dad. We cleaned." He waved his arm toward the room. "It looks better. And it even smells better."

"What did you do?"

Jan stood up and walked around the table next to Michael. "The cleaning lady broke her vacuum, so we had to clean everything ourselves."

Bruce looked down at his feet. "What happened to the floor?"

Michael walked over to his father. "After it killed Evette's vacuum, we took a closer look at the carpet and we determined it couldn't be saved. It's next to the garbage cans in the back yard."

"My mom loves hardwood floors." Jan said. "And look, they are beautiful. Wood floors like these are hard to find. It might be made from the type of old-growth timber that you don't see anymore. Look at the gorgeous grain."

"I can help you refinish the floor if you want, Dad," Michael said. "It will be great."

Bruce sat down on the sofa. "Your mother picked out that carpet. She loved that green. It wasn't too long before she got sick."

Michael sat down next to his father and put his arm around him. "I know, Dad. But the carpet was so full of sand, we couldn't get it out. Ripping it up wasn't much fun, either. I have sand in crevices I'd rather not talk about. It's like I went surfing and had a really bad wipe out."

Bruce turned his head to survey the room again. "The place sort of looks like it did when I bought it. Maybe that's not so bad. Those were some good times."

Michael smiled. "And you'll have good times again with Angie, I'm sure. So how was your day? Did you meet up with the guys?"

Bruce's face lit up. "Yeah, we had some fun. My buddy Dave is the best. I love that guy. We got some coffee and then hung out at his place. Played some poker. Watched the game. Drank some beer. It was a great day."

"I'm glad. Jan and I will clean up our pizza, then we should head out. Maybe you could call Angie and let her know the place is clean."

Bruce nodded. "I will. Thanks for doing this. We'll see what she thinks."

Jan and Michael put everything away, collected Swoosie, and said goodnight to Bruce, who still looked sort of sad. As Jan closed the door behind her, she said, "Maybe I'm just tired, but I'm wondering if we did the right thing. I feel a little bad for him."

"Don't. He's been in a sort of emotional limbo since my mom died years ago. He never even went out on dates with anyone. Your mother is the first person I know about. That's why their wedding was a surprise. Maybe he's finally moving on."

Jan leaned on the side of her rental car and faced Michael. "I hope so. He seemed so sad. It's weird, because before, I only knew him as the guy with the purple hair and blue jumpsuit."

"All of his troubles didn't go down the drain."

Jan smirked. "Oh please; that's not the Toilet King song; it's the Roto-Rooter jingle and you know it."

Michael smiled. "Just checking to see how tired you really are." He reached over and tucked a wayward curl behind her ear. "I was serious about dinner, too. I've got tomorrow off because of that audit at work. Do you have plans? If I have to take vacation time, it would be nice to do something fun."

"I should make sure my mother doesn't need anything. That's why I'm here, after all." Jan grimaced. "And gosh, what could be more fun than cleaning up detritus from the late 70s?"

"I'm sure I can think of something."

After that astonishing lust-inducing kiss earlier, Jan was pretty sure he was right.

~

Angie assured Jan that everything was fine with Bruce and encouraged her to go out and have a good time. "You never do anything fun. Live a little!" Although Angie's comment about her lack of social life was a little insensitive, Jan was secretly relieved not to be spending more time with her mother and her crystals. Unfortunately, being with Michael was becoming more complicated. She was starting to enjoy being around him a little too much. Shouldn't she be mourning the loss of her relationship with Steve more? Going out and having fun with Michael (whatever that meant) seemed somehow sacrilegious.

Michael asked Jan to meet him the next morning at a coffee shop that was far enough away from his house that he could give Swoosie a proper walk and tire her out. Jan arrived at the cheerful, bright yellow Victorian building and found Michael and Swoosie already sitting at one of the tables on the wraparound deck. As she walked by the door into the building, the scent of exotic spices tickled her nose.

"You both look relaxed. This is a beautiful building."

Michael handed a piece of croissant to Swoosie and stood up. "It's actually a restored train station. And the coffee is excellent."

"It certainly smells good. Swoosie seems to think the croissant is tasty, too."

Michael passed Swoosie's leash to Jan. "Hang on to her while I'll go get you some coffee."

Jan sat down and looked down at the dog. "You're going to behave yourself, right?" Swoosie wagged her tail and turned to watch as Michael disappeared through huge train station doors into the cafe area. Then she put her paws up on the table and snatched the rest of the croissant off the plate.

"Swoosie, NO!" Jan yelped as she jerked back on the leash. But it was too late; Swoosie was hurriedly snarfing down the remains of the pastry. What an amazing food thief. Looking around, Jan couldn't see Michael anywhere. She should tell him to get himself a new croissant, but the coffee shop was extremely crowded, and it wasn't worth risking losing this choice seating location on the deck. Maybe Michael would think about getting himself something else to eat, given his dog's tendency to consume everything within reach. After all, this certainly wasn't the first time the dog had snarfed something while he wasn't looking.

Having finished her croissant, Swoosie sat up again and peered at the table. And then stared mournfully at Jan.

"Oh please. Spare me the puppy-dog eyes. You are not starving. That was probably 500 calories, you little swine."

Swoosie perked up her ears, wagged her tail, and smiled in response.

Jan bent to stroke the dog's soft pointy ears. "You are just absurdly cute, though. I'm sure that helps you get away with everything."

She turned as a female voice behind her said, "Please, please can I pet your dog?" The tall, athletic woman was wearing skin-tight bike shorts and a rainbow top that matched the bike helmet she had cradled in her arm. "What kind of dog is it?"

"She's not my dog, but yes, she's very friendly. Swoosie is a Samoyed." Swoosie wagged her tail more vigorously, looking forward to enjoying some more affection from a new human.

The woman crouched and put her helmet down on the wooden deck so she could cuddle Swoosie's face with both hands. "Oooh, aren't you just the cuuuutest little thing!"

Jan rolled her eyes melodramatically at Michael as he walked up with a tray of coffee and pastries. "Welcome back. I hope you got extra. Swoosie decided she needed a snack."

Michael leaned over and put the plate as far from the edge of the table as possible. "Swoosie knows you're new at dealing with her. Constant vigilance is required with this dog. She totally played you."

Having finished loving up Swoosie, the woman stood up, took one look at Michael, and thrust out her hand. "Hello! I'm Veronica. Is this your dog? I love her!"

Michael smiled and shook Veronica's hand. "Yes, she is. Thank you. It's nice to meet you."

Michael stood, waiting for Veronica to leave so he could sit down. He nodded in the direction of the cafe. "The line is getting longer. You might want to get over there before all those people crammed into that yellow microbus in the parking lot make it over here. Then the line will be out the door."

Veronica looked at the line, then at Jan and said, "Oh. Okay. Yes, I'd better go. Maybe I'll see you again sometime?"

Michael moved to sit down at the table, "Maybe."

Jan reached for her coffee. "Good grief. Being around you and Swoosie is just a love fest. You'd think that woman had never seen a cute dog or a good-looking man before."

Michel grinned. "You think I'm good-looking?"

"Way to fish for compliments. Men who know they are good-looking seem less attractive, by the way. I'm guessing that one of your ardent groupies may have mentioned that before."

"Maybe once or twice."

"Kat's friend Maria says you look like the Marlboro man back when he was hot."

Michael peered over his steaming coffee mug as he took a sip. "I don't know who Kat or Maria are, but does that mean you were talking about me with your girlfriends?"

Jan felt the color rise on her cheeks. "Well, I don't know if they are my girlfriends, exactly. Kat is taking care of my dog Rosa while I'm here. They invited me to a little party of sorts, after they found out about the whole thing with Steve at the library."

"Oh yeah. That." Michael leaned back in his chair, cupping his mug in both hands in front of him. "The thing I like about this place is that it's right on the 101. You can watch every prototype Southern California person go by. For example, Veronica is one of the Spandex People. They are very serious bikers and they have to be aerodynamic, so their clothes show every possible nuance of their form, whether you want to see it or not."

Jan inclined her head toward the cafe. "You seemed to appreciate Veronica's assets."

"Well, yes, but I don't want to see Harry the Welder's junk over there." Michael shifted his gaze toward a burly man wearing a tank top and bicycle shorts who was walking up the steps into the cafe. "I mean that's just way more than I need to know."

Jan giggled and glanced toward the man at the next table. "Okay, what about that guy?"

Michael turned and looked quickly at the man. "Oh that's easy. That's your basic Biker Dude. The leather vest is a dead giveaway. I'll bet you fifty bucks that the vest has the classic Harley logo on the back."

Jan shook her head. "Not taking that bet. What about the guy over there? He looks pretty normal."

Michael swiveled in his chair to take a look. "Hmm, that's Mr. Pressed Jeans. Ultra yuppie. Probably drives an extremely expensive car. And he's very proud of it. That big keychain with the wad of keys on the table probably has the logo on it. Maybe Porsche? Lamborghini? Ferrari?"

"Hard to say."

He turned toward a woman at another nearby table who was reading a book. "And then you have this woman. She's one of the Solo Book People. She wants to get out and be around other human beings, but she brings a book to ensure no one will actually talk to her. The book is like a death ray for introverts who want to be left alone."

"Hey, now you're talking about *my* people! I don't know if I'm an introvert exactly, but people who read need to eat too, you know." Jan picked off a piece of croissant and popped it in her mouth. "Your descriptions remind me of high school. Like *The Breakfast Club*, where you have the brain, the athlete, the princess, the basket case, and the criminal. This may not be a surprise, but I was a brain in high school. What were you? I'm guessing you were a jock, right?"

Michael looked thoughtful for a second. "Eventually, I guess. But if we're classifying based on the movie, for a lot of high school I was more like the Judd Nelson character, although I don't think I actually ever told anyone to eat my shorts."

Jan smiled. "Ahh, so you were a bad boy? I'm trying to envision you in the grubby torn denim jacket."

"More like a smart ass. As a brain, you may not realize this, but most teachers don't appreciate that type of humor. My mom's death messed me up for a while, and my dad and I weren't getting along. I skipped a lot of classes, took up smoking and other undesirable habits, you might say. Then my junior year, a buddy convinced me that if I took up track I could meet girls. So I had to quit smoking or succumb to serious respiratory distress out on the field."

"You cleaned up nicely in the end. Well, according to Veronica, anyway."

"Wait! I forgot one more type of Southern California person." Michael sat up straight and looked around the cafe. "I don't see them here today; maybe it's too early. But we can't forget about the Stroller People. They're the parents who have the gigantic, $350 running strollers that they have trouble controlling, so they bump into everything. It's like bumper cars, except with screaming toddlers."

"You spend a lot of time here, don't you?" Jan said.

"Hey, there's outdoor seating and Swoosie needs her exercise." Hearing her name, Swoosie wagged in agreement, but didn't take her eyes off the pastry remnants that were still on the table.

Michael waved in the general direction of the coastline. "This is only the beginning. From the sound of it, you didn't do much of anything fun when you lived here, so it's time to go see the sights of San Diego. We can stop by my place, drop off Swoosie for a nap, and then go from there."

"Where are we going?" Jan asked with a bit of trepidation.

"You'll find out."

Chapter 7

Fun in the Sun

After they dropped off Swoosie, Michael took Jan to a street fair. He regaled her with stories about her fellow tourists while she looked at crafts and knickknacks. They stood in front of a huge display of tie-dyed shirts, skirts, and tapestries. The colorful cloth flapped merrily in the ocean breeze, the rainbow flags celebrating peace, love, and herbal enjoyment.

Michael gave her a friendly nudge. "You need a sarong."

"Because librarians so often wear sarongs?"

"No, because you'd look good in it. Maybe even better than the ruffles."

Jan gave him a sidelong glance. "You're just not going to let go of the ruffles, are you?"

"They were memorable. I think I'm starting to understand Bob's thing for sexy librarians. Plus, this is San Diego. You should try to dress the part."

Jan fondled the fabric of one of the tie-dyed sarongs between her fingers. "You mean Bob, the drunk guy at the wedding? Ugh. For the record, not everyone wants to dress like a Dead Head, you know."

"Hey, the light's all shining on me," Michael said. "I'm just saying you don't have to wear so many clothes." He stroked the small section of her forearm that wasn't covered with cloth. "Sunlight could touch your body and it wouldn't be the end of the world."

Attempting to ignore the involuntary increase in her heart rate when he touched her, Jan said evenly, "Thank you for that small homage to Jerry Garcia, but have you noticed that I have freckles? We fair-skinned people need to watch out for skin cancer. I hope you're wearing sunscreen."

"Yes, I am. I'm a responsible sun worshiper." He raised his right hand. "Like a Boy Scout. Always prepared and all that."

Jan turned away from the sarongs, toward him. "Why don't I believe you were a Boy Scout?"

"Okay. I wasn't. But I like their cookies."

"That's the *Girl* Scouts."

Later, they went to the Indian restaurant as Michael had promised.

"This has been a great day," Jan said as she ripped a piece of naan into small pieces. "You were right. I never saw much of San Diego when I was here. It's different to experience it as an adult. And this curry is delicious. You were right about this place, too."

"Tomorrow will be even better. Now I have a question for you."

Jan's eyes widened. Where was this going? "What kind of question? Should I be worried? I don't have to dance in front of people again or something, do I?"

Michael leaned forward and the flickering candle flame reflected in his eyes. "No. Nothing bad. What is something you have always secretly wanted to do, but were too afraid to do?"

Jan put down her piece of naan and leaned back in the chair. "I don't know. I'm not sure what you mean. You don't want me to go bungee jumping or something do you? Because I really don't like that kind of thing."

"No. I'm serious." Michael reached across the table and took her hand. "Is there something that you dreamed about when you were a little kid? What were your favorite things?"

"Books."

"Okay, that's not helpful." He squeezed her hand gently. "What were the books about? When you were little, what did you read? What did you dream about?"

"Lots of things." The warmth of his hand was disconcerting. Dreams? Mostly she dreamed about having a normal life with a normal mother. But that wasn't particularly interesting. "Okay, I guess I did go through the typical horse-crazy-girl phase. I probably read *Black Beauty* ten times. And I loved *Misty of Chincoteague*. And of course all the Walter Farley books."

Michael released her hand and took a drink of water. "You lost me on the last one. Who is Walter Farley?"

"He wrote *The Black Stallion* and a bunch of other horse books. There were dozens of them. The first book is called *The Black Stallion*, and in that one a little boy named Alec ends up stranded on a desert island with a huge, wild, beautiful black Arabian horse. After they are rescued, they end up racing. A lot of the other books involved horse racing too, like *Man o' War*, which was based on a real horse. I liked that one a lot, too."

"Hmm. Was there a movie made from the first book?"

Jan leaned forward in her chair and smiled. "Yes! It had Mickey Rooney in it."

"Did you ever ride horses when you were a kid?" Michael asked. "Or did you just read about them?"

Jan shook her head. "No, we never had the money, and as you know, my mom and I moved around a lot. I'm not sure my mother even knew about my horse-crazy phase. I've seen horses from a distance and watched racing on TV. Horses are so beautiful, but I've never actually touched one."

"Okay. Tomorrow we'll do something about that."

"What?"

Michael smiled. "You're going riding."

"I can't do that."

"Why not?"

Jan waved her naan at him. "How about because I don't know how to ride?"

"You have to start somewhere. The first step is to actually get on a horse. Wear long, comfortable pants like jeans. And no flip-flops or sandals, either. You need to wear closed-toed shoes."

"So I guess heels are out."

"In any of those books, did you ever see a picture of someone riding a horse in high heels?"

"No."

"That's your answer."

After dinner, Jan drove Michael to his house. Although they'd exchanged the steamy kiss the day they were cleaning Bruce's house, Michael had been a perfect gentleman all day, to the point that Jan was starting to wonder if he'd just been too tired to know what he was doing before.

The awkward end-of-the-night is-he-going-to-kiss-me question was looming large in her mind. She pulled up in front of the house. Was she ever going to see the inside of his place? Did she want to see the inside? Maybe she was just one of his many flirtations. She was leaving to go back to Alpine Grove in two days, anyway. It was stupid to even consider starting something with him. And he was her step-brother, after all. When you got right down to it, that was gross in a sordid daytime-drama kind of way.

Jan was startled from her swirling thoughts when Michael said, "You're awfully quiet. Are you fretting about getting on a horse tomorrow? I promise it will be fine. People who own horses don't want people getting hurt. It's bad for publicity."

"No. Sorry, I was thinking about something else. I'm purposely avoiding thinking about the fact that the average riding horse weighs around 1,200 pounds."

Michael put his hand on her shoulder. "It's good to do things that scare you sometimes."

Jan looked at him and covered his hand with hers, enjoying the warmth of the contact again. "Is that supposed to be some type of inspirational quote?"

"No. Just my experience," Michael said, giving her shoulder a gentle squeeze goodbye. "Okay. Swoosie and I will meet you tomorrow at eight in front of the coffee shop. I'll be caffeinated and she'll be tired, so we'll be ready to head south for your equine adventure."

As he walked up the sidewalk toward the house, Jan could hear Swoosie yipping furiously inside. Should she have initiated the kiss this time? Was there some type of dating protocol? After so many years with Steve, she wasn't sure. Plus, even with Steve, that wasn't the type of thing she ever did. She thought she wasn't supposed to. Didn't everyone say nice girls didn't do that kind of thing?

Initiating a kiss certainly counted as something that scared her. Turning the key in the ignition, she shook her head. Maybe her life would have been more interesting if she weren't such a nice girl. Being the responsible grown-up all the time definitely had some down sides.

~

Clad in a t-shirt and some old jeans and tennis shoes she had dredged up at her mom's house, Jan met Michael and Swoosie in front of the big yellow Victorian coffee house again. Michael loaded the dog into the back seat and got in the front. "Hi there! Are you ready to ride?"

Jan started the car. "I guess so. Where are we going?"

"First to my house to drop off Swoosie in her crate. With two runs in two days, she should be extra tired." He peered around the headrest at the back of the car. Swoosie had curled up into a tight furry ball on the back seat. Her eyes were squeezed shut and she was quietly snoring. "Look at that. She's already crashed. I wish she were always like this. The dog walker who comes in during the week when I'm at work doesn't really wear her out."

Jan glanced away from the road to look at him. "Vacation seems to agree with both you."

"I talked to some folks from work. Next week is going to be rough. I'm not sure what is going on, but it sounds like the audit isn't going well. I haven't taken a vacation in years. Lately, there's always been too much going on. So it's great that you're here to distract me. Keeping busy has helped me avoid thinking about all the work that's piling up."

"How nice that I can be a distraction. My mom has been packing, so I think she may finally really move in with your dad. I'm hoping that happens. Then I'll feel like my mission here was accomplished. It's been an odd visit for me too, since I thought I'd be tending to her in a state of illness, not cleaning furiously and then visiting San Diego attractions with you."

"Life is what happens when you're busy making other plans."

"Quoting lyrics now are we?"

"You know who it is, right?"

Jan smiled. "I love John Lennon. That song was written for his son Sean."

"Still batting a thousand. Impressive."

Michael directed Jan to a riding stable that was south of San Diego, close to the Mexican border. She parked the rental car in the muddy parking area. As they got out of the car, a horse whinnied. The earthy scent of dust, horse, and manure filled the air.

Jan waved her hand toward the barn. "Where is everybody?"

"They're probably inside saddling up the horses. We're the only ones riding today. Since it is your first time on a horse, I thought it might be better if we weren't riding with a big group of people."

"I appreciate that. If I fall off or freak out, I'd rather not do it in front of a crowd. How did you pull that off?"

Michael smiled. "My agency has worked with these folks in the past. They owe me. Remember that trained horse in the commercial? It was one of theirs. We paid them a fortune to truck Trigger up to Alpine Grove and tend to him."

"Yes, I remember you were worried about the horse's time."

"I think Trigger's participation in the ad is helping put one of their kids through college."

They entered the darkened barn, where a short older woman with wild gray hair bursting out from under a cowboy hat was doing something to the saddle on one of the horses. Jan whispered to Michael, "Those horses are really big. You didn't tell me they'd be so large."

"Up close they look bigger; it's a perspective thing," Michael said as he waved to the woman. "Howdy, Connie. How's it going?"

Connie patted the horse's side. "Hiya Mikey. Just cinching up Friday here for ya."

Jan glanced at Michael and turned back to Connie. "The horse is named Friday?"

"She was born on Good Friday," Connie said. "And you'll never find a better horse. Right, Friday?" The horse waved its head up and down.

"What's the name of the other horse?" Jan asked. "She... or he...is very pretty."

"That one's yours darlin', and her name is Honey," Connie said. "She's named that because she is such a sweet ole honey-pot. We put all the little kids and beginners on her. She wouldn't hurt a fly. Just yesterday, we had a five-year-old little cowboy up there and he did great."

Jan walked up to Honey and tentatively reached out a hand to pet the horse's neck. "Hi, Honey. You're going to be nice, right?" The horse made a snorfle noise. "I hope that's a yes."

"Don't worry darlin', you'll be fine. So we're ready to go here. Let me get the mounting block for you."

While Connie disappeared into another room, Jan tried to will the butterflies in her stomach to settle down. "What if I fall off? I could break something."

Michael put his arm around her shoulders. "Allegedly, a five-year old did just great yesterday. You'll be fine."

After some patient assistance from Connie, Jan sat atop Honey. "Things look different from up here."

Michael rode Friday over to stand next to her. "Pretty cool, huh?"

Jan smiled. "We haven't moved, but so far, so good."

Connie explained a few basics and instructed them on the rules of the trail. "I'll be right here. All you have to do is follow me. The horses know what to do and they know where we're going. Okay, let's go, folks."

Jan's stomach clenched in fear as Honey moved underneath her. But she had listened closely and then attempted a few tentative experiments in equine direction. The horse actually was paying attention to her instructions. She looked back at Michael, who was following her on Friday, "I'm riding!"

Michael grinned. "I knew you could do it. Watch out for that tree branch; we're heading down that trail over there."

Jan focused on the trail and Connie's horse in front of her, who was named Anna. They walked through a swampy woodsy area with branches overhanging the trail. Jan ducked to avoid getting smacked in the face by various shrubs. They exited the trees, which opened out to a wooden bridge that crossed the dunes toward the Pacific Ocean. Jan gasped as the panoramic view of an almost empty beach that seemed to stretch for miles opened up in front of her. "I didn't realize we were so close to the beach!"

Connie turned around in her saddle. "Yep. This is the good part. You get to ride in the ocean. The horses like to splash around a bit and get their feet wet to cool off. If you have a camera, I'll take your picture, too."

"I have one," Michael said. "Here you go." He handed the camera to Connie and rode around toward the ocean and indicated that Jan should follow him.

Honey was enthusiastic about the *go* command and launched toward the ocean at a slow trot, instead of the placid walk that Jan had enjoyed on the trail. Panicking at the sudden movement, Jan clutched the horse's mane and the saddle horn and bumped in the saddle as Honey moved forward. "Ow! Easy Honey, slow down!"

Michael grinned. "Try pulling back on the reins."

Recovering her equilibrium, Jan did as instructed and Honey returned to a walk, sloshing through the waves. Jan laughed as the water splashed up on her jeans and the wind whipped her hair around her face. "Wow, this is amazing!"

～

After the horseback ride, Jan was on an adrenaline high. According to Michael, the next stop on the San Diego tour was the Hotel del Coronado for a late lunch. He directed her to the red-turreted Victorian seaside resort that Jan had seen only in pictures. They sat at an outdoor cafe under a big white umbrella.

Jan sighed as she looked out at the expanse of white sandy beach and the ocean. "This is so beautiful. I always wanted to come here after I saw the movie *Some Like it Hot*. The movie was filmed at the Hotel del in 1958."

"Marilyn Monroe was hot."

Ignoring the movie-star commentary, Jan said, "Did you know the hotel is supposed to be haunted? A woman named Kate Morgan died here in 1892. She died on a staircase from a gunshot wound that was determined to be self-inflicted. But some people think it was murder, and that now she's a ghost who haunts the hotel room where she stayed."

"Are you worried?" Michael waved a potato chip at her. "A haunting can really ruin your lunch."

"Kate sounds fairly harmless, really. Guests who've stayed in the room say that sometimes she turns the TV on and off or they feel breezes going through the room when the window isn't open."

Michael took a sip from his water glass. "There are a lot of historical photos in the hallways with plaques full of information like that."

Jan's eyes sparkled. "I can't wait to see them! Are you almost done?"

After they left the hotel, Jan drove north toward Michael's house. He needed to let out Swoosie, so it seemed her two whirlwind days of being a tourist were coming to an end. As they sat quietly and watched the scenery go by, Jan reflected on all the places she'd seen and things she'd done. She hadn't had this much fun in years. Maybe ever. But tomorrow Michael had to go back to work. Jan planned to spend time at her mother's place helping her finish moving, and then packing for her own return trip to Alpine Grove. It would be great to see Rosa again, but returning to her life and work was strangely depressing. Maybe it was just post-vacation letdown. She hardly ever took vacations, so she'd didn't have much experience with the disappointment of returning to regular, day-to-day life.

They got to the house and Michael moved to get out. Jan stayed in her seat. "Thank you for everything. I've had such a wonderful time."

Michael gave her an odd look. "Don't you want to come inside? I can hear Swoosie yapping. She's probably beyond ready to get out of her crate."

Jan smiled with relief. The day wasn't over after all. "Sure, that would be great."

Jan walked through the door of the bungalow and noticed the dark hardwood floors. No wonder Michael offered to help refinish floors in his dad's house. These floors had obviously been redone. They gleamed with what had to be dozens of coats of varnish.

Michael put his camera on a table and pointed to a well-worn overstuffed couch that was covered with a blanket, presumably placed there to ward off Swoosie fur. "Have a seat. I'll be right back."

Jan heard the clang of a gate and Swoosie came charging out of the bedroom and ran around the room twice before leaping up onto the sofa next to Jan and giving her cheek a slurp.

"Swoosie. Where are you?" Michael said from the kitchen. "Let's go outside."

The dog leaped back off the couch and raced around the room two more times before shooting toward the back door in the kitchen.

Jan wiped the slobber off her cheek. Swoosie had energy to burn. Even with all the walks, it was like having the Tasmanian Devil hurtling through the house.

She heard the back door slam and Swoosie and Michael returned. The dog seemed to have restored some degree of composure and daintily hopped up on the sofa and curled up in a corner.

Jan looked up at Michael. "What did you do to her?"

"Nothing. She just was expressing her displeasure at being left behind. I call it spaz-dog mode when she loses her marbles and runs around like that. She should be fine now that she's let me know that being stuffed in her crate is rude and offensive. Even though she loves her crate and chooses to sleep in there herself sometimes. But when something is not her idea, it's offensive. We actually go through this pretty much every day. So do you want something to drink?"

"That would be great," Jan said as she got up from the sofa. "I guess I'm not used to such a high-energy dog. Rosa is a lot less moody. She just hangs out and follows me around, hoping for food."

Jan followed Michael into the kitchen. The room was light and bright with white cabinets and appliances, but it looked almost unused. "I'm guessing you don't cook much."

Michael turned around, grabbed her around the waist, and pressed his body to hers, pushing her back against the counter as he gave her a crushing, hungry, bone-melting kiss. He released her and said, "I've wanted to do that for hours. Ever since you were out there with your hair all wild, riding in the ocean."

Gasping in surprise, Jan gripped his shoulders and looked into his eyes. "Oh, um, wow."

Michael grinned. "Are you actually at a loss for words?"

She wrapped her arms around his neck and then reached behind her head to pull out the hair tie that was holding her hair back. She pulled his head down toward her to kiss him back and murmured. "Maybe I should wear my hair down more often."

Michael put his hand at the nape of her neck, pushing his fingers into her hair as he nibbled on her neck. The roughness of the stubble on his jaw made her shiver as he moved across her shoulder and pushed her t-shirt aside. Good thing the counter was there, or she'd probably fall over. Steve had never made her feel like this. Ever.

Breathless, Jan pushed him away. "I hate to break the mood or your momentum, but I'm being rammed into a drawer handle here. It's starting to hurt."

"This house does include a bedroom. With a large soft bed in it," Michael said with a questioning look. "It's a queen size."

Jan smiled, "Well that's some serious salesmanship. If it's queen-size, how could I possibly refuse?"

Michael scooped her up in his arms and carried her back to the bedroom, kicking the door shut behind him with his foot. He placed her on the bed, stretched out next to her, and stroked her cheek lightly with his fingertips. "You look a little nervous."

"I think you have a lot more experience with flings than I do."

"Flings?"

"One-night stands, affairs, carrying-on, fooling around, dalliances, hanky-panky..." Jan's eyes widened. "Sorry, I'm out of synonyms."

Michael propped his head up with his hand and looked down into her eyes. "You mean sex."

"Well, yes. That seems to be where this is heading." Jan knew her cheeks were undoubtedly a mortifying shade of crimson by now. "It's not like I haven't done it before. I mean I was with Steve for a long time, but it was, well um, not always that great. Particularly recently. Maybe it was me. I don't know. Plus, we were engaged. I'm not the sleep-around kind of girl."

"So you're reassuring me that you're not a slut? That's good to know."

Jan cringed inwardly. What *was* she trying to say? "I was just thinking, that's all. You're going back to work tomorrow and I'm going back home. And what happens then?"

Michael gathered her into his arms and kissed her, "I think sometimes maybe you think too much. Why don't we just relax and see what happens now? Didn't someone say that tomorrow is another day?"

"Scarlett O'Hara. *Gone with the Wind* by Margaret Mitchell. Published in 1936."

Michael smiled. "I had a feeling you'd know."

He leaned over her and kissed her deeply. And then Jan stopped thinking about much of anything at all.

～

As the sun was setting, Jan laid curled up in Michael's arms with her eyes closed, feeling the rise and fall of his chest. She couldn't remember ever feeling this relaxed. Or satisfied.

Her pleasant sense of contentment was interrupted by odd noises outside the bedroom door. "Slurp, snorfle, slurp..." Then a pause. Then more slurping.

She pushed herself up on her elbows and looked down at Michael's face. "Is your dog making a gross noise outside the door?"

He sighed and opened his eyes. "I hope not. It rarely means anything good when she does."

"Does she slurp a lot?"

"Slurp?"

"Yes, *slurp*. Don't you hear it? But it's not like a normal dog cleaning noise. What is she doing?"

Michael sat up and looked toward the door. "I have no idea." He got up out of bed, giving Jan an opportunity to thoroughly peruse his naked form as he strolled toward the door. All that running with the dog was definitely paying off.

Michael opened the door and found Swoosie sitting on the other side, looking happy to see him. She wagged her tail and slurped. Michael crouched down and opened the dog's mouth. "What have you got in there?"

Swoosie wagged more enthusiastically and willingly let Michael peer into her mouth and poke around among her teeth to see if she was chewing something she wasn't supposed to be chewing.

Jan sat up in bed and held the sheet up over her chest. "What are you doing?"

"Looking to see if she ate something. As I may have mentioned, she tends to eat things she shouldn't."

"Like the contents of half a buffet table."

"Yes, that too. But she has been known to eat things that not everyone would classify as technically edible."

"Is she okay? She doesn't have anything stuck in there does she?"

Michael let Swoosie's mouth close and stood up again. "Not that I can see."

Swoosie slurped loudly and both Michael and Jan looked at her. The dog wagged her tail and slid into sphinx position, slurping some more.

Jan grabbed her shirt and threw it over her head. "Can I take a look?"

Michael shrugged. "Sure. She's used to people trying to remove artifacts from her mouth."

Jan walked over to Swoosie. "Say aaaah."

"I think you may have to take a more direct approach." He crouched down, grabbed Swoosie's muzzle again and opened it. "What do you think? See anything?"

"No. Maybe she's having some kind of allergic response to something she ate. I didn't see much of anything in the kitchen, but maybe she ate something else. I, ah, wasn't really paying attention."

Michael grinned at her. "I wasn't either. Let's take a look around." He stroked the dog's head. "She seems happy enough. Not like she's sick. Unfortunately, I know all to well the expression she gets on her face when she's not feeling well."

"I'll bet."

After locating and then putting on the rest of their clothes, the pair went around the house looking for anything missing that might meet Swoosie's broad definition of edibility. Swoosie followed them, slurping occasionally for emphasis.

Giving up, they sat on the sofa. Swoosie jumped up and sat in between them. Michael opened the dog's mouth again for another look. "I can't figure this out. There's nothing *in* there. Maybe you're right and it is an allergic reaction."

"Should you call the vet?"

Michael sighed. "I suppose. They're on speed dial. I have no idea what's wrong with her. It's getting late in the day and if she is allergic to something, I'd hate for her to die in the middle of the night because her throat closed up or something." He stroked Swoosie's soft head and said sadly, "You are such a problem child." Swoosie leaned on him, smiled, and wagged, pleased to be the center of attention.

After a short conversation with the veterinary clinic, Michael and Jan loaded Swoosie in the car for the drive to the office. They sat in the lobby, waiting for the vet and listening to Swoosie make her peculiar slurping noises.

Jan reached over and took Michael's hand. "I'm sure she'll be fine."

"I hope you're right. It's probably not very macho to say, but I love this dog. It will kill me if something happens to her."

"I understand," Jan said squeezing his hand. "I feel the same way about Rosa. She was my mom's dog originally, but now she's my best little buddy. Every time I think about the fact that dogs only live 15 years or so, I want to cry."

Michael shook his head, "Yeah, let's not go there. I can't handle the idea of Swoosie getting old. Of course, at this rate, she may not *get* old. We've spent a lot of time here at the vet. This dog is her own worst enemy."

A tall thin man with wavy blonde hair opened a door and motioned for them to come into the exam room. He was wearing a long light blue lab coat and the name embroidered on the front said John Jefferies, DVM. "Michael. Good to see you again. How is Swoosie today?"

Michael shook the veterinarian's hand. "I'm not sure. She's making an odd noise. At first, I thought she ate something that got stuck in her mouth, but I can't find anything. Then I thought she might be having an allergic reaction."

The vet put Swoosie up on the exam table and looked at her eyes and felt her body. "Did you see her eat anything?"

"No, I was in another room."

"Could you hold her?" Dr. Jefferies asked and then opened Swoosie's mouth. "So what is going on here, you little fluffy thing?"

Michael held Swoosie around her torso to keep her still as the vet ran his fingers throughout the dog's mouth. Swoosie started and pulled away and Michael grabbed her more firmly to keep her from launching off the exam table.

"What's this here?" the vet asked as he held up a black elastic hair tie. "This was hidden in her back teeth under her tongue." Swoosie looked disappointed that her prize had been discovered and moved her head to snatch it back from his grasp. The vet lifted the elastic away from her mouth, "Sorry, little dog. I'm not giving it back."

An embarrassed heat flushed Jan's cheeks. "I think that's mine." She took the elastic from the veterinarian's hand. "Thank you." She jammed the elastic into her pocket.

Michael relaxed his hold on Swoosie. "So she's fine, right?"

Dr. Jeffries smiled. "Yes, although in the future you may want to try and keep your hair accessories away from the dog."

After paying the bill and loading Swoosie back into the car, Jan drove back to Michael's place. The silence was uncomfortable. Obviously lost in thought, Michael stared out the window, the grim expression on his face subduing his normally animated features. She should say something to him. But what? Maybe he was regretting what they did earlier. She thought it was amazing, but who knows what *he* thought. Heaven knows he had a lot more experience, given how women had a habit of throwing themselves at him.

At last, right before she pulled in front of Michael's house, Jan blurted out, "I'm so sorry about what happened with Swoosie. I must have dropped my hair tie on the floor in the kitchen. I didn't think about it. I feel terrible."

Michael smiled slightly, but it didn't offset the sadness in his dark eyes. "I don't think either of us were thinking much. It's not your fault. Swoosie eats everything. I've got the vet bills to prove it."

"I know you have to work tomorrow and then I've got to go home. This isn't the way I thought we'd end the evening." She thought they'd be entwined in each others arms. Which they were. Until they weren't.

"Me neither. Most of Swoosie's vet trips are unexpected, though. I should start expecting the unexpected."

"Oscar Wilde said 'To expect the unexpected shows a thoroughly modern intellect.'"

Michael gazed out the window again. "At least I can be modern."

Jan slowed the car to a stop and turned off the ignition. The change in Michael's mood was so unsettling, she wasn't sure what to do. After an awkward pause, finally, she said, "I had a wonderful time. Well, except for this last part, which again, I'm sorry about. But all the places we went, and um, everything we did, it's all been great."

Michael looked toward the house then back at her. "I should go. I have to get up early for work. But I'll give you a call from there tomorrow to see how everything is going. You'll still be at your mom's place, right?"

Jan nodded. "Yes."

Michael leaned over and gave her a quick kiss. "I'll talk to you then."

Jan sat and watched as he gathered Swoosie out of the back seat and walked up the sidewalk to the house. What were the odds that he would actually call?

Chapter 8

Crystals & Chakras

Kat sat on the sofa with Rosa on one side of her and Lori on the other. Joel walked in, stopped, and pointed at Rosa. "Isn't that dog supposed to be out in the kennel?"

Kat looked up from her novel. "Yes. But she has been a good girl all week and she's going home tomorrow, so I wanted to give her a little special time. She looked so sad and she likes being a house dog here with everyone else. I hate to leave her outside in the Tessa Hut. See how she's being so sweet, just sitting here quietly next to me? Rosa is like Linus—she follows me around like a shadow. She's certainly not going anywhere."

Joel crouched down to pet Rosa and looked up at Kat. "You are such a softie. Special-dog time could get more complicated if you board more dogs. The house isn't that big. Speaking of which, I don't suppose that's a business book you're reading, is it? How's the business plan going?"

Kat covered the title of her novel with her hands. Joel didn't need to know how trashy it was. "No. It's not a business book. And I'm still working on the plan. You do realize you're being a nag, right?"

Joel grinned and stood up again. "I prefer to think of it as motivational support."

"By the way, Maria is coming up tonight."

"Again?"

"Yes. She's having issues with her apartment complex. The guy next door, Tony, is quite the, um, ladies man, I guess you'd say. The walls aren't very thick and there's a lot of noise from his apartment on the weekends." When she'd talked to Kat, Maria's description had been significantly more colorful and expletive-laced.

Joel put his hands in his pockets. "Really?"

"Yes. Maria said there was a big fight in her parking lot the other night. It was bad enough that someone even called the police. Tony has taken in some friend who was thrown out of his place by his pregnant girlfriend. The house guest's ex-wife is in town and she wasn't too excited about the girlfriend. Oh, and the house guest might have cancer, too. Anyway, Mr. House Guest drank a whole lot and then started a fight with another neighbor. It sounds like he was seriously unhinged and caused a big incident. Maria refers to it as living in Melrose Place."

"Wow. That's quite a soap opera. Things are pretty tame by comparison here in little ole Alpine Grove. No wonder she wants to come here. At least it's quiet. Has she considered finding a new place to live?"

"She's working on it. I think the whole thing with the police increased her incentive to move. Maria talks a good game, but I know she's not fond of feeling unsafe in her own home."

"Let me know if there's anything I can do."

Kat got up off the couch and wrapped her arms around Joel's waist. He enveloped her in a hug and kissed the top of her head. She tilted her head back to look up into his face. "Thanks for being cool about letting her stay."

"Well, she stays in your office, so you're the one who won't get any work done."

Kat put her head back on his chest, enjoying the sound of his heartbeat. "It's the weekend. Days of rest. All the business books say you're supposed to take a break from work because when you work from home it's too easy to end up working all the time. I don't want to turn into a workaholic. Stress is bad for you."

Joel released her from the embrace and looked down into her eyes. He pushed a stray tendril of dark hair behind her ear. "You were looking pretty relaxed just now. And it's Friday. I don't think you have much to worry about."

"I'm multi-tasking. See how I am tending to the needs of my boarding dog while reading a junk novel at the same time? I'm working and relaxing simultaneously, thus enhancing my work-life balance."

Joel laughed. "That's some impressive rationalization."

"It's a gift."

The sound of a car rumbling down the driveway caused all of the dogs to leap up and head for the door, barking furiously.

Kat waved toward the door. "According to our brave canine defenders, Maria has arrived."

Joel took Kat's hand and they walked outside to the landing outside the front door. The dogs thundered down the steps and greeted Maria, who was standing next to her little red Miata.

"Listen here, you big, hairy thing," Maria said, pushing Linus's nose away from her skirt and shaking her index finger at him. "You should know my rules of personal space by now. No poking me *there*. That's considered rude."

As Kat and Joel walked down the front steps, Maria looked up from her lecture and waved at them. "Hey there, lovebirds! Did you miss me? I see the full-figured dog is back here again, too. How come she is running free? Did she escape again?"

Kat shook her head. "No. Rosa has been really good, except for a little bath-time trauma. But after that it's been fine. I think we bonded. Now she won't leave my side. Well, except to say hi to you, I guess."

Joel took Maria's suitcase out of the car and started dragging it toward the house.

Maria hugged Kat. "So how are you doing, girlfriend? How's life with the sexy engineer?"

"No complaints. I'm doing better than you are, I think. How's the apartment hunt going?"

"Not so good. I wish you'd bought your apartment when it went condo. Then you could rent it to me. That was a nice complex."

"Sorry. At the time, buying wasn't much of an option. As you may recall, I was destitute. You had to sell all my furniture for me."

Maria flipped her hair back with her hand. "That's true. And that money went to a good cause: shoes for me. But now that you're an heiress, you've got the cash-o-la."

"Sorry, but that train has left the station. The condo purchase option was a one-time offer. And the building manager was not my biggest fan after she found out I had a cat, so it's not like they'd give me a special deal."

Maria sighed. "I gotta get outta Melrose. I mean, don't get me wrong. I like a fine soap opera. I've been watching *Days of Our Lives* for years. The sands in the hourglass just keep going for me. But I can't handle living with a bunch of losers fighting in my parking lot. If I want to see that level of male stupidity, I can see it at work. I don't need it at home, too."

"Yeah, you look kind of tired. We'll have a good weekend and maybe you can get some rest."

Maria put her hand on her hip. "Are you implying that I am not looking my best?"

"I may not be Miss Cover Girl, but I do know heavy-duty concealer when I see it. I'm guessing under all that makeup, you have dark circles under your eyes."

"That does it," Maria said. "I need a plan of action. I don't feel good, and now I don't look good. That's totally unacceptable! My job and my home life are both in the crapper and I haven't wanted to deal with it. But now I'm pissed."

Kat put her arm around her friend's shoulder. "Maybe tomorrow another Wine and Whine is in order. We'll figure out a plan. But first, maybe you should just get some sleep tonight."

Maria sighed and leaned her head against Kat's. "Yeah. I guess it's pretty obvious that I need to get some beauty rest. I am really tired. Thanks, girlfriend."

∼

After a frustrating day of dealing with her mother's endless dawdling about packing to move in with Bruce and her all-too-frequent questions about what she had been up to with Michael, Jan was relieved to get on the plane and return to the quiet of Alpine Grove.

Her mother had assured her that she was finally getting the last of her stuff moved and would be spending the night at Bruce's house. Whether or not that would really happen was anyone's guess. The day had been so frustrating that it was only that morning that Jan realized Michael had not called her from work.

Thanks to Rosa's digestive disturbance on the way to Kat's place, the drive back from the airport was just as stinky as Jan had feared it would be. Even with all the windows rolled down, the offensive odor still pervaded the car. The stench of aged sun-baked dog vomit might never come out, unless she paid for expensive professional detailing. Or fumigation.

As she drove up to her tidy 1940s cottage in Alpine Grove, she smiled. Even if the drive had been unpleasant, it was still good to be home. She pulled her mail out of the little green mailbox out front and thought about seeing Rosa again. Maybe her life seemed boring to other people, but she loved this little house at the end of the street in her quiet neighborhood. It was a relief to be away from the crowds in Southern California. Not to mention her mother's New-Age-speak and turmoil. Being around her was exhausting, partly because it was so difficult to tell what she was saying much of the time.

Jan put away her clothes and reflected on her week away. It certainly hadn't been all bad. Spending all that time with Michael had been downright magical, in fact. Now being here in her familiar, comfortable home, the whole experience seemed far away and unreal, almost like it hadn't actually happened. But it had. She wrapped her arms around her waist and remembered the warm, passionate sensations of being in his bed. And all their conversations at restaurants and coffee shops. Time had melted away so quickly when they'd been together. Even the awful, sandy cleaning exercise had been an adventure. And then of course the horseback ride. It was like a dream. Even if she never heard from him again, she'd still have the memories.

After Jan unpacked, she got back in the car to pick up Rosa. She couldn't wait to see her round black dog again; the house seemed extra empty without Rosa's furry presence. Jan sang along to bad 80s music as the smelly car bumped down the long driveway toward Kat's house. She approached the house and noticed Kat and Maria were sitting on the steps in front of the house. Rosa was with them on a leash, lying at their feet. At the sound of Jan's car, the dog stood up and began barking.

Jan parked the car, got out, and ran toward Rosa. She crouched down and rubbed the dog's head. "Oh, look at you! How are you? I missed my girl!"

Kat smiled. "I guess you're glad to see her."

Jan stood up. "Yes, I missed her so much. Thanks for taking care of her on such short notice. And she's so clean. You must have washed her. I wish my car smelled that good. Thank you for doing that. I hope she was good."

"Well, not exactly," Kat said. "But I dealt with it. I was glad to hear your mom was okay too, and you didn't have to spend your time there at the hospital."

"Yes, I ended up having a much better time than I expected, although I'm not sure my mom's marriage is really going to make it. But then, that's nothing new, either."

Maria got up from the step. "Hey Jan, it's good to see you again. San Diego must agree with you. You look different."

Jan looked down at herself. She was wearing a fairly standard outfit. White blouse and navy blue slacks. "Different how? I always look like this, I think."

"Hmmm. I don't think so. You had some fun with a man, didn't you?"

Jan looked at Maria, then at Kat. "What?"

"I think Maria is delicately implying that she suspects you had sex," Kat said. "She can tell these things. I don't know how, but she can."

Maria nodded. "Doesn't the Marlboro man live in San Diego? Did you do the deed with him? I hope so. Because he sounded totally hot."

Jan's cheeks reddened and she bent down to pet Rosa with the hope that maybe Kat and Maria might not notice. "I did see Michael. There was a problem with our parents living together. Technically he's my step-brother, since his dad married my mom." She stood up again. "So yes, I saw him again."

Maria raised an eyebrow. "Naked?"

Jan dropped her hands to her sides. "Okay fine. Yes, naked."

"Excellent," Maria said, clapping her hands together. "I knew it. And I'm guessing by that little smile on your face that he was looking good. And that *it* was good."

Jan grinned. "Yes. Really good. Far better than expected, in fact."

Maria nodded. "And better than that low-life boyfriend you had too, I'm guessing."

"Way better. No comparison." Just thinking about it gave her a little thrill.

"Good. If I can't be getting any myself, at least I can hear about it from you two." Maria nudged Kat. "That's another thing we need to talk about. How is it that someone as fine as myself does not have a man? That's just wrong. After Larry, there's been a whole lotta nothing and I'm getting cranky."

Kat nodded. "Yet another question to ponder. It could be a long evening."

Jan took Rosa's leash from Kat. "I should be going, since I have to work tomorrow. Jill covered my whole vacation at the library, and she's probably ready for a break. Thank you again."

As Jan's car clunked through the potholes in the driveway, she thought about what she'd said. There really was no comparison. She missed Michael in a way she had never missed Steve.

When Steve had left to go back to work after their weekends together, she pretty much forgot about him. But she couldn't get Michael out of her mind.

∼

The next day Jan and Rosa went to work at the library. It was great to be back in her familiar space. The library had always been her haven and she immersed herself in genealogy research related to one of the founders of Alpine Grove for a patron who was working on a written history of the town. Learning about the original settlers of the area was fascinating and the day flew by. Doing major research also was a great distraction from thinking about Michael. But once it was time to lock up the library and go home, her mind was swirling with memories and questions about San Diego again.

She opened the door to her cottage just as the phone was ringing. Rosa ran into the house and jumped on the sofa. Jan dropped her bag, slammed the door, and ran to answer the phone.

On the other end of the line, Michael's deep voice greeted her. A sparkle of excitement fluttered through her. "Hi Michael. How are you?"

"I'm fine. How's library life?"

"Great. I worked on research all day, which is my favorite thing to do."

"Did you learn anything good?"

"Oh yes. I got lost in stories about the Miller family. They were one of the original settlers here."

Michael cleared his throat. "So, I'm calling to let you know about my dad. I don't think your mother is going to tell you."

"Is he okay? Did something happen? He didn't have an accident or something, did he?" What had her mother done now?

"No, he's fine." Michael paused. "But I'm pretty sure the marriage isn't going to work out."

Jan bowed her head and put her hand over her face. Not again. How did her mother manage to destroy marriages so quickly? "But we cleaned the house. That was supposed to fix their problem with living together. What did my mother do?"

"It's not really anything she did. It's who she is."

"Did the New-Age stuff finally get to him?" Jan rubbed her eyes. That would figure. "I know it drives me nuts. I definitely could see that driving him away. He's so much more down-to-earth and plainspoken than she is."

"No. It's because she's a woman."

Jan dropped her hand to her side and straightened. "What?"

"Well, I was talking to my dad and he was telling me that your mom has been trying to deal with the root of his chakra problems. She thinks his energy is blocked and brought over crystals. I guess she brought some stone that influences the sacral chakra."

Jan paused to think for a second. "Wait a minute. That's the chakra that affects sexuality and procreation. And pleasure. Is this about sex? Please, please say no. I really don't want to talk to my mother about that."

"Do you think it was fun talking to my dad about it?" Michael said in an amused tone. "I mean we had to have the birds and the bees talk when I was thirteen. That was enough for me."

"So, I'm guessing their sex life is not good?"

"After last week, I'd say ours is probably a whole lot better."

Jan was glad he couldn't see her blush. "I can't argue with that. But what did he say?"

"Well, it's not what he said exactly. It's what he didn't say. I think he might be gay."

"What? Gay as in he prefers men?"

"It would explain a lot."

"Did he tell you this? Did he come out to you?"

"Not exactly in so many words. I should have stayed longer, but the conversation was so awkward, I couldn't stand it anymore and I left. I ran over there with Swoosie to have breakfast like I always do. I feel a little bad, since my dad has never said anything like this to me before. I think he really needed someone to talk to, but it was too weird. I was thinking about my mother and...I don't want to go into all that. But it was strange, so Swoosie and I left."

"Telling someone you're gay is a pretty big deal. You are such a chicken."

"Hey, you're one to talk. You're the one who doesn't want to talk about sex crystals with your mother."

"You're right. Sorry. Is he going to discuss this with my mom?"

"I'm not sure. Mostly I thought you should know. From what you've said, it sounds like failed marriages are nothing new with her, but I think this time the problems with their relationship are not her fault."

Jan smiled. "If this is true, we cleaned that sandy house for nothing. And killed Evette's fine machine."

Michael chuckled. "I'm sure she has had the fine machine fixed by now. But some things you can't control. Or fix. I think this situation may count as one of them."

"Should I try to talk to my mom? I know I don't want to. And if your dad really is gay, he needs to tell her. But maybe I should find out if she's okay."

"That's up to you. I also wanted to let you know that I have to come back up to Alpine Grove next weekend to do some more shooting for the commercial. We need some background, establishing shots of the area. We spent so much time dealing with the actor and horse problems that we ran out of time to do them."

"Maybe I can return the favor and show you the sights of Alpine Grove."

"I think that would take all of about ten minutes. But I would like to see you."

"That would be great." Jan said, trying to modulate her voice so she didn't sound like a love-starved teenager. "I'll be here. So will Rosa."

"I should go. But good luck talking to your mom. I'll see you soon."

As Jan hung up the phone, she closed her eyes. She had really wanted to invite him to stay here at her house. But he wasn't the only one who was a big chicken.

For the rest of the evening, Jan debated calling her mother. But what would she say? "So, I hear your sex life with the Toilet King isn't so good." Ugh. No way.

In the end, she decided to put off any call until tomorrow. Or the next day. Maybe if she had some time to process the information, she could think of something to say that wasn't utterly stupid.

Two days later after much deliberation, she had a plan. Instead of talking, she'd just listen. Yes, Mom was hard to understand, but maybe she'd let Jan know what was going on in her own oblique way. And then Jan could at least try to be supportive of what was going on. Whatever that might be.

She picked up the phone and dialed Bruce's house. Her mother picked up the phone.

"Hi Mom. I'm just calling to see how everything is going."

"It's lovely to hear from you, dear. I'm fine, but I'm about to go out to an astrology class. Did you need something?"

Jan paused, desperate for something to say. "Not really. I just wanted to see how things were going with Bruce now that the house is clean." Sheesh. That was lame. Maybe mom wouldn't notice.

"The energy in the house is much better. But Bruce's energy is not good. His root chakra is blocked. I think it is causing dysfunction in areas of his body because the energy is not flowing properly."

Uh-oh. Jan wasn't sure she wanted to hear about those areas. "Um, that doesn't sound good. I hope he's not sick."

"No dear, it's not a sickness. His sexual drive is not what it should be. The human sex drive is strong. With a man like him, it should be a powerful energy. But it isn't."

Jan cringed inwardly. She so, *so* didn't want to hear any of this. "Oh, uh, well, that doesn't sound good, either."

"I'm sure it's not me. My heart is united with my sexuality and I am a passionate person. I need to have both love and sex in abundance. Fortunately, I have rose quartz, garnet, and other crystals to help stimulate the creative expression of love."

"Well, um, I hope the, uh, stimulation works out. You always say crystals are...um...powerful."

"You were spending a lot of time with Michael when you were here. I assume you spent time in the bedroom, too. How is he sexually? Perhaps there is a hereditary dysfunction. I can give you some crystals if you need help."

"Fine, mom. Michael is fine. No hereditary...anything." Help! She was not going to talk about sex with Michael with her *mother*. No. Way.

"Sex should be more than just fine, dear. I hope you know that. Perhaps you are just missing Steve. You were together for a long time, after all. Is everything okay? You sound nervous."

"Yes. I'm great. It's all great. Really, everything is just fine. But I should go...I...I have to feed Rosa. She's hungry."

"Give her a big hug from me. She's such a sweet girl."

Jan hung up the phone and sank down on the sofa. She had a lot more sympathy for the conversation Michael must have had with his father. If she never talked about Bruce's chakras and sex drive with her mother again, it would be too soon.

~

Jan stood at the counter at the library checking out a book for a patron. She smiled as Michael walked through the door, the outline of his broad shoulders silhouetted in the late afternoon sunlight. He met her gaze with a flash of recognition and warmth in his brown eyes that made her heart beat faster.

After handing the book to the woman, Jan leaned forward, putting her elbows on the counter as Michael walked up. "Welcome back to the Alpine Grove library. How did the commercial go?"

Michael leaned across the counter so his face was only inches from hers. "It was much easier without the horse."

The warmth of his skin so close brought back a number of thrilling memories, but Jan didn't move. She looked into his dark eyes and said, "So many things are."

Michael moved his hand to touch her arm and Jan gasped slightly as her skin tingled from the contact. He said, "So how have you been?"

Without shifting her gaze from his eyes, she said. "Good. How about you?" Jan moved her hand to stroke his forearm. He started slightly at her touch and smiled.

A loud cough echoed across the high ceiling of the library. "*Ahem.* You two need to get a room. But first I need to check out this book."

Jan jumped back from the counter. She could feel the heat on her cheeks and knew her face must be flaming red. Oops. "Sorry, Mr. Grumbacher. I didn't see you there."

"Well that's obvious. I need to get this book for my wife."

Jan looked down at the cover. "Hmm, *Sex Can Keep You Slim.*" She opened the back cover to pull the card out of the pocket, so she could stamp the due date. "It's certainly a popular title. I hope she enjoys it. Well, and you too. Anyway, the book is due back in a month. Thank you."

The short, grizzled older man took the book and tucked it under his arm. "I don't think a month will be enough, but it will have to do."

Michael grinned. "More proof that the library has something for everybody. So are you ready to get out of here? You're supposed to show me the sights of Alpine Grove, remember?"

"Yes. Mr. Grumbacher was the last person here. Sometimes people hide out back there in the 600s because it's the medical section and they don't want other people to see what they're looking up. I just need to get Rosa from the back and lock up."

Rosa toddled out of the office after Jan and went over to Michael. He bent down to pet her head. "Hi Rosa. How have you been?" Rosa wagged, and having completed her social obligation, followed Jan toward the door.

Jan turned toward Michael, "Is it okay if we stop by my house? I need to feed Rosa. She takes dinnertime quite seriously."

"I can see that. Sure, I'll just follow you. I'm in the tiny, silver rent-a-car thing that looks like a demented roller skate."

Jan pulled up in front of her cottage with the roller skate not far behind. She let Rosa out of the back seat and waited for Michael. He unfolded himself from the compact car and joined her at the front door of the little yellow house.

"Welcome to my humble abode."

Michael smiled as he walked through the door and looked around the entry area and kitchen. "I note you have cooking utensils and even apples sitting out on your counter. Apparently, your dog is not a world-champion counter surfer like mine."

"No, Rosa is mellow by comparison." Jan patted the dog's head. "Aren't you, Rosa?" Panting, Rosa wagged because there was talk of food. "Make yourself at home. Do you want something to drink?"

Michael leaned on the kitchen counter and put his hands in his pockets. "No thanks."

Jan moved around the kitchen getting Rosa's food together as Michael and Rosa looked on. Bending to put the bowl on the floor, Jan said, "Here you go." Rosa rushed over and began gobbling.

Jan stood, turned around, and found Michael standing right in front of her. Uncomfortably close. She smiled. "Hi."

Taking half a step forward, he enveloped her body in an embrace and bent down to kiss her, pausing to murmur "Hi" before pressing his lips to hers. Jan ran her hands across the muscles on his back, enjoying the familiar contours. All of the tension and anxiety of the last week left her body and she reveled in the sensation of being in his arms again.

Oblivious to the groping going on above her, Rosa belched loudly. Pausing to come up for air, Jan said into Michael's ear. "You seem to have a thing for kitchens."

He nuzzled her neck, sending a tingle down her spine. "Don't you think kitchens are erotic?"

"I do now. Although in the past, I mostly used mine for cooking."

Michael trailed his fingertips from her neck down the side of her body. "Mmm, you can cook?" The feel of his breath against her ear was making her crazy. And whatever he was doing with his hands wasn't bad either.

"Yes," she whispered, wrapping her arms around his neck in an effort to avoid collapsing on the floor in a molten puddle. He was way, way too good at this. "Are you hungry?"

"Yes. You haven't noticed?" He nibbled on her earlobe for emphasis.

"I mean for food." If he didn't stop that, they were going to end up tearing each other's clothes off within the next three minutes.

Michael's hands roamed under her shirt. "That too."

Jan pulled away. "You're going to have to stop for a second because this is my last shred of willpower. It's your last chance. I know you had a long day, so do you want me to make dinner?"

Michael smiled. "You weren't kidding? You really can cook?"

"I like to eat and my mother didn't cook much of anything. As Julia Child pointed out, 'no one is born a great cook, one learns by doing.' So yes, I can cook. It was that or eat nothing but those nasty instant ramen noodles."

"Yuck. I hate that stuff. Plus, real cooks quote Julia Child. You must be good."

Jan straightened her blouse. "Also, I wanted to talk to you since you seem...interested again. I thought you might be angry with me about what happened at the vet." She looked down at the floor. "To be honest, I wasn't sure I'd ever see you again. I thought I might be another one of your one-night stands."

Annoyance flickered in Michael's eyes. He turned and walked over to the sofa, sat down next to Rosa, and crossed his arms in front of his chest. "Is this going to be a 'relationship' conversation? Because I'm not a big fan of those."

Jan's eyes widened. "Do we have a relationship? We spent time together in San Diego, but I still don't know you very well."

"You know some things about me pretty well," he said with a half smile.

"Well, yes. But I was wondering what happened the other day. You seemed upset. I thought you might be angry with me for dropping my hair elastic."

Michael shook his head. "I thought my dog might die and it was because I wasn't paying attention. You know exactly why I wasn't paying attention. I felt guilty. And I hate going to the vet. I don't like doctors much, either. Oh, and hospitals. Those are the worst."

"You weren't angry at me?"

Michael leaned forward and put his elbows on his knees. "No. I told you. Swoosie is her own worst enemy. I love that stupid dog, but she drives me insane. Right now, I'm here with you, but in the back of my mind I'm worried about her eating something at doggie boot camp, even though I've given them 39 instructions on what she can and can't have and do."

Jan smiled, pushed Rosa aside, and sat down next to him on the sofa. She put her hand on his arm. "That's so sweet."

He turned to her and pushed her hair back, exposing her neck. "I notice you left your hair down for a change."

"I'm trying out a new look."

"I like it," he said, then bent his head toward her neck to give a particular spot behind her ear some attention.

Jan jumped up off the sofa. "Stop! You know what that does to me. I'm going to make dinner now."

Michael smiled, "You're no fun."

"I'll be more fun later."

"I'm counting on it."

～

The next morning, Michael rolled over in bed. As his fingertips grazed her cheek, Jan opened her eyes. He smiled and said, "This is a lot nicer than the H12 motel."

"I haven't stayed there, but from what I hear it wouldn't be difficult to top the ambiance." She leaned over to kiss him. "You look relaxed."

"It has been stressful at work, and it's nice to be away from it."

Jan smiled. "Health experts say that sex helps you sleep and handle stress better. I'm glad I could help." She propped her head up on her hand and looked down into his eyes. "I thought you liked the excitement of ad-land. Did something happen related to the audit?"

"I'm not sure. There are some things that don't make sense. I know my boss Derek can't be involved. He just wouldn't do that. I had to get information together for the audit. I'm not an accountant, but when I look at the numbers, stuff is missing. And let's just say the IRS auditor noticed too."

Jan shifted to see his face more clearly. "Do you mean you think he's embezzling?"

"That's what the audit seems to show. But no. There's just no way he'd do that. This guy has been my mentor for years. And a friend. I've always kidded around, saying that when I grow up I want to be just like him. I can't imagine him stealing from the company."

Jan sat up and put her arms around her knees. "Have you talked to him about it?"

"Not really. Everyone else at the office is talking about it with each other, but at this point it's all rumors. I don't think anyone has the guts to confront him."

"But you looked at the audit, right? Shouldn't you address it with him? Particularly if you're friends. Maybe there's an explanation."

Michael pulled her back down on top of him and wrapped his arms around her. "You're stressing me out again. I think I need to relax."

Jan bent her head to kiss him. She stroked the stubble on his cheek, "Watch out. You could end up with wild neurotransmitters like dopamine skipping around all over your body, making you so relaxed you can't move."

"That sounds like fun. I'm willing to take that risk."

Later after feeding Rosa breakfast, they decided to take the dog out for a hike. They drove to a parking area near a trail that led to a water fall.

Michael got out and looked around. Jan's car was the only one in the lot. "Where is everybody?" The only sound was the twittering of birds in the trees.

"I usually don't see many other people when I go hiking. It's very peaceful and this is a lovely trail."

They started up the path, their feet shuffling through the sun-dappled leaves that had fallen to the forest floor. The soft breeze whispered through the pines overhead and occasionally a squirrel chattered, scolding them for disturbing his winter preparation projects. Jan bent down and unhooked Rosa from her leash, so she could wander and savor the earthy scents of the trail.

Michael looked down at Rosa as they strolled along. "I'm impressed you can just let her off the leash like that. Swoosie would be in the next county by now." He paused to take a picture of Rosa examining a large bracken fern.

"Rosa doesn't want to leave. She knows I'm her meal ticket. She doesn't chase deer or other wildlife and we're the only ones here. She's never left my side or done anything bad before. Plus, she's pretty slow. You're a runner, so you could probably catch her."

Michael laughed. "And I've had lots of practice chasing after wayward canines."

"Yes, there's that, too."

They reached the overlook for the falls and stood by the railing, gazing down into the stone canyon. Water cascaded over the cliff into a pool below. The air was rich and humid, the mist clinging to their skin. The sound of the rushing water echoed off the jagged granite boulders and a shimmering rainbow bridged the expanse between the trees on either side of the pool.

Michael put his arm around Jan's shoulders. "You were right. This is a great spot. Thanks for bringing me here."

Jan turned to face him. "The Alpine Grove sights aren't as well-known as places like the Hotel del Coronado, but there are fewer people."

"I think you mean no people."

Jan waved toward the canyon. "These falls are named Lilly Falls after a woman named Lilly Miller, who was one of the early settlers here. This area where the canyon is located was homesteaded in the late 1870s by a man named Christopher Miller. Lilly was his wife. In the 1920s, Jim Green and his wife Helen Green purchased the Miller ranch and built a house near where the parking lot is now. In 1961 Helen Green donated the entire 4,800-acre property to the state for a park, stipulating that the waterfall be named for Lilly Miller, one of the first Alpine Grove pioneer women."

"You certainly know your local history."

"I do a lot of genealogy research for people at the library. It's really interesting. This was not an easy place to live in the late 1800s, particularly in winter."

Michael nodded and took her hand. "But it is beautiful." They stood in silence for a few moments, taking in the sound of the waterfall, the singing of the birds, and the wind through the trees. Finally, Michael turned and tugged Jan after him, "Let's go over here."

They walked away from the overlook to a clearing that was covered with a carpet of moss and surrounded by trees. Michael said, "I had one of those John Muir quote books. He said to climb mountains and also to lie down among the pines." He crouched down on the ground, dragging Jan down with him.

"That's from one of the compilations of his letters."

Michael got down, sprawled out on his back, and stared up at the trees above. "I've climbed a few mountains, but I haven't done the lie-down-among-the-pine-trees thing. It's one of those life experiences I haven't had. Here's my chance."

"Okay." Jan smiled and settled in on her back next to him. Rosa came over, sniffed her shoe, and curled up in a ball next to her feet, apparently figuring it was as good a spot as any for a nap. "Muir said that if you climb mountains 'nature's peace will flow into you as sunshine flows into trees.'"

Michael closed his eyes, sighed, and clasped her hand. "I think I see what he meant."

Chapter 9

Meetings

The next day, Michael left Alpine Grove to head back to San Diego. As the roller skate puttered away down the street, Jan scritched Rosa's ears. "It's just us again, girl." As usual, Michael hadn't said anything about ever seeing her again. After his obvious annoyance about any type of relationship conversation, she certainly wasn't going to bring it up. It was stupid to be falling for a guy who not only lived far away, but who also probably had a whole slew of spandex-clad women lining up to sleep with him.

Disgusted with her train of thought, Jan turned away from the doorway. "Come on, Rosa. It looks like it's going to rain. I think curling up on the sofa and watching a nice light, fluffy movie might be a good way to spend the rest of our Sunday. I'll even make popcorn. What do you think?" Rosa wagged and turned back to the house.

The next day, Jan and Rosa went to the library. Jill had returned to work after her days off, and that afternoon she was busily getting ready for story time. Small children and their parents started filing into the library. Jan stood behind the counter and watched as they all gathered around, settling in on pillows and the tiny chairs that were set in a circle in front of Jill's adult-size chair.

Jan waved at Cindy Ross, who bent over her son as she helped him find a chair. She gave him some instructions and then turned to walk over to the counter. Jan was struck by how much the tall woman looked like her brother Joel. In addition to her height, Cindy had the same sandy-colored dark blonde hair. "Hi Jan," she said in a stage whisper. "So I want to know about the hunky guy you've been seen with lately. That guy is definitely not Steve. What gives? I thought you were engaged."

It was easy to see how Cindy found out everything happening in Alpine Grove. She simply took the direct approach and asked. Jan couldn't think of a way to politely tell her to mind her own business. Oh well. She crossed her arms in front of her chest and said primly. "As I understand it, you already know about the fight. I broke up with Steve."

Cindy leaned over the counter. "Yeah, I figured. But who is the hottie? I saw him come by the library again the other day when you were closing. He's just as gorgeous as everybody said."

Jill sighed. "He's my step-brother."

"What? Eww. That's gross." Cindy said a bit too loudly.

"Shhh. Please keep your voice down. And no. Not eww." Jan said, putting her elbows on the counter and leaning forward so she could whisper more quietly. "I said, *step*-brother. His father married my mother."

Cindy laughed and practically shouted. "Oh my God, it's like the Partridge Family!" All the little kids turned and looked at her.

Jan bent her head down and leaned her forehead on the cool counter. She heard Jill say "Shh" and could envision her glaring at Cindy. Jan raised her head and mumbled, "I think you mean the Brady Bunch."

"And your name is Jan!" Cindy clapped Jan on the upper arm and whispered. "This is so awesome. It's about time you dumped that guy Steve. Everyone knew he was cheating on you. So is the hunky guy good in the sack? Or just nice to look at?"

Jan stood up. Obviously, being polite wasn't going to work. "I'm not telling you that."

Cindy leaned back from the counter and gave her a knowing look. "Ha. That means he is good. I knew it. If you weren't sleeping with him or he was awful in bed, you'd deny everything." She looked over at the circle of children. "Oops, my kid is making a break for it. Gotta go!"

Jan watched as Cindy collected her son and planted him back in his seat. It was best not to dwell on how Cindy was going to interpret and share the new intel she had just received. The Alpine Grove gossip grapevine was going to be buzzing tonight.

~

Later that week, Jan was finishing washing her dinner dishes when the phone rang. A jolt of excitement went through her when she recognized Michael's voice at the other end of the line.

"How's my favorite step-sister?"

Jan smiled at his amused tone of voice. "As far as I know, I'm your only step-sister, but I'm fine, thanks. Just kind of tired from work."

"I got my film developed. I didn't know you took that picture of me lying under the pines."

Jan smiled. It was inevitable that he'd discover she'd taken the picture. "I'm quite stealthy. It seemed like you should have a record of your new life experience, so I grabbed the camera."

"It doesn't look like me."

"Of course, it looks like you. I was there. And it's a photograph. Who else would it look like?"

He sighed. "I look in the mirror and I look at that photo and it's like it's a different person."

Jan shook her head. What the heck was he talking about? "You seem the same to me. Or you sound the same, anyway. Did something happen?"

"I feel old."

"The last time I saw you, you seemed, well, rather healthy. All of you seemed to be functioning quite well from my perspective."

Michael laughed. "Well, I'm glad to hear that. It was a relaxing weekend. I miss feeling that way. It has been an awful week at work and lying under the pines listening to the wind and the waterfall seems like a lifetime ago. I guess I just wanted to say hello and say that I miss you."

Jan's jaw dropped. That was a surprise. Maybe they did have a relationship, after all. Or at least maybe the beginnings of one, anyway. "I miss you too." A whole lot. More than she wanted to admit. And certainly more than she was going to tell him. "You are welcome to return any time. People have come to Alpine Grove for recreation, vacation retreats, or rest cures for more than 100 years."

"Rest cures?"

"There was a tuberculosis sanatorium here in the 30s. The fresh air was supposed to be good for patients battling the white plague."

"Your mind amazes me. How do you remember these things?"

"I remember certain types of things, like stories and facts. It helps that I see a lot of Alpine Grove history books repeatedly. So I'm exposed to the information more than once."

"So you're a brain trapped in the body of a game show hostess."

Jan laughed. "Okay, now you're quoting *Say Anything*, which is too easy, because I just watched it the other night. John Cusack makes me swoon and I'd had a bad day."

"What happened?"

"It wasn't a big deal. It's just that when you live in a small town, everyone knows your business. And the ladies of Alpine Grove have noticed your presence here."

"Oh really?"

"Yes. You were referred to as a hottie, I believe. You may feel old, but apparently you're still looking pretty good."

"That's reassuring I guess, assuming you feel the same way."

Jan twisted the phone cord around her finger. "Yes. I do." Particularly when he was naked.

"So do you have plans this weekend?"

"Not really. Do you want to come up and stay here again?"

"Yes. I would like to get away from here. But there is a little problem. Doggie boot camp doesn't have any space for Swoosie this weekend. Would it be okay if I bring her with me? It's kind of a long drive, but I need to clear my head. I'll bring her crate, too."

Jan had a bad feeling about Swoosie's participation in the road trip, but there was no way she was giving up a chance to see him again. "I guess that would be okay. Rosa has always been fine with other dogs. She got along with all Kat's dogs when she stayed there. It should work out, assuming Swoosie plays nice." Maybe. She needed to seriously Swoosie-proof her house.

"I'll see you late Friday night, then. I'll bring the photographs, too. There's one I want you to see."

Jan hung up the phone and spun around in a circle. "Woo-hoo!" Rosa stood up and wagged. Jan danced around Rosa and the dog hopped up and down a few times in a show of solidarity about whatever was making Jan so happy.

~

Friday night, Jan was reading a novel and just dozing off when she was startled back to consciousness by a knock at the door. She found Michael standing on her doorstep looking unshaven and somewhat bedraggled. He grabbed her around the waist, pulled her to him, and kissed her. Jan's body melded to his and she returned the kiss with passionate enthusiasm.

At length, Michael released her. Jan stood up straighter and asked breathlessly, "Where is Swoosie?"

"In the car. I was thinking it might be best if she met Rosa out back. But I wanted to say hello to you first."

Jan ran her fingers through the hair behind his ear. "I like the way you say hello. Let me get Rosa. You can go through that gate over there. I'll meet you around back."

Jan opened the back door and Rosa toddled down the steps to the backyard. She slowly wandered toward some shrubs near the back fence, poking her way around her favorite spots in the yard.

Michael opened the gate with Swoosie on a leash. The dog looked around, spotted Rosa, and yipped happily. Michael closed the gate and bent down to remove the leash. "Be good, Swoosie."

The fluffy white dog ran over to say hello to Rosa, who looked a bit concerned about the furry interloper running around in her yard. The pair sniffed and circled. Swoosie bowed and wagged her curly tail, trying to invite Rosa to a game of tag around the yard. Rosa looked up at Jan. "It's okay Rosa, you can play if you want to."

Rosa walked over toward Jan and sat down next to her. Jan stroked the dog's head and turned to Michael. "I know you must be tired, but I think Swoosie isn't. Do you want to take them for a little walk?"

"Okay. That's probably a good idea. It was a long drive and Swoosie is squirrelly."

"In my experience, that's generally not a good thing."

A corner of Michael's lips turned up in an exhausted half smile. "You're right about that."

They leashed up their respective dogs and went out the gate to the street. The dogs seemed content to walk next to each other and sniff the neighborhood as the humans strolled along behind them.

"I tried to dog-proof my house, but you might want to look around. I think Swoosie may have a better imagination than I do as far as committing acts of canine badness."

"You took everything off the counters, right? No apples or stirring things?"

"That was the first thing I did. It's all stored away. As long as she can't open the refrigerator, we're fine."

Michael shook his head. "Don't give her any ideas. That's the last thing I need."

Jan glanced over at his face. He did look terrible, which for him was saying something. No wonder he said he felt old. Today, he definitely looked older than he had last weekend. "What happened at work? You look kind of, ah, tired, I guess."

"Yeah, I know. I look like crap. I feel like crap. I didn't sleep much this week. Insomnia is an evil thing."

Jan stopped, reached out to grab his arm, and turned to him. "You should have told me that. Driving when you're sleepy is extremely dangerous."

"I know. I drank about 700 cups of coffee on the way here. I think I know every all-night truck stop between here and San Diego."

Rosa sat down next to Jan and looked up at her with a worried expression. "It's okay Rosa; we're just having a conversation."

Meanwhile, Swoosie had wrapped her leash around Michael, effectively trapping him in place. He bent down to try to disentangle himself from the dog. "I've been working late and then when I do get home, I can't sleep. The deadlines just keep coming. I think the clients are figuring out that something is really wrong. My boss Derek is totally out of commission. I'm not sure what he's doing. Not working, that's for sure. I thought he was a friend, but now part of me is worried I've been working for a crook all this time. It's a mess. I shouldn't even be here. There's so much work to do."

Jan reached over to touch his face. "I'm sorry, but I'm glad you came."

"Me too. I think I'll feel better in the morning." He looked around the dark street that was bathed in moonlight. "At least it's quiet here. No phones ringing or people yelling."

"Quiet is one thing Alpine Grove has going for it. As far as I can tell, no one here loves the night life."

"And no one has got to boogie?"

Jan smiled. "It's good to see you're still alive in there somewhere."

Michael gripped Swoosie's leash more tightly and wrapped Jan in a hug. "I'm feeling better all the time."

~

That night, after Michael had stashed Swoosie in her crate and they'd finally gone to bed, he'd curled up next to her with his head on her chest. Considering he had to be exhausted, Michael was still extremely tense. Jan could feel his taut muscles and sense his anxiety and restlessness as he feigned sleep. She lightly stroked his back with her fingertips until he finally did fall asleep. Lying in the dark bedroom listening to his peaceful, rhythmic breathing, she no longer could avoid the obvious. It wasn't just lust or a fling anymore. She was falling in love with him. And that was a huge mistake.

The next morning, Jan was in the kitchen making breakfast when Michael and Swoosie returned from their run. The door opened and Swoosie ran into the house and leaped up on the couch with her leash trailing across the floor behind her. Jan was relieved to see that Michael looked more like himself again. She turned from the stove. "Did you have a good run?"

Michael crossed the room to Jan, cupped her chin in his hands, and kissed her enthusiastically. "The best. There was no one else out there. Just me, Swoosie, and a lot of trees showing off their fall colors."

"Swoosie looks happy, too." Jan turned and looked more closely at Swoosie and Rosa, who were concentrating on sniffing something on the couch. "What are you guys doing?"

Swoosie and Rosa looked up guiltily at Jan. Swoosie jumped off the couch and stood beside Michael. He looked down at her. "You're going to behave yourself, right?" Swoosie wagged.

Later, after Jan and Michael had breakfast, Jan put food in the dog bowls and put them on the floor "Okay, time for you guys to have breakfast, too."

The dogs came running and collided with one another trying to get at both bowls.

"What's that noise?" Jan said.

Michael shouted, "No!" startling both dogs away from the food. He shoved them aside, reached down and picked up the bowls. "Rosa is growling I think."

"Wow, I've never heard her growl." Jan looked down at her dog. "I didn't think she knew how."

"I think we may need to approach canine feeding time in a more organized way. Does Rosa know how the *sit* command?"

"Sort of." When she felt like it.

Michael walked across the kitchen. "Swoosie, come." Swoosie bounded after him, bunched up her furry body, and spun in a circle. "Swoosie, sit." The dog settled her rear on the floor and smiled up at Michael proudly. He gave her a morsel of dog food. "Good girl. Stay."

He handed a food bowl to Jan. "Take this one over to that far corner of the kitchen. Make Rosa sit. Don't let her get up until you say the magic word."

Jan did as instructed. Rosa sat and stared at Jan, looking horrified that she wasn't getting her food. She turned to Michael. "Wait. What's the magic word?"

"It starts with 'o' and ends with 'k' or technically, if you spell it out, the word ends in a 'y.' Either way, the word indicates agreement." Michael said, glancing at Jan to make sure she understood. "Here's the plan. We put the food bowls down in front of the dogs. They sit until we say the magic word. Then they eat. When they are done, we pick up the bowls and make them sit again until we say the magic word again."

"I think Rosa is going to faint with hunger over here. She's drooling all over my foot. That's gross, Rosa."

"Go for it," Michael said, and put Swoosie's food bowl down in front of her. The dog stared at the bowl, anticipating the big moment when she could eat.

Jan had to convince Rosa that diving nose-down into the food bowl wasn't going to happen until she said so. After Rosa seemed to have the idea, Jan said "Okay."

Swoosie and Rosa launched to their bowls and snorfled their food eagerly. After thoroughly cleaning out her bowl, Swoosie sat and stared up at Michael expectantly. When Rosa finished, she tried to wander off to go check out Swoosie's bowl, but Jan put her back in her corner and told her to sit again. Rosa sat, looking offended. Even though it involved food, she was not convinced that this game was any fun at all.

Jan said, "Okay!" Swoosie leaped up and ran over to the sofa. The dog jumped up on the couch, spun around, and settled in for a post-breakfast nap. Rosa looked confused and slowly wandered over to her dog bed, glancing back at Jan.

Jan looked at Michael. "I think my dog hates me now."

"Don't worry, she'll forgive you. Feeding her again will help. The last thing you want is dogs fighting over food. And by not letting them eat until you say so, you are showing them who is in charge."

"I think it's too late for that. Rosa already knows I'm a pushover."

Michael smiled. "You've never owned a challenging dog, have you? You think Swoosie is bad now? Believe me, she was worse. She's one of those dogs who is always testing you to see what she can get away with."

"I think Rosa takes a simpler, more single-minded approach to life. As far as I can tell, mostly she seems to think about food." Jan pointed at the dogs. "At least they seem to get along, for the most part. They're just sitting there looking sleepy."

Michael walked over to Jan and reached out to touch her cheek. "I'm not sleepy for a change. Sorry I wasn't much fun last night."

Jan put her arms around his neck. "You seem quite a bit more lively today. Sleep has many health benefits, you know."

"I was thinking about exploring more of the health benefits of sex you mentioned the last time I saw you."

Jan giggled. "I guess you *are* feeling better. Perhaps we should leave the dogs to their napping, then."

Michael grabbed her hand and pulled her toward the bedroom. Jan uttered a little shriek of laughter as they flopped down on the bed. She reached under his t-shirt, wanting to feel the warmth of his skin again, but there were way too many articles of clothing in the way. Then most of the clothes were on the floor and everything was a blur of sensation.

A loud tearing noise came from the living room. Jan paused in mid-kiss and pulled her head away from Michael. "What was that?"

He grabbed the nape of her neck pulling her back to him. "Who cares?"

There was another shredding noise and Jan rolled over and sat up. "Your dog is doing something bad."

"How do you know it's my dog?"

"Because it's always your dog."

Michael sighed heavily and threw his legs over the side of the bed. "I'd be annoyed if that weren't so true. I'll go see."

Jan pulled the sheet up over her body and sat up to admire the view of Michael walking out of the bedroom. Nice.

He shouted, "No! Bad dog!" and Rosa came rushing into the bedroom with a piece of paper hanging out of her mouth. She scuttled under the bed.

Jan heard Michael tell Swoosie to go to her bed. He put her in her crate and the gate clanged shut. He stomped back into the bedroom and crawled back into bed, drawing Jan into his embrace. "What was the last thing you were you reading when you were sitting on the sofa?"

Jan rolled over and peered under the bed to look at Rosa. She said over her shoulder, "Some mystery novel I got from work."

"Not any more. The dogs ate it."

She looked back at Rosa's eyes under the bed. "Oh Rosa, you too?" Rosa dropped the incriminating page of text from her mouth.

212 🍀 *Susan C. Daffron*

Michael leaned back on the pillow and put his arm under his head. "Apparently your dog has a taste for literature now."

"Given how much time she spends at the library, that could be a problem. I think your dog is a bad influence."

"I have no doubt about that."

Michael pulled her toward him again. "Where were we?"

Jan bent her head to kiss him and the phone rang. "I think this idea may be doomed."

She got up to answer the phone and looked back at Michael, who was grinning. "At least there's a nice view," he said. Rosa scurried out from under the bed to follow her.

As she walked through the area, Jan surveyed the disaster in the living room. It looked like her library book had been run through a paper-shredding machine that had subsequently exploded. Sighing, she picked up the receiver on the kitchen phone. Her mother's voice greeted her.

"Hi Mom. How is everything going?"

"Quite well, dear. I wanted to talk to you and Michael. His father said he might be there. I'm sorry to call so early. Are you having sex?"

"Mom! Really!" But she was naked. And cranky because she was missing out on sex. Not to mention getting cold. "I don't want to talk to you about that."

"But Michael is there, isn't he?"

Jan wrapped her arm around her waist. Brr. "Yes, he is. Do you need to talk to him?"

"Not specifically. I want to invite both of you to a family celebration on Tuesday evening."

Jan sighed. "Do you know how much work I've missed lately? The other librarian here is getting grumpy about filling in for me."

"Things in life don't always happen on a timetable, dear. It's important to surrender to the mysteries and uncertainties of life. You need to be in the moment. Bruce needs to heal an element of his life and I want to help him celebrate the transition."

"Getting paid is more challenging when you're living in the moment. Libraries have timetables."

"Don't be rigid, dear. Please talk to Michael, too. Or ask him to call Bruce. I think it would be good if he talked to his father."

"I'll talk to Michael about this, but I think he has some things going on at work, too."

"Please make an effort, dear. You need to be in a place of celebration."

"Okay, Mom."

Jan hung up the phone and scampered back to the warmth of the bed. "Fall is definitely in the air. It's freezing out there. And it looks like a paper tiger threw up in the living room."

Michael snuggled up to her and began nuzzling her neck. "Clothes would help, although I have to say I prefer the nudist look."

She maneuvered away from him. "Sorry to kill the mood, but this involves you, too. My mother wants us to go to a family celebration on Tuesday."

"Tuesday? I have to work."

"So do I. I guess it's at night. After work. But in San Diego, so it's not exactly convenient for me."

Michael sat up. "You could ride back with me and Swoosie tomorrow." He grinned. "Road trip!"

Jan groaned. "Why is this reminding me of the movie *Animal House?*"

Michael reached over and tickled her ribs. "To-ga! To-ga!"

Jan convulsed with laughter and squirmed to get away from him. She grabbed his wrist and tried to wrestle it away from the ticklish part of her tummy. He flipped her over and silenced her laughter with a crushing kiss. Moving his lips against hers, he murmured. "So where were we?"

Chapter 10

Deadlines

Sunday morning, Jan sat next to Michael as they bumped down the driveway toward Kat's house. Rosa and Swoosie were in the back.

Jan had made sure not to feed Rosa this time and the dog was looking somewhat less nauseated than usual about the bumpy ride. "Please don't throw up, Rosa. It's a long way to San Diego, and we have to spend a lot of time in this car."

Rosa wagged and stepped on Swoosie, who looked nonplussed about sharing her travel space with a black dog that felt compelled to endlessly wander back and forth across the back seat.

Michael looked at Jan. "This place isn't exactly convenient, is it?"

"No, but Kat has been really nice about taking Rosa on short notice. She doesn't really have a dog boarding kennel yet; they're building it in the spring, so she just lets Rosa stay in the house. It's sweet that she treats Rosa like one of her own dogs."

Michael pulled the car up under a tree and Jan hustled to get Rosa out of the back. "Swoosie, you stay here. We'll be right back."

Kat opened the door and walked down the front steps of the house toward the car. "Hi Jan. How's my buddy Rosa?"

Michael got out of the car and Jan waved toward him. "Kat this is my...friend...or step-brother, I guess, Michael."

Kat reached out to shake his hand. "Hi. I'm Kat. And I'm really happy to see that Rosa is clean. Thank goodness. It's getting colder and I was hoping to avoid another bath."

"Don't you have heat?" Jan said. "I hope so."

"Yes, but there were issues with bathtime that involved some outside time." Kat waved her hands in front of her. "Never mind. You really don't want to know. But I think we're going to have to build a grooming area, too."

"Jan said you're starting a boarding kennel," Michael said. "What are you going to call it?"

A distressed look crossed Kat's face. "I don't know. It's part of the marketing plan I'm supposed to be writing, but am not. How do you write a plan about a business that has no name?"

Michael nodded. "That is a stumbling block."

"You have no idea," Kat said. "I think I'm developing a complex about marketing."

"Marketing isn't so bad," Michael said. "It's just explaining what you have that people need. In your case, you have a solution to a big problem: no one to take care of the family dog."

Kat waved her arms in a gesture of frustration. "You make it sound so easy! But I start trying to write things down and it all sounds stupid. I'm a technical writer. Or I was. All my writing was about facts. Verifiable facts. When I write about marketing stuff, I feel like I'm making things up. Or trying to foist something on people like some creepy used-car salesman."

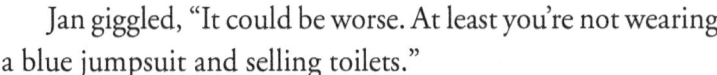

Jan giggled, "It could be worse. At least you're not wearing a blue jumpsuit and selling toilets."

Kat looked confused. "What?"

"Jan's step-father aka my father is the Toilet King," Michael explained. "If you lived in San Diego during a certain time period, you would have seen him in a lot of rather memorable local TV commercials."

Kat grinned. "Oh yeah; I heard about that when Jan told us about the wedding. That sounds like it was the best wedding ever! I wish I'd seen it. My friend Maria still talks about it." She looked over at the car. "Wait! Is that the dancing dog? The Samoyed who wears ruffles?"

"Yes, that's Swoosie," Michael said. "She's got a long ride ahead of her."

Kat clasped her hands together. "I know you've got to go, but can I meet her? She's so cute!"

Jan rolled her eyes and glanced at Michael. Really? Did every woman have a thing for furry white dogs?

"Sure, let me go get her," Michael said. He went to the car and clipped a leash on Swoosie, who eagerly leaped out onto the gravel driveway.

Kat crouched down and cuddled Swoosie's soft white fur. "You are adorable." She looked up at Michael. "Can you make her dance? Maria will never forgive me if I don't ask."

Michael smiled. "Okay. Just for a minute. Swoosie, come." He showed the dog a treat and then gave her a hand signal. She stood up on her hind legs and took a few steps forward. Michael took a few steps back and she followed him. He took one of her front paws and moved around her. Then he told her to bow and then to sit. Finally, he gave her the treat. Swoosie wagged and looked pleased with herself.

"That was awesome!" Kat said as she bent to pet Swoosie again and congratulate her. "Thank you so much."

"We should really get on the road," Jan said. "I hope this is the last time I have to leave Rosa with you for a while. I've seen my mother more in the last few weeks than I have in a long time. All these trips are getting ridiculous. At least a one-way flight will be a little less expensive."

"I should put Swoosie back in the car," Michael said. "It was nice to meet you, Kat."

Jan handed Rosa's leash to Kat. "I'll see you in a couple of days." She bent down to pet Rosa. "You be good."

Kat took the leash. "We'll be fine. Tell Michael I'll work on coming up with a name for this place. Drive safely!"

Jan walked back to the car and got in. She turned to Michael. "I still can't believe I'm doing this. It's the story of my life. I have to drop everything to do what my mother asks. But what else can I do? She's my mother."

"Well, I had to drive back anyway." He leaned over to kiss her, and then started the engine. "Even though it's a long drive, I'm glad I came up here."

Jan smiled. "So am I. And I'm glad we get to spend more time together. It seems like I'm always saying goodbye to you."

"Or hello." Michael looked thoughtful for a moment. "That reminds me; there are a bunch of CDs in the center console. It's a long drive. How about some Beatles for this magical mystery tour?"

Jan smiled, "That album was released in 1967."

"Groovy. Just so you know, I am not the walrus."

"I'll keep that in mind."

~

Kat brought Rosa inside and found Joel in the kitchen eating another snack sandwich. Rosa sidled up to him, looking hungry. He looked down at the dog. "I see Rosa has returned."

"Yup. I think Jan is getting tired of travel. But I can see why your sister had so much to say about Michael. The guy is gorgeous."

Joel smiled slightly. "Really?"

"Not that I noticed or anything. Because I am blind to the attractiveness of other men since I met you."

Joel just stared at her and continued to chew slowly.

"Okay, I lied. I noticed. But given the way he kissed Jan in the car I think he's taken." Kat fanned her face with her hands. "It was hot."

Joel grinned. "I think you've been spending too much time with Maria."

"He did point out something about my marketing problem. I think I've been looking at it the wrong way. I need to figure out what people need, not focus on what I'm selling. And come up with a name for the boarding kennel. When I was talking to him I realized that part of the reason I can't write about the business is because I don't know what it's called."

"What are you going to name it?"

Kat's shoulders slumped. "I have no idea. I haven't come up with anything. Could you help me think of something?"

"Maybe later. I have to go up on the roof now."

"How is the roof process going? It's getting cold. Ice on the roof would be bad for your vertical stability and long-term health."

"I'm almost done. Having to do it piecemeal, so you don't have a roofless house, has taken longer than I thought it would. It's been a tedious process. I'm looking forward to more time at ground level."

Kat wrapped her arms around his waist and leaned her cheek on his chest. "Me too. I'm glad you're almost done. You know that it freaks me out having you wandering around up there."

Joel put his arms around her and rested his chin on her head. "I know. Today should be the last day. Then tomorrow all the ropes and pulleys come down."

"It was an engineering marvel. It's the end of an era."

Joel squeezed her more tightly and then let her go. "Yes. The leaky-roof era. See you later."

Kat went downstairs to her computer and turned it on. She was supposed to be writing a magazine article about using design-software templates. Getting free software to play around with for the article was fun, but she was getting nowhere with the article itself. She sat and stared at the screen, waiting for inspiration to strike. Nothing. Her mind was blank. Where's a fairy godmother when you need one? Wait a minute.

She typed:

```
The computer screen is blank and so is the
expression on your face. You're wishing the
document would just magically appear on the
screen with all of its margins, column widths,
fonts, and styles already set up. If you
don't have a fairy godmother hanging around
to rescue you from a situation like this, you
might try template software instead.
```

Kat jumped up out of her chair and did a jig around the room. At last! She had written something. Words were on the screen. The article was started and she even knew what she was going to say next, because she had pages of notes about the software she was supposed to write about. It was only a little ironic that the opening was all about writer's block. Oh well. Whatever worked. She sat back down in the chair and began typing furiously.

A few hours later, she heard Joel stomping around upstairs with at least one dog. Probably more than one, since there wasn't a crowd in her office. The article was almost done. It was time to celebrate the fact that she was actually going to meet this stupid deadline after all.

Kat galloped up the stairs, and at the top landing spread her arms toward the room and announced, "I'm a writer!"

Joel looked up from the bread he was slicing, put down the knife, and turned to face her. "So I've heard."

"No, I mean I actually wrote something!" She ran across the kitchen and jumped into his arms, wrapping her arms around his neck and her legs around his waist. Looking momentarily startled, he grabbed her so she wouldn't crash to the floor. Then he readjusted his hold on her body and bent his head to kiss her.

Kat disentangled herself and stood on the floor again. "Wow. Thank you for your enthusiasm for my writing career."

"I'm all for supporting the arts. Does this mean you finished your article?"

Kat grinned. "Yes. Well, almost. But I finally figured out how to start it. That was horrible. Worrying about writing is worse than actually writing. Will you read it tomorrow? I need to send it to the editor this week."

"Sure. It's great to see you so happy."

Kat grabbed the slice of bread off the cutting board and took a bite. "I know. I've been grumpy."

"I didn't say it."

"Freelance writing sounds so easy. But no one tells you about writer's block. Now I need to figure out what to name this mythical boarding kennel. Are you up for brainstorming?"

Having finished assembling his sandwich, Joel moved to the table. "As long as we can eat lunch at the same time."

Kat brought a notepad and her slice of bread to the table. "You start."

"Alpine Grove Dog Boarding."

Kat tapped the pen on her notepad. "That's not exactly inspiring. But I'm writing it down anyway."

Joel put down his sandwich. "You're not supposed to criticize during a brainstorming session. The whole point of brainstorming is to let your mind go and generate ideas until you come up with something good."

"Maria calls this place *Chez Stinky*."

Joel frowned. "I don't think that's a good option. And besides, that problem has been resolved. Well, except for Rosa's last visit. But other than that, it's been fine."

"Now who is being critical?"

"I think boring is better than stinky. Let's try free association. What's the first thing you think of right now?"

"Fred Flintstone!"

"Really? Are you serious?" Joel wagged his index finger at her. "No more Saturday morning cartoons for you, young lady. Maybe we should try words related to dogs?"

Kat shrugged. "All right. Dog, fur, paws, tails, hound, puppy, bark, wagging."

"That's better. I'll add words to those. Hair of the dog, flying fur, paws for thought, hound of the Baskervilles, puppy love, bark to the future, wagging train."

"Bark to the future?"

"I think you're being critical again."

"No, I'm not." Kat crossed her arms across her chest. "The Hound of Music."

Joel walked around the table and bent down to kiss her neck. "Now you're not even trying. I'm going downstairs."

Kat pushed the plate forward on the table with her arms and laid her head down on them. Figuring out a name for this place could take a while.

Chapter 11

Picket Fences

After a few hours of road time, companionably chatting and singing along to Beatles tunes, Jan and Michael stopped at a diner to get some food and give Swoosie a break from the back seat. They sat outside at a sticky, round table that sported a bent plastic umbrella, which appeared to have barely survived several bouts of hurricane-force winds.

Swoosie rested her chin on Michael's thigh, hoping for a handout. He looked down at her sad, starving expression and gave her a little piece of bread. "That's it. No more." Swoosie lifted her head then pressed it down again on his leg to emphasize that she was still hungry.

Jan nodded at Swoosie. "Your dog is a pig."

"It's one of her defining characteristics." He gave Swoosie another small piece of bread. "But it's not all bad. If she didn't like food so much, she'd be impossible to train."

"There is that. I'm sure having a dancing dog that also looks a little like a stuffed animal is a great way to meet women. Not that you need that, since they seem to flock to you anyway."

Michael stopped eating his sandwich and put it down. "Is something bothering you?"

"Not really." Jan leaned back in her chair and clasped her hands in her lap. "Maybe. I don't know. I guess I was in a committed relationship for a long time and it feels strange to...well...not be. I thought I was getting married. I knew what my future would be like. Now I don't know." That was an understatement.

"I will admit to the fact that pretty much every female of virtually any age finds Swoosie adorable. But it's not like I've been sleeping with every woman who comes up and pets my dog, you know."

Jan shifted in her chair. "No, I don't know, actually. We've spent a lot of time together recently and you've never mentioned anything about any past or present girlfriends, relationships, or anything. But you know all about Steve. And what my plans were. I mean, I don't even know if you have ever been married before! Have you? Have you ever been in love? Did you go to your high school prom?" Picking a fight might not be the best way to find out these things. And yet here she was, doing it anyway.

"You want to know if I went to the prom?" He narrowed his eyes. "Okay. Yes. Her name was Charlene and we went out for about two weeks afterward. Happy?"

Jan shook her head. "I can see you don't want to talk about this. It probably falls into the category of a relationship conversation, and you have indicated you don't appreciate that type of discussion." Now he was definitely irritated. She may as well keep going, so she could stop thinking about it.

He rubbed the back of his neck. "I'm not sure what you want me to say. Do you want a list of every woman I've ever slept with? A number? An accounting of my whereabouts whenever I'm not in bed with you?"

Jan sighed. What did she want? "No. It's not like that. I guess I was trying to find out if I'll see you again after the next few days. We spent another weekend together and it was wonderful, at least for me. But I still don't know where I stand with you. Maybe you think that's stupid or I'm trying to push you into something you don't want. But I've realized I need to know. One way or the other." Preferably before her heart shattered into 10,000 tiny little pieces.

Michael leaned forward and put his elbows on the table. "Why can't you just enjoy the experience? I enjoy being with you and we've had some good times. What's so wrong with that? It's fun being around you and I like talking to you." He grinned suggestively. "And doing a lot of other things with you, too."

A tear escaped from her eye, and Jan brushed it away hurriedly, hoping Michael didn't notice. "Maybe you won't understand. But after the whole thing with Steve, I don't want to be hurt like that again. I know he had changed. And intellectually, I know it's a good thing we broke up. But when we first met, and for years, I loved him. Maybe I was just in love with the memories. Whatever it was, it doesn't matter. I don't want to be hurt like that again. It was awful."

"No one can guarantee anything like that," Michael said. "People get hurt. People get sick. People die. No one can predict the future. I certainly can't. I do know that my job is incredibly demanding. I work long hours. And with the exception of the last week or so, I love it. That's not going to change. So to answer your question, no, I've never been married. Or had any type of long-term thing like you did with Steve. If you are after the whole white-picket-fence deal, you may be disappointed."

Jan sat up straighter in her chair and shook her head slightly to get the hair out of her face. White picket fences?

Steve had said almost the exact same thing. "That's helpful. Very helpful." She yanked her hair back into a ponytail, pulled an elastic out of her pocket, and wrapped it around her hair. "We should get going." She pointed at Swoosie. "And I think your dog just gnawed some old gum off the bottom of the chair seat there."

Michael stood up and pulled Swoosie after him. "Let's go, Swoosie. I really can't take you anywhere, can I?"

The rest of the drive was quiet. Michael put on some music, but most of the road-trip enthusiasm had been quelled. Jan was by turns annoyed with herself for killing the fun mood of the trip and relieved that she finally had said some of the things she'd been thinking about for too long.

The only problem was that in the process she'd managed to make it even less clear if she'd ever see Michael again. How angry was he? Did they just break up? If so, from what? And where was she sleeping tonight? His place? That seemed unlikely, now that he hadn't spoken to her for what seemed like forever. Maybe Mom hadn't ditched her apartment yet and she could stay there, assuming it still had any furniture. Bunking with Bruce and her mom at his house would be beyond awkward. The thought of seeing sexual healing crystals everywhere made her cringe.

Jan's mind swirled with unanswered questions as she leaned her head on the window and stared blankly out at the passing farmland. It was going to be a long few days.

~

Michael pulled up in front of his house. Even after all the silence, Jan couldn't think of anything to say. She certainly had no idea what he was thinking. As she moved to open the car door, he grabbed her arm. "Do you want to stay here?" he asked.

Before her brain initiated any rational thought, Jan said, "Yes." Had he heard anything she'd said? This was such a mistake. What was wrong with her?

Michael tugged her toward him, the gearshift digging into her leg. He kissed her more tentatively than usual. "I'm glad. I would like you to stay."

Enjoying the familiar flutter of excitement and the sensation of his lips against hers, Jan smiled, then frowned. What was she doing? Did she have no control over her hormones at *all*? She moved toward the door again. "Maybe we should go inside."

They unloaded the car and brought Swoosie and their luggage into the house. Jan stood in the living room and watched as Swoosie raced around the house, her claws skittering across the hardwood floors.

Michael came up behind Jan and wrapped his arms around her, pulling her against his chest. He kissed the side of her neck and gently removed the elastic from her ponytail, so her hair cascaded around her face. "You might want to put that away."

Jan took the elastic, shoved it in her pocket, and turned to face him. She had every intention of telling him to stop. That she should sleep on the sofa. It would be better that way. But then he reached out and ran his fingers through her hair at the nape of her neck. His hands moved downward, pulling her body toward him. Jan opened her mouth to explain, but then his mouth was on hers and it was a lost cause.

The next morning, she rolled over in bed and reached out her arm for Michael. The house was quiet and she could tell he wasn't in it anywhere. When had he left? Sitting up, she looked around the room. Nothing had been moved, but the house seemed empty without Michael's presence. It was odd to be here by herself. She got up out of bed and walked out to the living room. Swoosie stood up in her crate and yipped with glee.

Jan crouched down and peered inside. "He left you with me? That can't be a good idea. How about you stay in there while I take a shower?" Swoosie sat, looking dejected, apparently realizing that she wasn't going to be released yet.

After her shower, Jan puttered around the kitchen, looking for something to eat. Swoosie was rattling around in her crate, making it clear that she did not appreciate missing out on any food preparation that might be happening.

Jan strode out to the living room. "Oh, all right," she said as she opened the gate. Swoosie shot out and ran toward the back door. "I guess you have to go outside?" She opened the back door and the dog ran out to the yard. Jan leaned in the doorway waiting for the dog to finish her morning routine. Swoosie raced back into the house and sat next to the stove.

"Sorry, little dog. Nothing for you. I refuse to be responsible for any more of your gastrointestinal indiscretions." She turned and looked around the kitchen. Maybe Michael had left a note. Presumably he had gone to work. Did she have that number? Did she even know the name of the agency where he worked? She was sleeping with the man. Shouldn't she know this by now?

Walking through the living room, she observed the bare table tops with no notes anywhere. Outside the front window, there was no car, either. How could Michael have just left her here without saying anything? He must trust her not to steal everything he owned. Or had he forgotten she was even there in the rush to go back to work? Maybe that was the protocol with one-night stands.

She peeked in a few drawers. Did he have business cards lying around somewhere? Given his dog's enjoyment of paper products, it shouldn't be surprising that the place was so barren. It was like a model home. The only decorations were the photographs on the wall. Apparently, Swoosie didn't have a taste for art.

Jan slammed a drawer on an end table shut. If he actually cared about her, he wouldn't have just left her here all alone without a word. It made her want to cry or throw something fragile at the wall. But there weren't any available knickknacks, so the house was safe for the time being.

At a loss for what to do next, she sat on the sofa and Swoosie hopped up next to her. "Hi Swoosie. You really are quite a social little thing, aren't you?" She wrapped her arm around the dog's furry body and Swoosie leaned over and licked her cheek. Jan ruffled the dog's fuzzy coat. In response, Swoosie flopped over on her back for a tummy rub.

As she rubbed the dog's soft fur, Jan considered her options. She could call her mother and ask for a lift. But she really didn't want to answer the inevitable questions, particularly given her mother's new interest in discussing sex and crystals. Ugh.

Or she could stay here and wait for Michael to call. Except that he undoubtedly would be wrapped up with whatever was going on at work, and she'd just sit here all day getting even more upset about the fact that he'd obviously completely forgotten about her.

Maybe she could take Swoosie for a walk and see if there were any places to stay nearby. This was a tourist area, after all, and Michael's house wasn't far from the beach. She definitely should not stay here again tonight. The idea of leaving made her feel sort of sick, since she knew she'd miss him again. But it was the right choice. Getting any more involved with Michael was senseless. He had made it clear he wasn't interested in anything beyond a fling, which was bad for her long-term emotional health, since she wanted far more.

"Okay Swoosie, I have a plan. You need to help me go find a motel." Swoosie flipped back over like a turtle righting itself and bounded off the couch, ready to go.

She leashed up the dog, but she didn't have any keys to lock the door. After searching around the kitchen, she discovered a set of keys to the back door wedged in the back of a drawer. "Okay, let's go!" Swoosie launched out ahead of her.

Jan walked down toward the beach with Swoosie and then stopped. She had to make a decision. North or south? No clue. She turned right to head north, since it seemed like Swoosie wanted to go that way. As the sun beat down on her back, warming her tense muscles, she finally started to relax. Walking through the residential neighborhoods made her think of Michael's habit of people-watching. What would he say about those surfers loaded down with gear, headed for the beach? Or the older couple strolling slowly hand-in-hand?

A woman wearing a floppy red hat, carrying a big beach umbrella and dragging a little girl behind her, ran toward Jan and Swoosie. "Ooh, what a cute dog!" The little girl said,

"Doggie! Pet doggie!" and reached out her free hand to point and wave at Swoosie.

Swoosie sat and looked ready to be accosted by the small girl, who kept pointing at her and shrieking, "Doggie! Doggie!"

The woman bent down to pet Swoosie. "Can Anna pet her?"

Jan nodded. "Swoosie is very friendly."

Dropping the umbrella, the woman directed the little girl's hand toward Swoosie's head to pet her. "She's so pretty! How do you keep that fur so white? Don't you have to brush her all the time?"

Jan shook her head. "Ah, well, she's not really my dog. But as I understand it, she stays pretty clean."

The woman stood up and collected her umbrella again. "Thank you so much. What a sweet dog!"

"You're welcome." Jan paused and then added, "Do you know of any motels around here? I need a place to stay."

The woman nodded. "We're staying at the inn right up the street. Turn on 15th Street. You can't miss it."

"Thank you."

Jan kept walking and found the motel. The large white building looked nice enough and the neon *Vacancy* sign was flashing. "Well Swoosie, I guess this is where we turn around. I'll drop you back at home and then say goodbye." Swoosie turned and wagged at the sound of her name and then started marching forward toward home.

At the house, Jan put Swoosie in her crate, collected her things, and threw her bag over her shoulder. She put the keys back in the drawer, locked the back door behind her, and walked around through the gate to the front yard. A young, thin, leggy woman with long, straight brown hair wearing a bright yellow t-shirt was walking up the sidewalk toward the house with a portly golden retriever in tow.

Jan nodded in acknowledgment. At least Swoosie the female attractant wasn't with her. She just wanted to get out of here.

The woman stopped in front of her and told the big red dog to sit. "Who are you?"

"My name is Jan."

"I'm Joan. Did you walk Swoosie?"

"Yes." Who was this person? Were women stalking the house now? "I guess you know Michael?"

"Yes. How do you know him?"

"He's...he's my step-brother. I'm visiting for a family get together."

Joan put her hand on her hip. "You don't look related to him."

"We're not. He's my *step*-brother." Did nobody ever listen to that part? "His father married my mother."

"Oh, I get it," Joan said, snapping her gum. "Are you staying here? Because if I don't have to walk Swoosie, it would be nice if someone told me, you know? He's *supposed* to call me if Swoosie doesn't need a walk, so I don't come all the way over here for nothing."

"You're the dog walker?"

Joan looked irritated and pointed at the golden. "Yeah. Duh. Who did you think I was?"

"I don't know." Jan looked down the street in the direction of the motel. "Anyway, please do walk Swoosie. I'm just leaving. She could use more exercise."

"All right. Whatever. I'm here, anyway." She pulled the panting golden toward the door, "Come on, George. We gotta go get your girlfriend now."

Jan readjusted her bag on her shoulder and scurried down the sidewalk away from the house. How embarrassing. It was time to get out of here.

~

After checking into the motel, Jan went for a long walk on the beach and stopped for dinner at a restaurant that faced the water. The ocean view was beautiful, but once she got the food, she realized she wasn't particularly hungry. She picked at the meal and gazed out at the surf, wishing she didn't feel the way she did. Missing Michael made her feel almost physically ill. Even worse was that she was going to have to see him tomorrow at her mother's party.

After dinner, she walked along the beach back to the motel feeling sorry for herself, wishing things were different. All the walking and mental gymnastics had been exhausting, so it was a relief to get back to her generic little beachfront motel room, curl up with a book, and fall asleep.

A pounding noise startled Jan awake and she sat bolt upright in bed. She looked at the clock. It was 2:33 a.m. She pulled the covers up to her neck and waited. Maybe the people next door were having a good time. That would figure, since she was definitely not having that kind of fun all by herself here in her sad, lonely little room. The pounding repeated more loudly. The noise was actually coming from the door to her room. Was there a fire? She jumped up out of bed and peered out the peephole. Michael was standing outside with his fists clenched.

She hurriedly unhooked the security chain and opened the door. "What are you doing here?" she whispered.

"Can I come in?"

Jan opened the door wider and he stalked into the room. She closed the door and leaned back against it. "Why are you here? Do you know what time it is?"

"Yes. My dog-walker told me when I woke her up after I got home from work."

"What? Why are you calling your..."

He dragged her to him and enveloped her in a hug. "I thought something had happened to you. You weren't there."

Jan pushed him away. "I know I wasn't there. I was here. And I'm fine."

"Why did you leave?"

"I told you. I can't do this...whatever we're doing... anymore. I shouldn't have stayed with you last night. That was my mistake. And then you disappeared this morning. I assume you were at work, but I don't know where that is. I don't even know the name of the company. You never told me. And then it seemed like you actually *forgot* about me." She raised her hand. "Wait a minute. How did your dog-walker know I was here?"

"She didn't. But she said she saw you and that you said you were leaving. This is the closest motel. I bribed the guy at the front desk to tell me your room number. He was kind of drunk and I made up a story about how we were newlyweds and you were a runaway bride on our honeymoon. He bought it."

Jan crossed her arms. "That was quite enterprising and creative of you. So why did you want to find me so badly in the first place? In the middle of the night."

Michael shook his head. "I don't know," he said in a low voice. "Work was really bad today. I think the company is actually going to completely implode. Or my boss may go to jail. Or both. Anyway, I went in early and was there until one this morning dealing with it all. Then I got home, expecting to see you. When you weren't there, I guess I kind of lost it."

"I don't see why. You obviously didn't care that I was there this morning. I don't understand you at all. How could you just leave me without saying anything?"

Michael took a deep breath and sat down on the bed. "I didn't forget. But I couldn't sleep last night and I didn't want to wake you. I thought I could get some work in early, then come back home and see you. But I got wrapped up at work and I couldn't get out of there."

"You could have called. You do know your own phone number, don't you?"

"I know." He shook his head slowly. "I got dragged into meetings. Then calls with clients in Russia. I kept thinking it would be just one more call, and then before I knew it, it was one o'clock."

"So you decided to come to my motel like some kind of stalker? This is kind of creepy, you know. Everything is creepy in the middle of the night. You couldn't wait until morning?"

Leaning forward, he put his elbows on his knees and stared at the floor. "I haven't told you about when mom died, have I?" He turned and glanced at her face. "Okay, I know I haven't. I never talk to anybody about it."

Jan sat down on the bed next to him. "What are you talking about?"

"It was the middle of the night. She had cancer. My dad wasn't there. She...died. I was holding her hand. Have you ever actually watched someone you love die? And then I had to call the funeral home. And they took her away. Sometimes I still dream about it."

"I'm sorry about that. But what does it have to do with me?"

He looked into her eyes. "It was the middle of the night and I thought you were gone. It's not the same. I know that. But I wasn't really thinking straight."

Jan wanted more than anything to reach out and hug him again. But it was not going to happen. No. She stood up and stepped back, away from him. "I think I understand what happened tonight, and I am sorry. But I had a lot of time to think today after you left. I don't think I should see you. We don't want the same things. It's not good for me and you seem to have some stuff you need to deal with at work. And it seems like you should talk to your father, as well. You should probably go home and get some rest, since we have to go to that party tomorrow. If we don't show up, both of our parents will not be pleased."

He looked up at her. "Are you sure?"

Jan waved toward the door and made an effort to adopt her business-like librarian tone. "Very. I'd appreciate it if you could pick me up and drive me to the party. I don't have a car and I'd rather not pay for a cab all the way up to your dad's place. This trip is already costing me a fortune."

Michael stood up and walked toward the door slowly. He turned and said, "I'll see you tomorrow then."

The door closed behind him and Jan took two steps toward the bed and flopped down on it, pressing her face into the pillow. As a tear slid down her cheek, she tried to will herself not to cry. Not anymore. Crying about this whole thing was senseless. Why did she have to fall in love with him? They'd never had a real relationship anyway. What was wrong with her? She should just get over it. Only one more day and then she'd never have to see Michael again.

Chapter 12

Rainbows

Jan spent most of the morning moping around her motel room, missing and thinking about Michael way too much. Frustrated with her roiling emotions, she went for another long beach walk to try to tire herself out. Michael was supposed to pick her up at five, so she stopped by the restaurant for lunch again.

After the walk, she had resolved again that she would stop seeing him for good. It was the only logical choice. Everything always seemed so tragic at two thirty in the morning. Her habit of running away from drama like her mother's wedding had never been an issue before. How was she supposed to know it would trigger some horrible memory about Michael's mother's death? And yet it was still awful to see him so distraught.

Today in the bright light of day, returning to Alpine Grove and going back to her simple, peaceful life didn't seem quite as depressing. All she had to do was get through the party. Then she was getting on a plane and leaving for good. She was sitting on a bench outside the motel lobby clutching her purse when Michael's car drove up. She opened the passenger door and got inside.

Michael smiled at her and she noticed the dark circles under his eyes. He looked terrible again. Had he gotten any sleep at all? Putting the car into gear, he turned and said, "Are you ready to deal with our parents?"

"Yes. I guess so. My mother wasn't terribly clear what all this was about. Just that we have to be there. She does like any excuse for a party."

They drove up the freeway in silence. Michael seemed to be lost in thought. Jan looked out the window at the many condominiums that lined the hills like little armies of pink houses staging attacks along the canyons.

As the car pulled up to Bruce's house, Jan flashed back to the sand-infused green carpet sitting on the front lawn. The great cleaning adventure seemed like a long time ago.

They walked up to the front door and stood on the doorstep. She smiled at Michael, "This could be interesting."

He took her hand in his. "I have no doubt about that."

The door opened and Jan's mother Angie opened her arms wide to welcome them into the house. She was wearing a rainbow-colored diaphanous caftan with huge sleeves that swirled around her. "Come in, come in!" She whirled back into the room and then stopped and appraised Michael's appearance. "Your aura seems cloudy and congested. Something is wrong." She turned to Jan. "Is this related to what we discussed? Is there a problem? I have some crystals that might help, you know."

Jan's eyes widened. "No, Mom. *No!* Michael has just been working a lot."

"I'm fine," Michael said. "Just tired, that's all."

Angie looked unconvinced and put her arm around Jan's shoulder. "I have to go do some things in the kitchen. Have a lovely time, dear. I'll talk to you later."

Michael bent down and whispered to Jan, "Your mom is dressing like Stevie Nicks."

Jan tried to ignore the shiver of excitement that ran through her as his warm breath hit her ear. "My mother went through a big Fleetwood Mac phase. Maybe she found that outfit again when she moved."

They walked into the room, which was strewn with crystals and shimmering rainbow ribbon everywhere. Many people were milling around. Once again, Jan knew hardly anyone; it was like the wedding all over again. Except with fewer flowers and more of a floaty, colorful motif.

Michael looked around. "Wow, this is different. The floors look really good. Somebody waxed them or something. I think your mom must have convinced my dad to get rid of some of the most disgusting furniture, too. I'm going to miss that ugly orange couch. So will Swoosie."

"Your dog is a sofa connoisseur. Speaking of which, I had a nice walk with her the other day. She was really good and so sweet with a little girl we met who wanted to pet her."

"I told you little girls love her. She isn't always a bad dog, you know. Do you want something to drink?"

"That might help. And you're driving. How about something with a lot of vodka, if they have it. Mom tends to embrace the idea of an open bar."

"Okay. I'll investigate." He put his hand on her arm and looked into her eyes. "I'll be right back."

She watched him stride toward the bar, his long legs covering the distance quickly. Staying away from him tonight was going to be challenging. One more evening. That's it. Retain common sense. Stay the course. She needed to rein in her hormones for a change, so she could get out of here with her heart still (mostly) intact.

Angie stood up on a dining room table chair and tapped a spoon on her glass. "May I have your attention, everyone?"

A server put his tray down on the table next to Jan and stood back against the wall, so he could attend to a wayward contact lens. The poor guy probably got sand in his eye. The tray was covered with colorful shot glasses. Surveying the rainbow-hued beverages, Jan took a pink one and peered down into it. Jell-O shots? Really? She slurped it down in one big gulp. Yum.

The chatter in the room settled down a little and Jan noticed Michael was standing near the kitchen at the other side of the living room, holding two large hurricane glasses full of fuchsia-colored liquid. He put them down on the sideboard and looked up at Angie.

"Thank you all for coming to our celebration." She pointed at Bruce, who was standing near a window looking like he might want to jump out of it. "Many of you were at our wedding, so I wanted you to be here to celebrate a new phase of our relationship. After exploring our friendship and love for each other, we have found that Bruce has been holding back in an important area of his life because of fear. It is important to face our fear and free ourselves from the chains that bind us. So we want to celebrate turning over a new leaf." She waved toward Bruce. "Come here, darling."

Bruce walked over to the chair and held Angie's hand. He cleared his throat. "Okay, well, here's the thing. I've been avoiding something and Angie here has helped me see that it's time to be honest. With myself and all of you. We're going to get a divorce."

Several people in the room gasped and urgent, hushed whispers flitted around in the space like butterflies. Jan looked over again at Michael, who was standing with his hands clasped behind him, almost in a military stand-at-ease posture, watching his father.

Bruce waved at the crowd. "It's not because I don't love Angie. Because I do. She's a wonderful lady. But I need to be true to myself. I'm, well, here's the thing. I'm gay. And I'll probably be spending more time with Dave." He pointed at his friend, who raised his hand and waved slightly from his position in the corner of the room.

Michael smiled at Jan and their gazes locked. He silently mouthed the words, "Told you so."

Jan looked away quickly, embarrassed that she'd been staring at him, instead of paying attention to the announcement. She grabbed another shot glass from the tray and cradled it in her hands.

Bruce looked uncomfortable for a second and then Angie spoke again. "Thank you all again for being here and helping Bruce release some of the past pain he has been dealing with for many years. Please don't worry. We have discussed the importance of safe sex and HIV testing. This is not the stigma it once was. It is love and we all must embrace love in all its forms."

Jan glanced quickly at Michael. An extremely well-endowed server with large curls of auburn hair was whispering something in his ear. Jan looked down and shook the chartreuse contents in her glass. No lime in nature was truly that color. She tipped the glass back and sucked it down. Tasty. After replacing the glass on the tray, she focused again on Angie, who had raised her glass for a toast. Oops. Now, she needed another glass. The server was moving to pick up the tray. Maybe a red one this time.

"I hope you all consider what you want from life and rid yourself of negative energy as Bruce has. Be true to yourselves. We love you all." Angie stepped down from the chair and the room erupted in conversation. Many people went up to the couple to talk to them. Jan slurped her cherry Jell-O thoughtfully, then put the glass aside.

Michael maneuvered his way through the crowd toward Jan with the drinks. She took the frothy-looking fruity beverage from him. "I hope this has a lot of vodka in it."

"I had a feeling this was coming, so I asked the bartender to pour it a little heavy."

Jan took a long drink, "Whoa. I hope you gave him a big tip." She looked up into Michael's dark brown eyes. "I know you told me about your dad, so this whole announcement thing is not completely unexpected, but it's still a little weird for me. Are you okay with all this?"

"It's great. I just want my dad to be happy. I mean, look at him. He looks like a giant weight has been lifted from his shoulders. And he's hanging out with Dave without having to pretend to do guy things like play poker. I've known Dave was gay for years."

Jan gulped her drink. "That guy from the Olympics just came out, too. Maybe it's the thing to do. I can't imagine keeping a secret like that for so many years. I guess I can't blame my mom for *this* divorce, anyway. And it sounds like she was helpful, for a change. Some of the past breakups have been pretty bad. But this was actually...nice. Really nice."

She clutched her drink in both hands and poured some more fruity beverage down her throat. Looking into

Michael's eyes, she said, "It was all so sweet. The part about love in all its forms. And being true to yourself. That was really extraordinary. Particularly for my mom. I mean, if you knew her years ago, you'd be surprised. Or maybe not. I don't know." Jan held the empty glass up in front of her face and tipped it back, trying to extract the last drops from the bottom. "That was really good."

Michael sat in the chair next to her and leaned toward her, taking the glass and putting it on the side table. "You drank that pretty quickly."

"It was kind of like a Slurpee, 'cept at the end. That part tasted like vodka. Does vodka sink? I haven't had a Slurpee in a long time. There aren't any 7-11s in Alpine Grove."

"Why does that not surprise me?"

Jan looked down at the floor. The pattern on the Oriental rug seemed a little fuzzy. And maybe like it might be moving. Standing up would be a bad idea. Maybe she'd just sit here for a few minutes until the dizziness went away. She turned and looked at Michael again. "I think I have negative energy too. Why do I have negative energy? I think my chakras aren't flowing right. My chakras are broken."

Michael smiled. "In my experience, your sacral chakra is doing just fine. I don't know much about the other ones, but they're probably okay, too."

Jan pushed his shoulder. "That's all you think about, isn't it? You're such a guy. I'm having a serious, um. Well. It's serious. I'm having a life crisis. Yes, that's what it is. It's an existential crisis. That's what I'm having."

"Okay. I'm not sure what you mean, but..."

Jan leaned back in the chair to get a better look at Michael. "Wow. What happened to your hair? It looks like your dad's. Well, except not purple."

"That's reassuring."

"You look different. Wait. Why do you look like your dad all of a sudden? Whoa. That's wild. It's like you got old. Actually, no. It's icky. Yuck. It's like I was sleeping with the same guy my mom was. Wow, that's so gross. Ewww."

Michael furrowed his brows. "You don't drink much, do you?"

"I never drink. Ever. I'm a teeeeeetotaler. My mother says I'm too rigid and I never have any fun." Jan bowed her head and stared at her hands in her lap. "I'm boring."

"You're not boring. But I think maybe I should take you home."

Jan leaned her head on his shoulder. "I miss Rosa."

Michael helped her stand up. "Okay, let's go."

～

Jan opened her eyes. She was lying in a bed in a darkened room. Somewhere. Where was she? After a bit of experimentation, she determined that if she moved her head, searing pain shot through her skull like a grenade. She tried to lie as still as possible and stared at the ceiling. What happened? What was she wearing? She padded her hands around her body gingerly. It seemed to be a soft cotton t-shirt. Wherever she was, there had better be a bathroom nearby. Her bladder was not going to take no for an answer much longer. She heard breathing nearby and carefully reached out an arm and determined she was not alone in the bed. Uh-oh.

She turned her head and cringed at the pain, along with a new and horribly unpleasant nauseous twirling in her stomach. What had she done to herself?

Trying to move very slowly and carefully, she crawled out of the bed and across the floor toward the bathroom. Given that Michael was the one asleep next to her, at least she knew where the bathroom was in his house. And it was mercifully close to the bedroom.

After giving her poor long-suffering bladder a break, Jan was pretty sure she might throw up if she moved again. Returning to the bed was not an option. It was way too far away. But the tile floor was nice and cool. Pretty tile. Nice tile. Very nice.

A few hours later, Jan opened her eyes and found Michael looking down at her. He crouched down and said, "Wow. This isn't a pretty picture. Are you alive?"

Jan rolled over on the tile. "Sort of."

"You might be more comfortable in the bed."

Jan groaned, "Can't. Get. There."

Michael scooped her up, carefully laid her in the bed, and pulled the covers over her. "Are you going to be okay here for a few minutes?"

Jan groaned and pulled the covers over her head. "Go away."

Much later, the bed moved and she peeked out of her sheet cave. Sun was streaming in the window and Michael was sitting on the edge of the bed. Southern California sun was bright. Ow. And it tasted like something had died in her mouth. She ran her tongue across her teeth. Gross.

Michael touched her shoulder. "Are you going to live?

A few feeble neurons fired. What day was it? Wednesday? A work day. She pushed the sheet down to her chin. "What are you doing here?"

"I live here."

"I know that. Could you close the shade? That light is awful."

Michael stood up, closed the curtains, and returned to the bed. He stroked her hair, pushing it back from her forehead. "Can I get you anything?"

The idea of food made her stomach do a few creative acrobatics. "No. Please no. I don't think I'm ever going to eat again. Ever. And definitely not drink."

Michael smiled. "Yes, you give the term lightweight new meaning. Have you ever had alcohol before at all?"

Jan rolled over. "Yes. But it tends to make me sick."

"So I noticed."

"You didn't answer me. What are you doing here?"

"Yes, I did. I live here, remember?" Swoosie trotted up to the bed, sniffed at Jan, and wrinkled her brow. "Swoosie says hi and I'm pretty sure she thinks you smell bad."

"Thanks. I feel the same way about you too, dog. And no, I mean why aren't you at work?"

Michael crawled onto the bed and stretched out next to her. He leaned back on a pillow with his arm behind his head. "Well, two reasons. One, I wanted to make sure you weren't going to die."

"How thoughtful."

"You're welcome. And two, because yesterday afternoon, right before I had to leave to pick you up for the party, the indictment came down against my boss. This morning I went in and cleaned out my desk before they locked the doors. I'm on involuntary leave until further notice."

Jan tried to straighten up and clutched her head. "Ugh. I thought they already did an audit."

"My boss was arrested this morning. Now they have to figure out if any of the rest of us were involved."

Jan slumped down on the pillow. "Wow. You weren't involved, right?"

"No. Of course not. But I've been working for a criminal, which is depressing. I think everything will work out okay in the end. I'm not sure what is going to happen to the company, though." He pointed at a newspaper on the nightstand. "There's an article about it if you want to know the details."

"I'm not really up for reading anything."

Michael brushed his fingertips across her cheek. "You *must* feel bad. When the librarian doesn't want to read, there's something very wrong."

She pushed his hand away weakly and closed her eyes. "Ha-ha. Very funny."

"Maybe you want to sleep some more?"

Curling her arm around the pillow, she mumbled, "Uh-huh" before rolling over and falling asleep. She had a series of bizarre dreams. Fleetwood Mac was playing a concert. And then Westley from *The Princess Bride* was there, talking about rodents of unusual size. But they were on a plane, which made no sense and led to a confusing dream about Edna, the lady who was in the seat next to her on the plane when she went to the wedding. The aisle was twisting and the plane was going down. What if she missed her connection? Wait. What flight was she on? Was there a connection? When was the flight? Her flight. The one she was supposed to be on at ten o'clock. Today.

Jan opened her eyes and sat up and then cringed at the sudden movement. What time was it? She looked at the clock, which said 12:34. Ugh. Could this day get any worse?

She reached over and looked at the newspaper article. At least she could find out where Michael worked now. Or used to work. Great. She skimmed the article and then staggered out of bed toward the bathroom. After splashing some cold water on her face and rinsing out her mouth, she determined that she was now able to at least walk to the kitchen. Michael was sitting at the table eating a sandwich and Swoosie had her head resting on his leg so she could studiously observe his movements.

Michael looked up. "Good afternoon, sunshine. Nice t-shirt."

Jan waved weakly and sat down in the chair across from him with a groan. She looked down at the light blue shirt with a logo on the front. "Windows 95?"

"I get a lot of free t-shirts. I thought you might yak on it."

"I'm sure Bill Gates is relieved that I'm feeling better."

"No doubt."

Jan put her elbows on the table and leaned her forehead on her palms. "I missed my flight. And I should go back to my motel. I was supposed to check out at eight." She looked up at Michael. "What do you suppose they did with all my stuff when I didn't show up?"

"I don't know. How about if I call the motel and ask while you take a shower. It would probably make you feel better."

"Thanks. By the way, where are my clothes?"

"I left them on the dresser."

Jan shook her head slowly. "I didn't see them there."

Michael got up and went to the bedroom. Jan followed him. "Here's your skirt on the floor," he said, holding it up. He looked at Swoosie. "What did you do with the rest?" Swoosie wagged and ran out of the room.

Jan scowled. "Did she eat my underwear? I'm going to be annoyed if she did. That bra was expensive."

"She ate clothes and towels when she was a puppy, but she hasn't eaten fabric in a while. Now she likes to sleep on it, instead."

"So my clothes are all covered in dog hair somewhere?"

Michael pointed toward the back of the house. "Probably in the backyard. She likes to dig a hole and line it with fabric. Because you were asleep, I left the back door open so she could go outside without making a lot of noise. That may have been a mistake."

"Your dog missed her calling as a landscape designer. Can I borrow another t-shirt?" Jan pulled at the front of the one she was wearing. "I'm going to take my shower and I'd like to change out of this one."

"Sure. They're in the dresser over there. Take your pick. I'll go out back and see if I can find your underwear."

"That would be great." Just great.

$\sim$

After Jan had showered, dressed and brushed her teeth, she did feel better. No one needed to know that she had borrowed his toothbrush. Ick. Or that she was wearing an old pair of

Michael's boxer shorts under her skirt. Boxers certainly did provide a lot of ventilation.

She went into the living room where Michael was hanging out with Swoosie and sagged down next to him on the sofa.

He looked up from his book. "That's an interesting fashion statement you're making."

"I tried to shake it out, but my bra still feels crunchy. I'm trying not to think about it. In the process of redecorating the yard, your dog chewed a hole in my panties, so I borrowed a pair of your boxers.

Michael grinned widely and reached over to lift a corner of her skirt. "I gotta see this."

She pushed his hand away. "No. I'm just glad your dog didn't eat my belt, too. Did you call the motel?"

"Yes. They have your things at the front desk, but they want you to go and pay them. There are no vacancies, so you have to check out, too. You can stay here if you like."

"I don't think that's a good idea."

"Why not?"

"We already had this conversation."

"But then you got drunk and told me you were boring." A corner of his mouth curved into a smile. "If you want a little excitement, I have some ideas."

Jan leaned back on the sofa. "No doubt. I don't think you're paying attention to what I'm saying. We live hours away from each other. You're attached to your job and like you said, you work long hours. There's no way we could ever have any type of relationship. I just don't want to get any more...involved than we already have."

He leaned back next to her on the sofa and turned her face toward him, cupping her chin with his hand. "Why is that such a bad thing? We don't live *that* far apart. And we've already determined that we can have some seriously fun weekends."

Jan smiled and pulled his hand away from her face. "Yes. But I don't want to be just another one of your weekend girlfriends."

Michael leaned his head back on the sofa and closed his eyes. "So that's it, then?"

"Yes. I've thought about this a lot and it's the only rational choice."

He turned to face her again, propping his head on his hand. "I hate rational choices. What's wrong with a little irrationality? I know I don't want to say goodbye to you again right now. And I hate having you here and feeling like I can't touch you. How about if I make you a deal? We have one more weekend together." He paused. "Although it's Wednesday. But whatever. A last hurrah, if you want to call it that. You have to get back to work. I could drive you back, since it's sort of my fault you missed your flight. Although for future reference, asking for alcohol when it makes you sick really isn't a good idea."

"I know. That was stupid. I was upset. And by the way, Jell-O is the devil's food."

"I'm not sure Jell-O counts as food." He reached out to move a wayward curl of hair back behind her ear. "I could stand a vacation after not sleeping again because of the whole indictment thing. I haven't gotten a good night's sleep since I left Alpine Grove, in fact. Maybe that's why they call them sleepy little towns. Because you can sleep." He leaned forward so their lips were almost touching and gazed into her eyes. "And I know you want to kiss me."

He brushed his lips lightly across hers. The sensation was electrifying. She should push him away. Instead, she wrapped her arms around his neck and pressed her lips to his. Warmth and relief and confused emotions swirled through her as she sank down into the sofa, reveling in the feel of his body on hers again. She'd missed this. Missed him.

He pulled his head back and said, "So do we have a deal?"

"Fine. You're taking advantage of my weakened state. I'm going to get hurt again. I just know it. By the way, I think you might want move your elbow. I still feel sort of nauseated."

Michael moved away from her on the couch and then reached out to take one of her hands. He interlaced her fingers in his. "Maybe you should eat something. Some crackers, maybe?"

She leaned over and rested her head on his shoulder. "I can't figure you out. You have been so nice to me today and you even scraped me up off the floor last night. But the other day, you just disappeared like I didn't exist."

"I told you. I went to work."

"I know. I've come to the conclusion that I don't like your job."

"But I don't have to work today. A fact I'm trying not to think about, since I may be unemployed." He stood up and stretched. "Are you going to be up for traveling today? Even if we left now, we'd get to Alpine Grove pretty late."

Jan groaned and curled her arms around her stomach. "Ugh. I need to call Jill. She's going to kill me. I can't face the idea of a moving car right now. I can't imagine what would have happened if I'd tried to get on a plane."

"Nothing good. Maybe we should just walk down to the motel, get your stuff, and call it a day."

"As long as we walk very slowly."

He leaned over, put his hands on either side of her head, and kissed her again. "Deal."

~

Michael and Jan strolled hand in hand to the motel. Swoosie was with them, happily sniffing, panting, and smiling at the passersby.

Michael looked down at Jan. "Are you feeling better? You look less green."

"Yes. Thank you for taking care of me when I was indisposed. That was not my finest hour."

Michael squeezed her hand as a show of solidarity. "Do you remember anything about last night?"

"I remember the party. But not much after you handed me the drink."

"You said you were having an existential life crisis."

Jan shook her head. "I did not." Did she? Maybe.

"Then it was like in the movie *E.T.*, where he finds the beer and gets drunk. You sucked down the drink, stumbled around, and tipped over."

"Nice. I'm sure my mother was very proud of me. Did you know, Steven Spielberg wrote most of that script when he was on location filming *Raiders of the Lost Ark*? He wrote it during the breaks between filming."

"No, I didn't know. I wonder how much beer he drank."

After picking up her clothes and paying off the motel, she and Michael had a relaxing afternoon hanging around his house. Not surprisingly, he had a vast movie collection and after dinner they watched *Ferris Bueller's Day Off*.

When the movie ended, Jan was leaning on Michael with her back against his chest. He had his arms wrapped around her and she was enjoying being in the moment, trying not to think about the future. "I like that movie." She turned to look up at him. "You seem to benefit from days off, too."

"I have been told that I work too much. I suppose I should stop and look around more often, like Ferris suggests."

"I always identified with his sister, Jeanie. Having to cover for him all the time. I had to do that for my mom."

"Does that mean I'm the guy in the police station she makes out with?"

"Well Charlie Sheen *is* cute. But no. You're Ferris. I can imagine you up on a parade float. You'd do that."

"Except I'd have my dog with me." He pointed at Swoosie, who was upside-down, snoring on the floor, her paws curled against her chest. "Because you know I can't leave her alone. I don't think you're Jeanie though. She's too angry. You're not wound that tight."

Jan giggled. "Maybe you should tell my mother that. She thinks I'm too rigid and that your aura is cloudy."

"That reminds me. I forgot to show you the picture I took of you." Michael untangled himself from Jan and crossed the room. He returned with a package of photographs and began riffling through them. "Here it is." He sat down and handed it to her. "This is how I see you."

Jan looked down at the photo. It was taken when they went on the horseback ride on the beach. Her hair was swirling around her face from the wind and she was obviously laughing. The late-afternoon lighting was stunning and there was a glow behind her reddish hair. "I had no idea you were such an amazing photographer. This doesn't even look like me."

"I think it does. Sometimes when you get really lucky, you capture a moment perfectly. Photography has been a hobby of mine for a long time. I just don't do it anymore much because of work. When I started in advertising I did a lot of the photo and graphic-design work because we didn't have many people. Then I moved up into creative direction and account management, so I stopped doing the hands-on stuff. Now so much of it is done on the computer, it's totally different. So I hung up my X-acto knife and Rubylith."

"Do you have other photographs that you've taken?"

"Sure. You've seen them." He waved his hand toward the room. "They're hanging up all over the place."

Jan sat up straighter on the couch. "Those are yours? I had no idea. I thought you'd bought them at galleries."

Michael grinned. "I have my own little art show right here. There are more photographs in the bedroom, you know."

Jan rolled her eyes. "If you ask me if I want to see your etchings, I may really throw up this time."

He gathered her in his arms and kissed her. "You can't fool me. I know you're feeling better now. You're using multi-syllabic words again."

Chapter 13

Home Again

The drive back to Alpine Grove was far more enjoyable than the drive down to San Diego had been. No more serious conversations, picking fights, or even thinking about the future if she could help it. Whatever was going to happen would happen without her analysis. There would be plenty of time to cry later. And she was going to cry a lot. Because she certainly wasn't falling *less* in love with Michael. After her unfortunate drunken adventure and subsequent hangover hell, he'd been so kind to her, it was hard not to feel anything but affection for him.

They pulled up in front of Jan's house and again, she was relieved to be back in her own space. She opened the door and Swoosie ran into the house, rushing around the small space doing her spaz dog routine.

A wave of contentment flowed through Jan as she put down her bag and walked around her home environment again. "It's so good to be home!"

Michael flopped down on the sofa. "It's good to be out of the car." Swoosie leaped up next to him, and settled in, apparently equally happy to be out of the back seat.

"We have to go pick up Rosa, though. I told Kat we'd come by as soon as we got here."

Michael stretched out on the sofa, pushing Swoosie out of the way. He yawned and Swoosie readjusted her position so she could take a nap alongside him.

Jan gazed at his relaxed form draped all over her sofa. "You drove all the way up here. Maybe I should go get Rosa myself."

Michael smiled. "Remember how I didn't get any sleep because of work? Well, I didn't get any sleep last night, either. But that was your fault. And since you slept approximately 16 hours previously, I'd say you're well-rested."

Blushing slightly at the memory, Jan said, "True. I didn't really think about that. I'll stop by the library and tell Jill that I'm really here. She's probably dreading that I'm going to call her and tell her I'm not coming in again."

Michael closed his eyes. "Uh-huh."

Jan left Michael and Swoosie to their napping and headed off down the road. She enjoying the familiar trees and fall colors as she wound her way back to Kat's place deep in the forest.

She drove up to the house and found Kat and Joel outside with many dogs gathered around them. Slowing the car to a crawl, she parked under a tree. Kat walked over, trailed by the gigantic brown dog, the black-and-white dog, and Rosa.

Jan jumped out of the car and crouched down to say hello to Rosa, "Oh, how's my girl? Look at you, being part of the pack!" She stood up and turned to Kat. "Hi again. I apologize again that I didn't get here earlier."

"I'm glad you seem to be feeling better," Kat said.

"How was your flight?" Joel asked.

"I didn't fly back after all. Michael drove me."

"So he's visiting again?" Kat said. "He seemed really nice. Oh, and you need to tell him that what he said to me about thinking about what clients want really helped. I actually wrote something on the business plan."

"It's a miracle," Joel said with a smile.

Kat turned to him. "Hey, who met her article deadline? And has a check in the mail? Oh yes, that would be me."

Joel grinned and said to Jan. "Writing is a mercurial thing. When it's good, it's very good. And when it's bad, I leave the room."

"Sometimes I read a novel and I'm in awe that someone actually sat down and wrote it," Jan said. "My mind doesn't work that way. I remember facts and history. It's hard to imagine being able to just write something out of thin air."

"Is Michael going to be around for a while?" Kat asked.

Jan looked up at the trees. "I'm, ah, not sure. He's off from work at the moment."

"Cool." Kat clasped her hands in front of her. "I know he's supposed to be on vacation, but maybe if he has a little extra time, he could give me some more marketing advice. Could you ask him if he'd be willing to help me come up with a name for the kennel? I'd pay for his help. Or you can board Rosa for free. Or his dog, too. You have no idea how bad Joel and I are at brainstorming. I think we're too analytical."

Joel shook his head sadly. "We tend to get bogged down in details. It's not good."

Jan nodded. "Okay, I'll tell him. From what he has said, I think he loves doing that kind of thing."

"Fantastic!" Kat said. "If he could help me figure that out, it would be a huge load off of my mind. Let me go get Rosa's stuff for you."

Jan leashed up Rosa and loaded her into the car and thought about what Kat had said. When she got back home, she told Michael about the conversation. "It seems like you're good at your job, even when you're not at work."

He wrapped his arms around her waist. "I suppose I can't help it. I've been doing this type of stuff for a long time. I look at a magazine ad and think of twelve ways it could be improved. A lot of it is just human nature. People hate to feel like they are being sold something, but they love to spend money."

"I never thought about it that way. I guess that's true. So will you help Kat? She said she'd even pay you."

"Sure. Although first I'd like to spend some time enjoying Alpine Grove again." He bent his head down to kiss her. "Starting with you. I feel much better after my nap." He kissed her lips and her neck, walking her back toward the wall.

Jan's back touched the vertical surface and he pressed his body to hers, running his hands under her shirt, up the sides of her body. Gasping for breath, she said, "Maybe we should move to the bedroom?"

He paused and looked into her eyes. "Good idea."

She smiled. "And maybe you could put your dog in her crate, too."

"That's an even better idea."

~

Over the next few days, Jan and Michael settled into a routine. Michael got up early and went running with Swoosie. After they returned and the dogs were fed, Jan made breakfast. They ate together and she went off to work at the library with Rosa. At some point during the day, Michael did the dishes. She didn't know exactly when, but the kitchen was always clean when she got home. He often went out with Swoosie and his camera for a hike somewhere. Sometimes he'd appear at the library in the afternoon and they'd eat lunch together. The dark circles under his eyes had faded and even Swoosie seemed more relaxed. She hadn't eaten or destroyed anything in days. Jan was even starting to like the fuzzy dog and looked forward to seeing Swoosie's happy, smiling polar-bear face when she got home at night.

After Michael had been there for a week, Jan started to get anxious about when he was going to leave. She'd promised herself not to think about the future, but he'd been there far longer than just the "last weekend" they'd discussed. And now she didn't want him to go anywhere. But she really didn't want to talk to him about it, particularly because they had been getting along so well. The fact was, she *never* wanted him to leave. But the sinking feeling in the pit of her stomach reminded her that it was only a matter of time.

They were curled up on the sofa watching a movie when the phone rang. Jan jumped up and ran to answer it. "Hi Bruce. Yes, he's here." She held the phone out to Michael. "It's your dad."

Looking startled, Michael got up off the couch and took the phone from Jan. "Hey Dad. Is everything okay?" He raised his eyebrows questioningly at Jan. "Yes, Angie told me

that, but I'm fine. I'm just taking a little vacation, that's all....
Really? I guess I should call them back, then. Okay. Yes, you
can do that if you want. Thanks for letting me know. Talk to
you soon."

Jan raised her hands, palms up. "What was that all
about?"

"He wanted to find out if I'm okay, since according to
your mom, my aura is cloudy. And I guess some of the agency
clients have been trying to reach me. I have an unlisted
number, so they called my dad to try to track me down."

"Really? I'm reminded again why I would never want
your job."

"He called to let me know they were looking for me and
to find out if it was okay to give out my home number to
people."

"Why is it unlisted?"

He shook his head. "Sometimes clients can be demanding.
Particularly if they're in other time zones. There was one guy
a few years ago who started calling me at home in the middle
of the night every time he had a new brilliant idea. I was
already working insane hours. So I changed my number and
made it unlisted."

"I think I'm liking your job even less than I did before.
And that's saying something."

Michael shrugged. "It's what I do. I'm good at it." He
looked thoughtful for a moment. "I really must be good if
people are calling my dad to find me. I should probably call
them back. Can I use your phone?"

"You're going to call people now? It's eight at night. Way
past business hours."

"It's eight in the morning in Moscow. They're just getting up."

"You want to call the other side of the world?"

"Yes. They make vodka." He grinned. "You know, the stuff that almost killed you? Not everyone has that reaction to it."

"Fine. Could you crate your dog? Rosa and I are going to the bedroom. I'll be reading. She'll be sleeping."

"Okay. See you later."

The next morning, Jan woke up and discovered Michael wasn't in the bed next to her. She heard movement in the living room, got up, and found Michael packing his things. Swoosie was circling around, excited about the prospect of another road trip.

Jan had read somewhere that the term heartache was based on a feeling of intense sadness that could cause a literal ache in the chest. It turned out to be true. She clenched her hands in front of her, digging her nails into her palms. "So you're leaving?"

"Yes. I need to go home and deal with some stuff. And the vodka people want me to fly to Russia."

"What?"

Standing up, he smiled. "I've always wanted to go to Russia."

"How can you work with clients if the agency is closed?"

"I'm going to work that out. That's why I have to go. These guys still need to sell their vodka. I need to help them figure out how they can get out of their contract with Derek."

"I see."

Michael reached out to take her in his arms. "This trip and this time with you have been incredible. I needed to clear my head. I feel so much better."

Jan hugged him and put her head on his shoulder. "It was a great weekend. Even though it was much longer than just a weekend. I'm going to miss you."

He gently pushed her away from him and looked into her eyes. "I'm going to miss you, too."

A tear slid down her cheek. She looked up at the ceiling. "I knew this would be awful. I should never have let you talk me into letting you stay here. I knew I'd never want you to leave and that's exactly what's happened."

"Maybe you could come down and visit for a weekend again."

Jan sighed and rested her head on his shoulder again. "No. That's not what I mean. I told you I don't want to be just a fling or the weekend girlfriend. I love you. I want to be with you all the time."

Michael didn't say anything and Jan raised her head again to look at his face. She couldn't read the look in his eyes, but if she were to guess, she'd say it was alarm. "I knew I shouldn't have said that. But it's the way I feel. You can't say I didn't warn you."

"I'm sorry. I really should go." He moved to pick up his suitcase.

Released from his embrace, Jan was suddenly cold. She crossed her arms across her chest. She watched as he loaded Swoosie's crate and then Swoosie into the car. He stood in front of her in the doorway. "Do you want me to call you?"

"It's a long drive. I'd like to know you made it home okay."

Michael turned to walk to the car and Jan moved to swing the door closed. She stopped and leaned on the edge, not wanting to close off her last glimpse of him. Suddenly, he turned around and walked back to face her. Cupping her face in both of his hands, he kissed her and then looked into her eyes. "You told me you were worried about a long-distance relationship. What if you moved to San Diego? Then we could see if things would work out."

Jan shook her head. "Don't you think I've thought of that? I'm not leaving here. Do you know how hard it is to get a job as a librarian? For years, the number of applicants has vastly outnumbered the available jobs. When I got my MLS degree, the only place I could find any job as a librarian was here in Alpine Grove. Then add in the fact that you're talking about finding a job in San Diego. The weather is good and the job market has historically been extremely tight. Apart from all that, I love my job and I love living in a small town. San Diego is a nice place to visit, but I'm not sure I'd ever want to live there again. I enjoy my life here. Maybe you find it boring, but it's my home."

Michael held her hands in his. "No, I never said it was boring here. But my job is in San Diego. And my home is there. You're not being very flexible. Maybe your mom was right. I mean, couldn't you do something else other than be a librarian?"

"Maybe. But I don't want to. I have a degree and I like what I do. What are you suggesting? Maybe I should take up surfing and sell bikinis on the Pacific Beach boardwalk or something? Have you considered giving up your job? You'd probably get more sleep, if nothing else. If you keep working long hours like you have, it will destroy your health. There's more to life than advertising."

He dropped her hands. "You know I can't do that. Advertising is what I do. I love it. And I'm perfectly fine. I run all the time."

Jan reached up to caress his cheek, "You spend two days away from work and it's like you're a different person. Relaxed. Happier. I really wish you could see the difference. Just please stay healthy. Even if I don't see you again, I don't want anything to happen to you."

Michael took her hand and kissed her palm. "I really have to go. I'll call you when I get back to San Diego."

As Jan watched him walk back to the car and drive away, tears streamed down her face. He was gone.

~

As Jan had predicted, after Michael left she cried. A lot. At this point, she was totally cried out and she had eaten more ice cream than was probably good for any human being to ingest. Michael had left a message saying he'd made it home, but hadn't called again. The unending lure of work probably made him forget she existed. Again. Jan heard from her mother that he was in fact still in San Diego, but Angie hadn't seen him since he'd been back and neither had Bruce.

After a week, missing Michael had become more of a constant dull ache, rather than searing pain, and Jan was getting back into the normal routine of her life. Kat invited her and Rosa to attend another Wine and Whine with Maria, and Jan vented about the confusing nature of men. She definitely did not consume any wine, however. Getting out and seeing other people did make her feel slightly better for a little while.

That Friday evening after a long day at the library filled with seriously annoying, ill-behaved children, Jan was settling in on the couch to watch a movie with Rosa. The sound of the dog's snoring was soothing and Jan was starting to doze off when a knock on her door startled her awake. She jumped up and pulled the curtain aside on the window next to the door. Michael and Swoosie were standing on her doorstep. The pang of surprise in Jan's chest quickly shifted to general annoyance. Didn't he *ever* call?

She opened the door and turned to watch as Swoosie zoomed into the house, obviously glad to be out of the car. Rosa jumped off the couch and Swoosie ran over to sniff. She play-bowed and Rosa wagged her tail, looking happy to see the fuzzy white dog again.

Michael walked in and closed the door behind him. Jan turned back to look at him. "What are you...?"

He wrapped her in his arms before she could finish her sentence and covered her mouth with his, kissing her in a way that obliterated all further thought. He released her and leaned his head against hers with a sigh. "I've wanted to do that for so long."

Jan placed the palms of her hands on his chest and pushed him away from her. "What I was going to say was what are you doing here? And FYI, in 1876 Alexander Graham Bell invented this little thing called the telephone. I know you know how to use one. You could have called me first."

"I knew you'd say no if I asked to see you."

Jan backed away and leaned against the door frame. She watched as Swoosie jumped up on the couch next to Rosa, who had already settled in for another nap. "You're right. That's very astute of you. I would have said no."

Michael reached out and took one of her hands, lacing her fingers with his. "When I drove back to San Diego from here, I had a lot of time to think. I convinced myself you were overreacting and being inflexible."

Jan pulled her hand away and turned to walk into the kitchen. "That's nice. And thanks so much. That doesn't explain why you're here, though. I'm going to make some tea. Do you want some before you leave?"

Michael reached out for her hand again and turned her around. "If you don't mind, I'd rather not leave."

"Are we having this conversation again? Because I don't think I can stand it. I'm exhausted. Tired of crying. Tired of thinking about you." She waved her hand toward the refrigerator. "I'm even tired of ice cream. And that's saying something."

Michael smiled. "I think I'm not being clear. You were right. I went back to San Diego and I fell into all the same patterns. Working too much. Not sleeping. Even Swoosie was pissed off at me."

"Your dog does require a lot of attention, you know."

"Yes. She stole one of my art boards and dragged it out into the hole in the back yard."

Jan smirked. "I'm glad to hear it's not just my underwear she's using for her landscaping projects."

Michael reached out to touch her cheek. "But the worst part was that I missed you. And being here. Talking with you. Hiking with Swoosie. Hanging out. I'd be sitting there at my dining room table by myself in the middle of the night working on stuff for the vodka guys and find myself staring into space and wondering why."

"Good question. I can't say I haven't wondered why you work such long hours. It's not healthy."

"I know."

Jan moved away, turned on the stove, and put the tea bags into mugs. "Really? It certainly doesn't seem like it. Did you think of trying something radical like sleeping? Even your dad said he hadn't heard from you."

"I didn't run up to his place with Swoosie last weekend. He called me to make sure I was okay."

Jan leaned against the counter and crossed her arms. "Apparently you are, since you're here. Bringing me back to the original question of why."

"You know me better than just about anyone, except possibly my dad. The night I went to your motel room, I told you about when my mother died. And you know about my—to put it nicely—troubled youth."

Jan shifted her stance. What was he talking about? "So? I got the impression you never spent much time actually talking to some of your prior dates. That is a downside of flings and one-night stands, you know. But it doesn't explain why you're here."

"If you work all the time, it's a great excuse. I've avoided getting serious with anyone because I didn't want to lose someone again. It's bad enough caring about a dog. Getting Swoosie wasn't my idea. But that's a whole different story."

"Yes, I think I was the one who pointed out that I didn't want to get hurt. And as noted, that didn't work out very well. I'm completely sick of crying, and I think even Rosa is wondering what is wrong with me. Where are you going with all this?"

Michael stepped closer to her and took a deep breath. "Sitting there in my lonely house, I came to a conclusion. The J. Geils Band was right. Love stinks."

"What?" Jan shook her head and looked up at the ceiling. "You're quoting 80s pop bands? Sorry I had to ruin your day with all my whiny feelings. But like I said, I warned you."

Michael reached out and extracted one of her hands, clasping it in both of his. "No. I mean I love you. Desperately. Stupidly. To distraction. Like every completely sappy love song you've ever heard. But it stinks to be in love when the person you love isn't with you."

Jan turned to him and looked into his eyes. "Are you saying what I think you're saying?"

He took her other hand and drew her closer. "I want to be with you. I'll move here if you still want me to. I like it here. I was happy and I want to feel that way again. With you. Right now my job is a mess, and I don't care. Even if I keep doing work for the vodka company, they're in Russia. And a lot of the other people who are trying to get me to work for them again are in New York City. So it doesn't really matter where I live. My dad is content and settled now with Dave. And after the last week or so, I know for sure that I am not happy when I'm not with you."

Jan wrapped her arms around his neck, not quite believing what she was hearing. "You're really serious? What would you do?"

Michael wrapped his arms around her waist. "I've thought about that quite a bit." He paused to kiss her neck. "The way Derek ran the agency was...I think the word you used was toxic. I figured that's just how advertising was. And I think some part of me was worried about failing. Letting my mother down somehow, particularly since I was such a screw-up in high school."

Jan shook her head. "I think by anyone's estimation, you've been successful professionally."

"I suppose. But now that I've been away from it, I've come to the conclusion that there was no reason work had to be so stressful. I got caught up in the competition because that's what everyone did in that environment. If I ran my own smaller company, I could take on just a few select clients. I could go back to doing more creative design work, which I enjoyed. And I could learn about all the new software programs. Not to mention, have a life again. Be with you. Go hiking. Take photographs. Go back to working with Swoosie again. I used to train her all the time when she was young. She loved it. I loved it." He pulled her into his embrace. "But not as much as I love you."

He gave her a kiss that was intense and all-consuming. As Jan began to melt in his arms, the kiss was interrupted by the sudden sound of the teakettle whistling. Pulling away, she turned to the stove to silence the obnoxious noise. She looked over her shoulder past Michael to the living room, where Swoosie and Rosa were happily sitting on the sofa shredding her book into tiny pieces. She smiled at Michael, "I think Swoosie and Rosa are forming a book club. Maybe you could start on that training program sooner rather than later."

He gathered her in his arms again. "It's a deal."

Chapter 14

Brainstorming

A few days later, Michael and Jan drove toward Kat's house. Rosa and Swoosie were in the back seat observing the scenery. The Alpine Grove gossip grapevine had gotten word that Michael had returned and Kat had invited them over for a brainstorming session.

Michael smiled at Jan. "I think my first marketing suggestion may be to get this driveway graded. I can feel the suspension of my car crying out in agony."

"Yes, my only advice is to go extremely slowly and try to dodge the biggest craters." The car slammed into a pothole. "Like that one."

"Sorry about that."

"It's your car." If Michael was moving to Alpine Grove, he was going to have to get used to bad roads.

"I may need to trade this thing in before I move. I'm guessing winter driving isn't going to be better."

"Not usually. But the snow does fill in the holes." Turning them into miniature skating rinks.

Michael pulled the car up near the house. Maria and Kat were outside examining something in the yard. Maria was wearing tight spandex pants and heels. She shook her finger at Kat. "I think we should squish it. That thing was on your head. When you were *in the house*."

Kat cringed and shook her hands in front of her in disgust. "So gross. So gross."

"Are you guys okay?" Jan asked as she walked up to them. It looked like they were doing some kind of rain dance with lots of waving and pointing.

Kat pointed at the insect that was crawling around on the ground in front of them. "That...that *thing* fell off the ceiling and landed on my head. Then it was crawling on me. I am *so* grossed out right now."

"She went screaming out that door." Maria inclined her head toward the house. "It wasn't pretty. I think Joel mighta blown a gasket, he was laughing so hard."

Michael crouched down to get a closer look. "That is one big beetle. What is it?"

Jan bent to examine the insect. "It's a Western Conifer Seed Bug, *Leptoglossus occidentalis* or WCSB. They're very common around here. In the fall, they tend to move inside to find a place to winter over. They're harmless, but produce a piney odor when provoked, so sometimes they're confused with stink bugs."

Kat shuddered. "Oh my God, they're moving *inside*?"

The insect buzzed loudly and took off toward the trees. Maria shrieked and Kat ran away from the bug toward the house.

Jan looked at Michael. "I guess I provoked it. Would you get the dogs?"

"Sure." He turned to walk back to the car, his feet crunching through the leaves.

After the bout of mild hysteria, Maria had composed herself and was checking her own hair for insect life. She leaned her head toward Jan. "There isn't anything in there, is there? Now I have bug paranoia. I hate that."

Jan peered at Maria's mop of dark hair and pushed a few curls around. "I don't see anything. I think you're fine."

Kat waved from the relative safety of the steps. "Sorry about that. It's nice to see you again. Do you want to come inside?"

Michael approached with Swoosie and Rosa on leashes. "Thanks." Rosa was walking sedately and Swoosie was trying to tie a square knot around Michael with her leash. He bent to try to extricate his left leg from the leash.

Jan said to Maria, "I don't think you've met Michael."

Maria extended her hand to Michael. "Hi. It's nice to meet you. I've heard a lot about you from Jan."

Michael stood and shook her hand. "Nice to meet you too." Swoosie was trying to yank him toward the house. "I think Swoosie is excited." He turned to follow the dogs up the steps.

Maria turned to Jan, gave her a nudge, and whispered. "Damn, girlfriend, you weren't kidding. He really is just smokin' hot." She fanned her face with her hands.

Jan blushed. "Yes. I, ah, think so too." Her skin's tendency to turn crimson at the slightest provocation was annoying. The last couple of days since Michael had returned to Alpine Grove had been better than she could have ever imagined.

Maria and Jan went into the house and they all settled inside around the kitchen table. Michael had brought treats to keep Swoosie's attention so she wouldn't sneak off and try to eat the house. The dog sat with her chin on his leg, hoping for a handout.

Kat said, "Thanks for coming out here to help me. I really need to name this as-yet-unbuilt kennel so I can board dogs. I am *so* not experienced with anything marketing-related. In fact, I purposely avoided anything to do with marketing when I was a technical writer." She turned to Michael. "I read about brainstorming and it turns out I'm terrible at it."

Michael smiled. "It's not a big deal. The main thing is to get a lot of different people together, so you get a wide range of ideas. You have to consider all of the ideas, even if they don't seem like they make sense."

"Even if they're stupid?" Maria said.

"No matter how weird or off-the-wall something is, you are supposed to write it down." Michael said. "Sometimes a bad idea will spur another better idea."

"Can we drink wine?" Maria asked. "I'm pouring, and after seeing that bug, I need a big glass. It was prehistoric. Like a tiny six-legged *tyrannosaurus rex*."

"None for me, thank you," Jan said. Never again.

Kat held her pen in the air. "Okay. I have a notepad and I'm writing stuff down."

Michael looked at Kat. "So what image do you want the name to convey?"

Kat bent and put her forehead on the table. "You're asking me questions? I didn't know there was going to be a test."

"How about words that reflect what you want people to think of when they are bringing you their treasured family pet?" Michael paused and stroked the fur on Swoosie's head. "When I brought Swoosie to doggie boot camp in San Diego, I was looking for a place that was reliable, professional, trustworthy, and so forth. See what I mean?"

Kat raised her head. "That's good. I'm trustworthy. I didn't lose Rosa, anyway."

"And she was an escape artist!" Maria said. "That dog is wily."

"That's reassuring," Michael said. "Jan may be going with me to Russia, so I wanted to see if you'd be up for taking care of Swoosie, too."

Jan shook her head. "No, I am *not* going to Russia." She had done quite enough traveling for a while.

Michael looked at her. "She's thinking about it." He turned to Kat. "Swoosie is a lot more, ah, difficult to take care of than Rosa."

Kat looked over at Swoosie, who still had her head on Michael's leg. The dog wagged and smiled. "She looks adorable right now."

"Swoosie has an eating disorder," Jan said.

"I'm sorry. Is she okay?" Kat said.

Michael smiled. "Jan means that Swoosie eats everything. Whether or not it's edible. So let's get back to the brainstorming. How about saying the first dog-related words that come to mind? I'll start. Hound, dog, woof, tail, wag, bark, puppy, paws, canine."

Maria said. "Cujo!"

"I think scary dogs may not be what Kat is after here." Jan said.

Kat said, "I prefer happy dogs, thanks. Not rabid ones. I think that might attract the wrong clientele."

Jan said, "Happy Hounds, Hound Haven, Happy Tails, Wagging Tails, Puppy Paradise."

"Hey, you're good at this." Michael said. "Some of those aren't too bad."

Joel nudged Kat, who was furiously writing down names. "At least *someone* is good at this."

Michael said, "How about the kennel aspect? In San Diego lots of pet businesses include the words resort or spa, for example."

"I think this is more like camping out." Maria said. "In a leaky tent."

Kat glared at her. "Hey, we're working on it. It's more like a bed and breakfast."

Jan said, "Or a bed and biscuit?"

"Exactly." Kat nodded. "We've got trails, too. Tails and trails."

Michael crossed his arms on the table. "Do you want to include any local reference? Many businesses include the name of the town or are named after some geographic feature like a mountain range."

"I already came up with Alpine Grove Dog Boarding." Joel said. "It was deemed too boring."

Kat said, "But what if we do grooming? Then it doesn't work, anyway."

"That's a good point." Michael said. "You might want to keep it general. Do you want to include your name?"

"Kat's dog boarding is just a recipe for confusion," Kat said. "My last name is Stevens which sounds like an accountant's name. Blech."

After another hour of questions and brainstorming, Kat had many naming options to ponder. She waved her notepad in the air. "I've got ideas. I totally owe you some free dog-boarding now!"

Michael smiled. "We might take you up on that."

Jan shook her head. "Not immediately, though. We have a lot to do to get Michael moved here and settled before winter arrives."

Kat gave both Jan and Michael a hug goodbye. "Thank you both." She bent down to pet Rosa and Swoosie. "It was good seeing you two, as well. You behave yourselves."

Chapter 15

Epilogue

After Jan and Michael drove home and fed the dogs, they were sitting on the sofa relaxing. Jan was leaning against Michael, reading the remnants of her library book.

"Your dog ate the ending of this mystery. I'm never going to find out what happened."

Michael bent to kiss her neck. "I'm afraid your dog participated. Buy a new one."

"The library book budget is being cut again. The board of directors wants to divert money to add computers. I think Jill may cry if they put more computers in the building. And she's already mad at me for taking so much time off."

Michael put his book down and cupped her chin with his hand to turn her head to his. "Speaking of time off, why won't you go to Russia with me? It's only for two weeks."

Jan turned around to face him. "I can't. It's too much time. I should be working and getting organized. There's so much to do to get you moved up here. You are going to sell your house and that means finding a real estate agent and listing it and pricing it. There are forms that will have to be signed. And when it sells, there's organizing movers. Going through stuff. Deciding what to keep and what to give away. And you need an office here. So that means looking at office space. More real estate agents and rental agreements. And I have to work. It's just too much."

Michael smiled and stroked her cheek with his knuckles. "You have 49 lists already. It will all happen. You don't have to have it all figured out right now. Come with me. We just agreed that we can't stand being a few hours apart. I certainly don't want to spend two weeks on the other side of the world without you."

Jan shook her head. "I shouldn't. I really shouldn't."

"Who says?"

Jan rolled her eyes. "Oh please. You sound like a ten-year old."

"You say that a lot, but I know you think it's endearing." He grinned and then kissed her. "I mean it. Who says you shouldn't go? Why are you should-ing all over yourself? Think about all the fun people-watching we could do. It could be incredible. Can you imagine? And I promise I'll keep you away from the vodka."

"You're very kind." Just the word vodka gave her a twinge in her stomach.

Michael looked into her eyes. "You could really help me on this trip. You were great at brainstorming at Kat's. And I've told you before that you are a one-woman research department. I don't think you understand how ad agencies would kill to have access to your encyclopedic knowledge. Just come with me. Take a chance. It could be fun. The library will still be there when we get back."

Jan kissed him. "I will admit you have given me a new appreciation for fun. But I have responsibilities."

"This is only the beginning of fun. We had fun in San Diego. We had fun here in Alpine Grove. There's no reason we wouldn't have fun in Russia, too. Fun is good. You should try it more often."

Jan bit her lip. "I can't leave Jill all by herself at the library for two weeks. I shouldn't just up and leave like that. Again. It isn't fair to her. She's already angry about all the time I've taken off."

"Don't librarians ever take vacations? Get sick? There are substitute teachers. Are there substitute librarians?"

"Well, yes. But like I said, the budget is being cut. I don't think there is any money to hire a substitute. I'm not sure it will work out." Although maybe some new graduates might be interested. She would have jumped at the chance a few years ago. Maybe she could make a few calls.

Michael smoothed a curl back from her forehead. "Tell the library big-wigs you'll give the substitute your vacation pay."

"What? Give them money? My money? I can't afford to do that."

"I can. Or more precisely the client can. They pay me. I pay you. You pay the sub. It all works out."

"You'd do that?" She took his hand in both of hers. "Really?"

He tilted his head. "Of course. So you'll go?"

Jan looked into his eyes. She was out of excuses. Now it was a matter of trust. So many years of avoiding her mother's out-of-control lifestyle had made her afraid of spontaneous decisions. But being with Michael had shown Jan that she could do things that scared her, like dancing the merengue in front of a crowd or riding a horse on a beach through crashing ocean waves. Nothing bad happened. In fact, it was great. Going to a foreign country was scary. But she trusted that Michael wouldn't drag her into something she'd regret. So there was no reason *not* to go to Russia with him.

Jan grinned widely. "Yes. I'll go. You're right. It's a wonderful opportunity and I would be a fool to miss it. It reminds me of that movie *Risky Business*, when Tom Cruise's friend says, "...sometimes you gotta say, what the..."

Michael cut her off with his kiss, pulling her against him. His hands were in her hair and then roaming the curves of her body. He whispered in her ear. "Exactly."

Thanks for Reading

Thank you for dedicating some of your reading time to *Fuzzy Logic*. I hope you enjoyed Jan, Michael and Kat's adventures and I wanted you to know that I'll be writing more books that will feature Kat, Joel and various other residents of Alpine Grove who bring dogs to the new boarding kennel. The third book, *The Art of Wag* is available along with ten other books in the series.

If you would like to be notified by email when I release a new book, you can sign up for my New Releases email list at SusanDaffron.com.

I know that not everyone likes to write book reviews, but if you are willing write a sentence or two about what you thought of *Fuzzy Logic*, I encourage you to post a review at your favorite book vendor site or share a message with your social networking friends.

If you would like to share your thoughts about the book with me privately, you can reach me through the contact page on the SusanDaffron.com web site.

I look forward to hearing from you!

~ Susan C. Daffron

Acknowledgements

Writing a novel is never easy and I'd like to thank my husband James Byrd for his support and encouragement throughout the writing and publishing process.

I'd also like to thank my alpha and beta readers for their eagle-eyed reading and great feedback:

- James Byrd
- Cynthia Daffron
- Dian Chapman
- Kathy Goughenour
- Kate Turner

Thanks also to Fiona, the original fuzzy white dog who was the inspiration for Swoosie. I'm happy to say that Fiona is not quite as naughty as Swoosie, but she is a Samoyed and she is just as sweet. People really do come up and ask to pet her all the time because she is THAT cute.

About the Author

Susan Daffron is the author of the Jennings & O'Shea series and the Alpine Grove romantic comedies, a series of novels that feature residents of the small town of Alpine Grove and their various quirky dogs and cats. She is also an award-winning author of many nonfiction books, including several about pets and animal rescue. She lives in a small town in northern Idaho and shares her life with her husband and three really cute dogs.